*Accla...............*

"Will remind readers what chattering teeth sound like."
—*Kirkus Reviews*

"Voracious readers of horror will delightfully consume the contents of Bates's World's Scariest Places books."
—*Publishers Weekly*

"Creatively creepy and sure to scare." —*The Japan Times*

"Jeremy Bates writes like a deviant angel I'm glad doesn't live on my shoulder."
—Christian Galacar, author of GILCHRIST

"Thriller fans and readers of Stephen King, Joe Lansdale, and other masters of the art will find much to love."
—*Midwest Book Review*

"An ice-cold thriller full of mystery, suspense, fear."
—David Moody, author of HATER and AUTUMN

"A page-turner in the true sense of the word."
—*HorrorAddicts*

"Will make your skin crawl." —*Scream Magazine*

"Told with an authoritative voice full of heart and insight."
—Richard Thomas, Bram Stoker nominated author

"Grabs and doesn't let go until the end." —*Writer's Digest*

# BY JEREMY BATES

# DARK HEARTS

*A Collection of Short Novels*

## Jeremy Bates

Ghillinnein Books

ISBN-13: 978-0994096029
ISBN-10: 099409602X

# DARK HEARTS

# BLACK CANYON

# THE PRESENT

I didn't want to kill them. I loved them. But sometimes you have to do what you have to do to survive. I think you'll agree with me after you hear my account of what happened twenty-five years ago. I had no other choice. It was either them or me.

\* \* \*

A quarter of a century seems like forever ago. That would make the year in discussion the year the Berlin Wall fell, the year Iraq invaded Kuwait, the year *The Simpsons* debuted on television, the year the first webpage was published on the internet, and the year the Cincinnati Reds defeated the Oakland Athletics in the World Series in a four-game sweep. It was, I guess, a pretty great year all in all—at least, a pretty important one. On a more personal note, it was the year I kissed my first girl, the year I got a mountain bike for my birthday, and the year I broke my collarbone when I fell off that bike while biking where I wasn't allowed to be biking.

It was 1990. I was a grade-six student at Dry Creek Elementary School in Englewood, Colorado, and the people I killed were my parents.

*  *  *

When you say Colorado most people think of skiing. Some think of Mesa Verde, or Garden of the Gods, or Estes Park, or Cañon City. Not many think of Black Canyon of the Gunnison National Park. But they should. They should go there too, see it with their own eyes. It's a breathtaking gorge half as deep as the Grand Canyon, though much, much narrower, which, in my opinion, makes it all the more spectacular. I try to return there once a year, partly for the scenery, but mostly for the memories.

# 1990

Black Canyon of the Gunnison National Monument (it wouldn't be upgraded to national park status for another four years) is located in the western part of Colorado State, a bit south of center, making it a two-hour drive from Englewood, where I lived. My dad was behind the wheel of the eight-year-old Chevrolet Citation. My mom, in the seat next to him, was smoking a cigarette and reading one of those supermarket magazines that give you all the dirt on celebrities. I didn't have any brothers or sisters, so I had the backseat to myself. I sat with my back against one door, my legs stretched out so my feet almost touched the opposite door. I didn't have my seatbelt on, but my parents weren't the type of parents who cared about seatbelts. In fact, they didn't care about a lot of grown up stuff that other parents cared about. Junk food was okay in our house, for example. And I was allowed to come home from school whenever I wanted, as long as it wasn't *really* late. I didn't even have to call if I was staying at a friend's for dinner, which I did a fair bit because neither my mom nor dad liked to cook much.

It was Friday, October 24. My dad had told me I didn't have to go to school this morning, which was awesome. Yet with both him and my mom around it didn't feel like a real day off, like when I got to stay home sick by myself. It felt more like a regular old Saturday. Even so, a Friday feeling like a Saturday was still better than a Friday feeling like a Friday.

We didn't leave the house as early as my dad had wanted because my mom was hung over and refused to get out of bed before ten, so we were just getting to the southern rim entrance to Black Canyon now, around midafternoon. I was staring out the car window, watching the golden aspens and other turning trees disappear behind us as we entered into a tunnel of dark, somber evergreens that blocked out much of the daylight.

When we stopped at a wooden gate, my parents started arguing about something. I tried to ignore them, but this proved too hard in the closed confines of the Chevy.

"What if someone checks, Steve?" my mom was saying in the same tone she used when she was cross at me.

"Who's going to check?" my dad replied offhandedly, annoyed, like he thought my mom was overreacting. "Camping season is over. There's nobody here but us."

"A ranger probably comes by."

"It's a waste of money."

"It's called the honor system."

"What are you, a Girl Scout?"

"Don't be so cheap."

Grumbling, my dad opened his door. "It's just going to sit there, you know?"

My mom didn't look at him or say anything; she already knew she'd won.

My dad climbed out of the car and stuck his head back inside. "Or some kids are going to come along and pilfer it."

"Kids?" my mom said, raising her eyebrows amusedly. "Look around, Steve. We're in the middle of nowhere. And you said there's nobody—"

He slammed his door shut and circled the vehicle. He stopped before a little wooden box sitting atop a pole. He took his wallet from his back pocket—he got the wallet as a free gift with a case of beer he'd bought during Labor Day weekend—and produced several one dollar bills.

"What's Dad doing, Mom?" I asked.

"Paying the camping fee, hon." She kept her attention on my dad, likely to make sure he put the money in the box and didn't fake it. My mom was right: my dad could be pretty cheap sometimes. I'd been bugging him for a raise in my allowance a lot lately, but he wouldn't negotiate. I got the same one dollar a week that I got when I first started getting an allowance two years before. It sucked. One small bag of salt and vinegar chips and a can of Pepsi wiped me out until the following weekend. My mom was a bit more generous. She usually gave me fifty cents, or sometimes a whole dollar when I asked her politely. I had to have a good excuse handy, like I needed to take the bus somewhere. Still, what I got from her added up, and I was no longer considered the poor kid by my friends. That dishonor went to Ralph Stevenson. His dad didn't work either, and he was always begging everyone for a spare dime or quarter. We never gave him anything, but we often shared our lunches with him. All his mom ever packed him was a raw carrot and a couple pieces of buttered bread.

My dad stuffed the dollar bills into the slit in the wooden box, cast my mom a you-happy-now? look, then returned to the car.

"Thank you," she told him as he shifted the transmission into first and popped the clutch.

He grunted, and we continued in silence to the campground. I never said anything when my parents were fighting with each other. I've learned it was best to simply "zip it," an expression my dad used a lot, and to wait the fight out. Otherwise chances were good I would become the focus of their anger and get grounded or spanked for doing nothing.

The campground, my dad had told me earlier, contained three loops of campsites. Loop A was open year round, while Loops B and C were open spring to early fall. Being late October, I figured we must be driving to a campsite in Loop A.

A few minutes later we parked in a small clearing and got out of the car and looked around at the crowding forest. "Smell that, Brian!" my dad said, inhaling deeply and clapping me on the shoulder roughly.

I sniffed. "Smell what?" The air was cool, brittle, reminding me that Halloween was next week.

"Nature!" he exclaimed. "You won't smell that back in the city."

"Worth four bucks, if you ask me," my mom said. She was standing on the other side of the car and cupping her hands around a cigarette she was lighting.

"Bitch all you want, Suz, you're not going to spoil my mood."

"Dad," I said, "can you open the trunk?"

"All I want," he went on, ignoring me, "is a bit of peace and quiet. That so much to ask? A bit of peace and quiet?"

"Dad?"

"*What?*"

"Can you open the trunk?"

He glared at me.

"I need my tent," I said.

Reaching inside the car, he pulled a trigger that released the trunk lid. I went to the trunk, lifted the lid, and collected my tent and backpack.

The clearing was little more than the size of a baseball in-field. The amenities included a vault toilet, a picnic table, and a grill. I stopped at a flat spot of ground a good distance away from the car and upended the nylon tent bag, dumping the poles and guy ropes and metal spikes onto the mat of spongy pine needles. There was no instruction booklet—or if there once had been, it had been long since lost—and it took me a solid half hour to set the thing up properly (and even then I wasn't sure I had con-structed it correctly as it seemed to lean drunkenly to one side).

Still, it wasn't falling over, and that was good enough for me. I glanced at my parents. They had set their tent up next to the car and were standing with their arms around each other.

Happy they were in one another's good books again, I joined them and said, "So what do we do now?"

"Huh?" my mom said. She'd been staring off into the distance with one of her thinking faces on.

"I said—"

"Sit back and relax," my dad told me. He released my mom's waist and snatched a bottle of beer from the blue Eskimo cooler chest that sat on the ground, next to the Chevy's front tire. He twisted off the cap, flicked it away into the trees, and took a long sip.

"I hope it's not going to rain," my mom said.

I looked where she was looking and saw that the sky had smudged over with dark storm clouds.

"It won't, baby doll," my dad said. "It'll blow over."

"Can I have a beer, Dad?" I asked.

"Even if it does," he said, hooking his arm around my mom's waist once again and kissing her on the cheek, "we'll just go inside the tent. It's waterproof. And I think we can figure out something to do there." His hand slipped off the small of her back to her rear.

She swatted it away. "Not in front of Brian, Steve."

"Dad?" I said.

"What?"

"Can I have a beer?"

"You hear that, Suz? The boy wants a beer."

"Can I?" I said.

"Hell no. You'll just waste it."

I frowned, but I wasn't disappointed, not really. My dad had given me sips from his beers before, and I didn't like the taste of them. I only asked for one to show him I wasn't still a little kid. He was always treating me like I was still in grade four or something.

"Have a Pepsi, hon," my mom said. "And bring me a bottle of wine while you're at it."

I removed the lid from the cooler. "Which one?" I asked. Three wine bottles floated in the icy water alongside brown bottles of beer and blue-and-red Pepsi cans.

"You choose, angel."

I selected the bottle with the fanciest label and brought it to my mom, along with a Styrofoam cup that had been in a plastic bag next to the cooler. Then I returned for my Pepsi and popped the tab before my mom changed her mind about letting me have one before dinner.

My dad's hand, I noticed, had found its way down to my mom's rear again, but this time she didn't swat it away.

I said, "What are we having for dinner?"

"Hot dogs," my dad told me.

"Yeah! Are we going to cook them on the grill or over the fire?"

I don't think he heard me, because he was asking my mom where she wanted the folding chairs.

"Right over there," she said. "By the fire pit."

He went to the car's trunk, which he'd left propped open so it resembled the mouth of a sunbaking alligator, and carried two slat-back folding chairs to the stone ring that formed the perimeter of the fire pit.

"Dad?" I said, following him.

"What, Brian?"

"Can we cook them over the fire? The hot dogs?"

"You can cook your wieners over the fire, if you want. But you're going to need to find a sharp stick."

"Can I go look now?"

"That's a great idea."

"Don't go too far," my mom called.

I spent about an hour wandering the woods surrounding the campground, looking for the perfect stick. I didn't know what characteristics the perfect stick entailed, but I figured it needed to be long enough so I didn't burn my hands in the fire, thick enough so it didn't snap beneath the weight of the wiener, and have a thin, pointy tip. In the end I found one that sported all these requisites, plus, as a bonus, it ended in *three* prongs, like a devil's scepter, which meant I could cook three wieners at once.

When I returned to the campground to show the stick to my parents, I found them lounging in the folding chairs, my mom laughing at something my dad was telling her. Loud music played from the portable stereo, some old-fashioned stuff, maybe Elvis, or The Beatles.

"Look at my stick!" I said as I approached them.

"That's lovely, Brian," my mom said. She had one of her funny smelling cigarettes pinched between her fingers. The filter was smeared with red lipstick.

"Dad? Look." Four empty beer bottles sat next to him on the ground.

"Let me see that." He held out his hand.

Beaming, I passed it to him.

He snapped off two of the prongs, then handed it back. "That's better."

I was too shocked to say anything. My eyes smarted with tears. I turned around and pretended to be interested in the stick.

"Brian?" he said.

"Yeah?" I said.

"Grab me another beer, will ya?"

Rubbing the tears from my cheeks—there had only been a couple—I opened the cooler and grabbed a beer. I considered asking my mom if I could have another Pepsi, but I didn't because I knew she would say no. I brought the beer to my dad, then sat on the ground a few feet away from him.

I listened to my parents' conversation for a bit. They were talking about their friends. My mom kept calling one of the women she worked with a skank. I wondered if maybe she meant "skunk." Sometimes when she was drinking she didn't always pronounce her words correctly. And I could tell she was a little drunk already. Her face was flushed, her eyes filmy. My dad wouldn't be drunk, not after four beers, but he probably had what he called a buzz.

He cracked open the beer I'd given him, then asked my mom for the cigarette she was smoking. He didn't smoke, not every day like she did, but he would have the funny smelling ones every now and then.

I leaned back on my elbows and breathed deeply. Despite my dad breaking my stick, and despite shivering a bit in the chill autumnal night, a swell of contentment washed over me. I liked times like these, when my parents were drinking alcohol. It was weird because in the movies parents drinking alcohol always yelled at their kids, or hit them. But mine were the opposite. They didn't fight as much, and they became nicer to me, more attentive.

"Hey, is there electricity here?" I asked suddenly, wondering if I could charge my Gameboy. I glanced at the stereo. There was no cord; it was running on batteries.

"Nope," my dad said. "But there's water in case you get thirsty."

I knew that. I had seen the rusty tap poking out of the ground.

"By the way, Bri-guy," he added. "We're going to need some tinder and firewood to make the fire before it gets dark. How about you go find us some?"

"Do you want to come with me?" I asked.

"Not right now. I've had a long day. You go along."

I went, even though I figured my day had been about as long as his had been.

Half an hour later I had built a good stockpile of tinder and kindle and firewood next to the fire pit. My dad came over and joined me and soon had a fire going. It was just in time too, as the last of the daylight was seeping from the sky, turning it a muddy orange that quickly bled to red, then to purplish-black.

My mom set the picnic table with paper plates and napkins while my dad got the grill going. I slipped two slimy Oscar Mayer wieners from the package and impaled one on my stick and kept the other gripped in my left hand. Then I extended the stick with the attached wiener into the fire and turned it slowly, like a rotisserie. When the wiener had blistered and blackened, I extracted it and took a bite.

"Ow!" I yelped.

"It's going to be hot," my mom told me from the picnic table. I could barely see her in the dark.

I blew on the wiener to cool it down, ate it quickly, then stuck the second one on the stick and repeated the cooking process. To my dismay, it slipped off the prong and dropped into the fire and ashes.

"Dad!" I cried. "My hotdog fell off!"

"Christ, Brian." He was seated next to my mom at the picnic table.

"Can I have another one?" I asked.

"You already got your two."

"But the second one fell off."

"What do you think we're going to eat tomorrow?"

"But I'm still hungry."

"You can have a bun."

My parents had lit tea candles, and I could see both of them in the jittery candlelight, chomping down on their hotdogs, shadows jumping on their faces.

"Just the bun?" I said, nonplussed.

"You can put ketchup on it."

My mom giggled, spitting food from her mouth. This started my dad giggling too. I didn't find that solution funny. In fact, now I knew what Ralph Stevenson felt like every day at lunch with his buttered bread.

Nevertheless, I was hungry, so I joined my parents at the picnic table and ate a bun with ketchup and drank the metallic-tasting water from the tap.

When we finished eating—my dad had had three hotdogs, I'd counted—my mom lit another one of her funny smelling cigarettes and shared it with my dad and talked about the stars. I looked up too. The moon was little more than a silver hook, but there must have been a gazillion stars twinkling down at us. I wondered what it would be like to get on a rocket ship and visit distant places in the galaxy. I decided it would be pretty great. I'd invite my parents and maybe one of my friends, maybe even Stephanie, the girl I'd kissed recently. Maybe we'd run into aliens. Maybe we'd even find God hiding somewhere.

When my mom ran out of things to say about the stars, my dad told some ghost stories. They weren't very scary because my mom kept interrupting him, saying, "He's just a child,

Steve," which effectively ended each one right at the gooey parts.

Later, when it was my bedtime and I had to go to my tent, I read an *Archie* comic book—a Betty and Veronica Double Digest —from cover to cover. Then I turned off my flashlight and lay perfectly still in the darkness. My parents had stopped talking and laughing some time ago, so I guessed they were asleep. The only sound I heard now was the chirrups of crickets. Then I made out a soft rustling in the leaf litter. It was quick, sporadic. I pictured a wood mouse rummaging for acorns, pausing every now and then to sniff the air to make sure nothing was about to swoop down from the black sky, or sneak up behind it. I ended up falling asleep reflecting on how crappy it would be to be stuck at the bottom of the food chain, living your life in constant danger of getting eaten by something bigger than yourself.

* * *

I woke at dawn. The fire had winnowed to nothing but a pile of smoldering coals. My dad was crouched next to it in the murky half-light, trying to set fire to some scrunched up newspaper pages by rubbing two sticks together really fast. He soon gave up doing this and used my mom's bronze Zippo with the picture of a tiny airplane on it. He set kindle atop the burgeoning flames, then larger sticks.

He was whistling and seemed to be in a good mood, so I approached and said, "What's for breakfast, Dad?"

I almost expected him to tell me he wasn't made of food when he grinned and said, "Pancakes." He grabbed a box of pancake mix from next to his foot and tossed it to me. I caught it and looked at a smiling Aunt Jemima. "Don't even need eggs or milk," he said. "Just add water. What will they think of next?"

"Can I have three?" Two of anything was usually all I was ever allowed.

"Aren't you listening to me, boy? It's just mix and water.

Have five if you want."

"Five!"

"Now come here and help me out."

I followed my dad's instructions, pouring half the box of pancake mix into a plastic bowl, then adding water from the tap. I stirred the mix until it became thick and gooey. Then I poured three circles onto the oiled grill.

"All right, all right. Give me some space here, Brian," my dad said. "I'll tell you when they're ready."

I retreated to my stump by the fire and continued to watch my dad cook the pancakes. He was a handsome man, I thought. He still had all his hair, which I knew he was proud of, because he always made fun of bald people. When he combed his hair and shaved, my mom often told him he looked like a movie star. Now his hair was scruffy and unwashed, and stubble pebbled his jaw. He wore a pair of Bermuda shorts and a red tank-top with a picture of a setting sun on the chest. His feet were bare.

Sometimes when my mom wasn't around, and it was just my dad and me like this, I didn't know what to say to him. I was worried about saying the wrong thing, upsetting him. He wouldn't yell at me or anything, not usually, but he'd go quiet, or ignore me altogether. That's when I knew I'd annoyed him.

He used to be an air conditioner repairman, my dad. But then last month he was fired. He got in a big fight with my mom about this. They still argued about it a lot. My mom wanted him to get another job, and he said he was looking. Once he told her he was going to drive trucks. I thought that was neat. But she didn't want him to, because it meant he would be away for long periods of time and there would be nobody home at nighttime to look after me when she went to the bar where she worked. She told me she was a waitress there, but I think she was a dancing waitress because my dad was always talking to her about quitting her dancing.

He cocked an eye at me now. "What are you looking at?"

"Nothing," I said.

"You ready for the hike today?"

"Where are we going?"

"The north pole, where do you think?"

I didn't know and got nervous.

"To the canyon!" he said. "Did you think we were just going to sit around here all day?"

"Awesome!"

"You bet it's awesome. You're going to keep up, right?"

"Yeah."

"Hope so. Now come get your pancakes."

I grabbed a paper plate and held it in front of me. My dad flopped three pancakes onto it. I doused them with maple syrup, then returned to my stump. While I gobbled the pancakes down, I noticed my mom stir in her tent. My dad had left the door unzipped and I could see inside as she kicked the sleeping bag off her, got up, and started to fuss through the clothes she had brought. She was wearing nothing but a pair of skimpy panties. Her breasts were medium-sized and nice-looking, like the ones you saw on TV sometimes. A tattoo of a unicorn decorated her right thigh. A much smaller dolphin circled her belly button. I frowned at the ugly bruise the size of an apple on her left biceps. She always told me the bruises were from bumping into things, but I knew that wasn't true. They were from my dad, when he hit her.

She was old, thirty I think, but she was still pretty. When we went to a restaurant for dinner, other men would look at her. Also, the waiters were always flirting with her, or at least my dad said they were. Some of my friends had weird crushes on her too. They told me she was hot. I told them they were gross.

A moment later she emerged from the tent dressed in a pair of short canary-yellow shorts and a tight white top that made it obvious she didn't have a bra on. Her hair was messy, and her face was free of makeup. I liked her face better like this. I thought she wore too much makeup sometimes. Without it she looked more like my mom.

"Hey, Mom," I said with a full mouth, smiling at her.

"Morning, hon. Mmm. That smells good. Did you help your

father with breakfast?"

"Yup! And he said I can have as many pancakes as I want."

"Hold on there, Brian," he said. "Three's plenty. There's not as much mix as I thought. We need to save some for tomorrow."

I glanced at the small triangle of pancake left on my plate and wished I hadn't eaten so fast now. My mom sat on a stump next to mine and lit a cigarette. She was rubbing the corner of her eyes like she did in the mornings when she drank wine the night before.

"Baby doll?" my dad said. "How many pancakes?"

"I'm not hungry."

"You have to eat something."

"Brian can have mine."

"All right!" I said.

"I just told him—"

"Please, Dad?"

He looked at me for a long moment, but I held his eyes, refusing to look away, and finally he shrugged. "One more, Brian," he said, turning back to the grill. "But that's it. What do you think, I'm made out of food or something?"

＊ ＊ ＊

According to my dad, there wasn't going to be much shade at the canyon, and the sun, even in October, would be intense at the high elevation we were at. So we filled our water bottles with water from the tap and slathered on sunscreen from an old brown Coppertone bottle that was almost empty and kept making farting noises every time I squeezed it. Then my dad clapped his favorite trucker cap on his head—"Fuck Vegetarians!" was written across the front in gothic lettering—and we set off through the forest. Along the way guideposts described the trees we passed. There were sagebrush and pinyon pine and Utah juniper to name a few, all of which were apparently well-adapted to growing in the thin soil and harsh climate.

I was walking next to my mom, searching the woods for the squirrels and chipmunks that seemed to be everywhere, when my dad said excitedly, "Look at those!" He was pointing at a pair of animal tracks in the dirt. "Reckon they might belong to a bobcat, or mountain lion."

"What did I tell you about scaring Brian, Steve?"

"I'm not scared, Mom," I said.

"I'm not trying to scare the boy, Suz," my dad said.

"Last night with the ghost stories—"

"He's not a goddamn baby."

"I'm not—"

"Quiet, Brian!" She frowned at me, touched her temple. "Sorry, honey," she added more softly.

"I'm not scared, Mom," I assured her.

"That's good." She turned to my dad. "I'm going to go back."

"Oh for fuck's sake, Suz."

"I have a headache, and I'm not going to spend the day arguing with you."

"I'm not arguing. I just said they were fucking bobcat tracks!"

"We're camping in the middle of nowhere. We haven't seen another soul since we arrived. Brian's eleven. He doesn't need to worry about bobcats and mountain lions."

My dad's eyes darkened, his face tightened. But then he said, "You're right, baby doll." He turned to me. "Brian, I made a mistake. They're probably deer tracks. You're not scared of deer, are you?"

"Steve," my mom said.

"Look," he said, coming over to her. "Today's supposed to be fun. I don't want it to be ruined. So I'm sorry for whatever I did." He cupped her cheek with his hand, then kissed her on the lips. "Okay?"

She hesitated.

"We'll stop in a bit, roll a spliff," he said quietly into her ear, but not so quietly I couldn't hear. "That'll clear up your headache."

"I suppose it might help..."

"Good," he said, and broke into a wolfish grin. Then he scooped her into his arms and ran along the path, ignoring her laughing protests to put her down.

I skipped to keep pace, and when my mom was back on her feet, I said, "What's a spliff?"

My mom ruffled my hair. "Just a cigarette, honey."

"The funny smelling ones?"

"That's right, angel. The funny smelling ones."

❊ ❊ ❊

Roughly ten minutes later we emerged from the shadowy forest and found ourselves standing under the bright blue sky and staring out over Black Canyon. My immediate impression was that the far side of the crevice seemed very close, and this made the two-thousand-foot rock walls seem all the more impressive. Large sections of them were blanketed in shadows, which, I guessed, was the reason for the canyon's name.

"Oh wow!" I said, shading my eyes with my hand to lessen the sun's glare.

"How's this for something?" my dad said proudly.

"Awesome, Dad!"

I hurried toward the edge.

"Don't go too close!" my mom called.

She didn't have to worry, though, because the ground didn't drop off suddenly. It angled downward from one rocky terrace to the next for some distance, each one covered with scrub and boulders.

I stopped at the edge of the first terrace and looked west along the canyon rim. "Hey!" I said to my parents, pointing to a promontory that stuck out over the lip of the canyon, almost like the tip of a ship about to sail off the end of the world. "Is that a lookout spot? Can we go there?"

"Sure, Brian," my mom said, coming up behind me. "But you're to stay with your father and me. No running off."

The lookout point was fenced in to prevent people falling to their deaths. I approached the fence hesitantly and looked down. I swallowed, and my stomach felt as if it had left my body. The bottom of the chasm was impossibly far down, the river that created it little more than a squiggly blue-white line.

I stared, mesmerized at how small everything looked. I'd never been this high above anything in my life, not even when my parents took me to the top of the Space Needle in Seattle for my mom's birthday dinner in March.

My dad, his arm hooked around my mom's shoulders, said the view was gorgeous and started laughing.

I frowned because I didn't get what was so funny.

Apparently my mom didn't either because she said, "What's so funny?"

"The view! It's gorges!" He spelled it out: "G-o-r-g-e-s."

My mom groaned.

"I don't get it," I said.

"Your father thinks he's funny, Brian. I just hope you don't develop his sense of humor."

"Why not? I think Dad's funny."

"Thanks, Brian," he said, leaning casually against the railing in a way that made my nonexistent stomach queasy. "Now, who's up for hiking to the bottom?"

"The bottom?" my mom said, her eyebrows lifting above the frame of her sunglasses. Her mouth made a pink O.

"Why not? People do it all the time," he told her. "There's gotta be a trail."

She joined him at the fence and peeked over the railing for the first time, hesitantly, like she thought something might streak up from the depth of the canyon and bite her nose off. "Are you serious, Steve? You want to hike all the way to the bottom?"

"We have all day. What else are we going to do?"

"We'll have to climb back up too, remember."

"I never forgot that in the first place. Look, Suz, it'll only take us a couple hours to get to the bottom, then a couple to get back up. The exercise will be good for us. You're always telling me to exercise more, right?"

"I'm never telling you to climb a mountain."

"It's not a mountain. It's a canyon."

"I don't know..."

"Brian's up for it. Aren't you, Brian?"

I wasn't. I was scared senseless by the idea. But I nodded my head.

"See?" my dad said. "Bri-guy's game."

"You sure you want to do this, Brian?" my mom asked.

I felt my dad's eyes on me. "Yeah, Mom. Totally."

She sighed. "I guess that means I'm outnumbered." She moved away from the railing, dusting her hands on the rear of her yellow shorts. "All right, Steve. Lead the way."

* * *

We continued the trek west, to the lowest saddle on the ridge, where we found a trail that descended below the rim into the inner canyon. This excited my dad, who increased his pace and kept shouting over his shoulder for my mom and me to keep up.

The trail switchbacked through Douglas fir and sunburst aspens before coming to a junction where a sign with an arrow pointing left read: "River Access. Permit Required."

My mom frowned. "You didn't say we needed a permit, Steve."

My dad shrugged. "I didn't know we did."

She harrumphed.

"It's true," he said. "Besides, you probably only need one during the summertime, when it's busier."

"How much did they cost?"

"Jesus, Suz. I just told you. I didn't know we needed one. So how am I supposed to know how much they cost?"

"What if a ranger catches us down here without one?"

"You and your rangers."

"We'll get fined. And the fine will be a lot more than the permit that you were too cheap to get."

"I didn't know we needed one!" he snapped.

I moved away from them and pretended to study a bush that had little red flowers sprouting among the green needles.

"If you had simply told me," my mom said, "I would have paid for it."

"Suz, I'm warning you..."

"What? You'll hit me?"

A long pause. Then my dad, softly: "You don't talk about that."

"Oh God," my mom said, and it sounded more like a moan than words. "What am I doing?"

"Don't say that..."

"Maybe we need a break..."

My dad's voice hardened. "You're going to do this? Right now?"

"It's not working, Steve. *We're* not working."

"You're going to throw away eight years together over a *camping permit?*"

"This isn't about a permit!"

Another long pause. I blinked away the tears welling in my eyes.

"Listen," my dad said. "I'm going to be working soon. I'll have money. We won't need to worry about shit like this. I'll take care of you."

My mom chuckled. "You're going to take care of me? Baby, I make more with my tips—"

"Honest money, Suz. Honest fucking money. You can get out of that shithole. You just give me a bit more time, you'll see."

My mom started making strange noises, and I finally turned around. My dad had his arms around her and was stroking her back. Her head was buried in his shoulder, and she was trembling. When she lifted her face, to wipe the tears from her eyes, she saw me watching them and said, "It's okay, Brian. Your father and I are just having an adult talk. Everything's okay. We're working some things out. Okay?"

"Okay," I said, and returned my attention to the bush.

* * *

The trail steepened immediately, weaving through more thickets of oak scrub and evergreens. Some sections squeezed between huge boulders, forcing my parents and me to progress single file. Other sections tiptoed along dangerous drops of ten or twenty feet. My dad walked bravely along the edges of these, tossing rocks over them now and then, while my mom and I kept our distance.

About three quarters of the way into the canyon we came across a flat rock outcrop where we stopped for lunch. Ravenous from walking all morning, we ate the peanut butter and jelly sandwiches we'd brought with us. We drank most of our water too. I could have easily finished the rest of mine, but my mom cautioned me to keep some for the hike back to the top of the chasm.

My parents were lying on their backs now, staring up at the sky, talking nicely to each other again. Adults are weird, I decided. I didn't know how they could hate each other one minute, then love each other the next. When I got in a fight with my friend Richard Strauss last month because he wouldn't give back the skateboard I'd lent him, I didn't talk to him for a full week. And I still didn't talk to Johnny Bastianello after he squeezed an entire bottle of glue into my pencil case, and that had been last year in grade five.

Anyway, I was glad my parents could make up so easily. I didn't want them to get a divorce. Sampson Cooper's parents divorced last year. At first it sounded cool because suddenly he had two homes where we could play, and his dad's place was in a new-smelling building with a swimming pool and tennis courts. But Sampson said moving between his parents' homes every weekend wasn't as fun as it sounded, and the swimming pool and tennis courts got boring after a while. Also, his dad had a girlfriend who was always trying to act like his mom, which he really didn't like.

My dad rolled onto his side and kissed my mom on the mouth. His hand rubbed her thigh up and down, then cupped one of her braless breasts. She moved it away, and he lay down again on his back.

I was sitting cross-legged about ten feet away from them, and I decided to lie down on my back too. I closed my eyes and enjoyed the warmth of the sun on my face. My mind drifted to Stephanie, the girl I'd kissed and was sort of dating. I couldn't wait to tell her that I'd hiked all the way to the bottom of a canyon. She thought I was super athletic, even though I wasn't, not really. She probably assumed this because she always watched me play fence ball at recess, a game that anybody could do okay at. Pretty much all you do is throw a tennis ball at a chain-link fence. If the ball gets stuck between the links you get five points. If it goes through, you get ten. If it rebounds without bouncing on the ground and someone catches it, you get out.

Stephanie and I had met last month in September. She was the new kid at our school and didn't have any friends. During morning and afternoon recesses and the hour-long lunch break in-between, she would sit by herself on the portable steps that faced where my friends and I played fence ball because the grade sevens always hogged the basketball court.

I knew what it was like to be the new kid, because I'd been in that same position only two years earlier when my family moved and I changed schools. So on the third or fourth day I'd seen her there, I worked up the nerve to go talk to her.

"Hi," I said, pounding the mitt of my baseball glove with my free hand nervously.

"Hi," she replied, smiling.

"Do you have any friends yet?"

"Not really."

"Do you want to play with us?"

"No, thank you."

"Oh."

I waited with her until the next fence ball game started, talking about nothing, making a bigger and bigger fool of myself. Then I went back and played my hardest in the new game, showing off. When the bell rang, I caught up to Stephanie and said, "Do you like this school so far?"

"It's okay."

Ralph Stevenson and Sampson Cooper and Will Lee ran by, singing "Brian and Stephanie sitting in a tree..."

I felt my cheeks blush. But I also felt special. I was talking to a *girl*—a pretty one too. They hadn't been brave enough to do that.

"Where do you live?" I asked her.

"On Amherst."

"I live on Cherokee. Do you want to walk home together?"

"Okay."

We started walking home together every day after that conversation. Stephanie's house was nice, much bigger than mine, white stucco with brown wood trim. On the third day she invited me inside. I was nervous. I had never been in a girl's house before. She showed me the kitchen, then the living room. We sat on the sofa for a bit, watching MTV. But all I could think about was whether I should sidle closer or take her hand, and whether her parents were going to come home and get us in trouble. Before I left she showed me her swimming pool in the backyard. I couldn't believe she had one. Sampson Cooper was my only friend who had a swimming pool, but he had to share it with everyone in his dad's building.

When Stephanie invited me to go swimming the next day in her pool, I said sure, but I purposely forgot to bring my swimming trunks to school. I was a skinny drink of water, as my dad called me, and I didn't want her to see me without my shirt on.

I'd been saving my allowance the last two weeks because I wanted to take her to the movies, and I figured I would probably need to pay for both of us. I currently had enough to buy the tickets, but I was going to keep saving until I could afford popcorn and Pepsis too.

My eyes fluttered open. The sun was getting hot on my face. Squinting up at the towering cliffs, the blue sky and white drifting clouds, I spotted a raptor wheeling back and forth on invisible air currents. Then, faintly, I heard what might have been rocks tumbling down the canyon walls.

I didn't mention this to my parents, because it might scare my mom. She might want to turn back. Then she and my dad might start fighting again. He might hit her this time; if I tried to stop him, he might hit me too, like he did two years ago, after my baby sister Geena died in her sleep. And if I'd learned anything from that experience, it was that fists hurt a heck of a lot more than the usual ruler or belt across your backside.

✳ ✳ ✳

With our stomachs full and our thirsts quenched, we embarked on the final leg of the descent. The canyon walls blocked out most direct sunlight now, and the sound of the churning river became louder and louder. Then, abruptly, the drainage channel we were following came to a steep drop-off.

"Give me a fucking break!" my dad said, arming sweat from his brow. "A dead end!"

My mom plopped down on a rock. "Can we rest here for a bit before we head back?"

My dad seemed surprised. "Head back? We're almost at the bottom."

"Do you plan on flying the rest of the way, Steve?"

"Maybe we can monkey down or something."

He started toward the drop-off.

"Steve, be careful!"

"Stop worrying so much." But he was indeed being careful, taking baby steps, testing each foothold before progressing forward. He looked like a man walking on thin ice who expected it to break beneath him at any moment.

Then he was at the edge, peering over it. He whistled. "Not too far to the bottom, fifty feet maybe. But it's a sheer drop." He turned back to us. "Let's look for a different route—"

Loose talus and scree shifted beneath his feet. A surprised expression flashed across his face. His arms shot into the air. Then he was gone.

My mom shouted. I would have shouted too, but every muscle had locked up inside me, so I couldn't move, breathe, make a sound.

"Steve!" my mom cried. She took a step forward, almost lost her footing, stopped. "*Steve!*"

He didn't answer.

"Oh God! Oh God! Oh God!" She repeated this litany over and over.

"Mom?" I managed in a tiny, breathless voice.

"He's gone!" she said. "He's gone!"

I'd never seen my mom so scared before, which in turn made me all the more scared. Finally my body responded to my thoughts and I started instinctively forward, to peer over the edge, to determine how far my dad had fallen.

"Brian!" my mom shrieked, grabbing my wrist and yanking me backward. She pulled so hard she tripped and fell onto her bum, pulling me down with her. Then she was hugging me tightly and sobbing and whispering a prayer, and when I got past the shock and bafflement of what just happened, I started crying as well.

\* \* \*

It took my mom and me an hour to find an alternative route to the canyon floor. At first my mom kept crying, albeit silently, like she didn't want me to know she was crying even though I could see the tears streaking her cheeks and could hear the occasional muffled sob. She kept telling me that my dad was okay, that he wasn't replying because he probably hit his head and was sleeping. I didn't believe her, the way I didn't believe her when she told me she wasn't angry at my dad after they'd had one of their fights. Which left one alternative: my dad was dead. But this proved impossible for me to comprehend. He was my dad. He couldn't be dead. He was *my dad*.

My mom was moving so quickly I had to half jog to keep up with her. To the left of us the canyon wall soared to the sky. To the right the river splashed and frothed, filling the air with a thunderous roar and a fine damp mist.

Soon the rocky ground turned to burnt grass, then to hardy shrubs—then to poison ivy, a huge patch that stretched from the chasm wall to the moss-covered rocks along the riverbank. I recognized what it was right away because I'd contracted a rash from it two summers before while my parents had been visiting their friends at a cottage in Colorado Springs. It had spread to every part of my body, from my face to my toes, and itched like crazy. The worst was when it got between your fingers and toes and began to bubble. I popped the bubbles, which leaked a yellowish puss and probably spread the toxin to other parts of me as well.

And those poison ivy plants had only come up to my shins. This stuff easily reached my waist and had leafs as broad as pages from a book. They ruffled in the slight breeze, almost as if they were beckoning me to come closer.

My mom had stopped before the patch. She was looking for an alternate path. Finally she said, "This is poison ivy, baby. We have to go through it."

"No way!"

"We have to, Brian. There's no way around it."

I glanced at the river. The poison ivy stopped at the rocky bank. "Maybe we can walk along the edge of the river?"

"Those rocks look really sharp, hon, and they're covered with moss. If you slipped on them, you could cut your leg wide open. Or get washed away by the river. Now, all you have to do is hold your hands above your head, like this." She demonstrated.

"If you don't let the leaves touch your skin, you won't catch anything."

"But the poison will still stick to my clothes."

"There's nothing we can do about that, honey. And I'm not leaving you here by yourself."

She pioneered a path through the poison ivy patch. I followed, holding my hands above my head as instructed. When we reached the far side, I examined my hands, half-convinced I could already see welts forming. I was wondering what Stephanie would think if she saw me covered in yucky red splotches and pussy bubbles when my mom stifled a yelp, then burst into a run. I looked up and saw the yellow of my dad's jacket in the distance.

✱ ✱ ✱

He was lying on his back beneath the skeletal branches of an old, twisted tree that looked as though it had been dead for a real long time. Bloody gashes and ugly purple bruises covered much of his body, almost as if someone had shoved him in one of those industrial dryers at the coin laundry alongside a handful of razor blades and put the machine on permanent press.

Nevertheless, he had a pulse. He was alive.

My mom had a fully stocked first-aid kit in her backpack, and we spent the next half hour plucking pine needles and clumps of dirt from his wounds, dousing them with iodine, then taping bandages over the larger ones. I thought we did a pretty good job, but my mom was worried about broken bones and other internal injuries we couldn't see.

"How are we going to get him back to the top?" I said, staring up the canyon walls. They looked impossibly high when you were at the bottom.

My mom didn't reply.

"Mom?"

"Do you know how to get back to the campsite, honey?"

"It's just up, then...that way." I pointed east.

She didn't say anything.

"Mom?"

"We walked for a long time, Brian. I wasn't paying any attention. I let your father take charge. I'm not sure I remember where we came out of the woods the first time."

"The first time?"

"When we saw the canyon for the first time. If I can't find our car..."

"I can find it," I said. "I'm sure I can."

"No, baby. You're going to have to stay here with your father."

"Without you?"

"You have to be here in case he wakes up. If he does, he's going to be scared and in a lot of pain. You need to keep him calm, tell him I've gone for help, I'll be back soon."

"You don't want me to come with you?"

"You have to look after your father. You have to keep a fire going too. I might not be back until dark, so you need to keep the fire going so I can find you. Can you do this?"

"I want to come with you."

"No, Brian, you have to stay here. Now, if your father does wake up, he's also going to be thirsty, so give him some water—but not all of it. Not right away. You have to make it last."

"But I can get more from the river."

She glanced at the river. I did too. It was roaring and frothing and moving really, really fast, reminding me of the rivers I saw people white-water rafting down on TV. Suddenly I wasn't so sure I wanted to get close to it. I didn't even know how to swim.

My mom took my hands in hers and looked me in the eyes. "You will *not* go near that river, Brian. Do you hear me? No matter what. It's a lot stronger than you think. It will sweep you straight away. Do you understand me?"

"Yeah, Mom."

"Tell me you won't go near that river."

"I won't go near the river."

"Promise me."

"I promise."

"I'm trusting you, Brian." She stood. "Now c'mon. Let's find some firewood and get that fire going."

* * *

We scavenged a good stockpile of sun-bleached deadfall, along with bark and fungi for tinder, and twigs and smaller sticks for kindle. Then my mom started a fire and gave me her bronze Zippo and showed me how to restart the flames if they went out. Finally she hugged me, kissed me on the cheek, told me to be brave and to stay away from the river, then left the way we had come, back through the poison ivy patch.

As soon as she disappeared from sight a heavy cloak of fear and loneliness settled over me as the seriousness of the situation hit home. I was on my own. My mom was gone, my dad unconscious. I was in a strange, unfamiliar place. I felt tiny and helpless next to the grandeur of the canyon and the power of the river. I didn't have any food and only a bit of water.

What if something bad happened? I wondered. What if my dad had a heart attack? What if there was an avalanche? I recalled the sound of the tumbling rocks earlier. What if one crushed my dad's head, or mine? My mom would return with help only to find us dead, our brains splattered everywhere...

*Stop it.*

I settled next to my dad, rested my chin on my knees, and watched him for a bit. His face appeared pale and shiny in the bright afternoon light, like the flesh of a slug. His breathing was slurpy, like when you sucked the last dregs of soda through a straw. His chest moved up and down, barely.

I touched his forehead. It was really hot, and I didn't think that was from the sun. I touched my forehead to compare, and his was definitely hotter.

Did that mean he had a fever? I pondered this, because I

thought you could only get a fever when you had the flu.

A fat black ant crawled up his neck and onto his chin. I picked it off, squished it between my index finger and thumb, then tossed its broken body away. Shortly after another industrious ant, smaller than the first, crawled up over his ear and along his jawline. I was about to pick it off as well, but then it beelined toward the wound below my dad's right eye. I decided to watch it, to see how it would react to the bed of exposed liver-red meat. Ants ate other insects, which made them carnivores. But this one simply stopped before the wound, its antennae twitching, feeling, then turned away. I pinched it between my fingers and dropped it on the gash. It shot straight off, like it was scared, though I didn't think ants could get scared. It ran up over my dad's closed eyelid, over the ridge of his eyebrow, and disappeared into his greasy, clotted black hair.

Feeling bad for letting it find refuge in his hair, I promptly squished any other ants that came close to him. There turned out to be a good number, and I searched the ground until I found the sandy-hole entrance to their subterranean dwelling. I stuck a twig in the hole, so the twig stood erect like a flagpole, effectively blocking any more ants from emerging.

I didn't want to look at my dad any longer, so I took one of my *Archies* from my backpack and tried to read it. After a few minutes of staring blankly at the same page, I forced myself to focus on the words in the speech balloons. They weren't funny or interesting. They were just words.

I closed the comic book and stared the way my mom had gone, willing her to come back soon.

❋ ❋ ❋

Night came first, and quickly. The strip of sky overhead turned yellow, then pink, then red, then purplish-black, like a giant had pummeled it with its fists, leaving behind a broken mess. The Milky Way glowed impossibly far away, but the starlight didn't reach the canyon floor, so it was pitch black outside the circle of firelight. I knew this because when I went to pee I couldn't even see my feet. Only darkness. Emptiness. A void. Like I was a tiny organism at the bottom of the ocean. That's how it felt anyway.

The drone of the now invisible river continued unabated, and my stomach kept growling hungrily. I hadn't eaten anything since lunch on the rock outcrop, and that hadn't been much, just the peanut butter and jelly sandwich, and the apple.

My thirst, however, was even worse. I had about three inches of water left in my water bottle. My dad had less. I'd taken a sip from mine after my mom had left, but that was all. It needed to last me until she returned...whenever that was.

And why wasn't she back already? According to my wristwatch, it was 10:07 p.m. That meant she had been gone for nearly eight hours. It should only have taken her two, maybe three hours to return to the campground, fifteen minutes to drive to that town we passed on the way in, Montrose, or whatever it was called. Another two/three hours to bring help to us. That was seven or so hours in total. So where was she? Had something happened to her? Had she fallen off a cliff like my dad had?

No, I wouldn't let myself think that. She was coming. She would be here any minute now—

My dad was staring at me.

I was so startled I cried out and toppled backward.

Then, just as quickly, I scrambled forward.

"Dad?" I said.

"Where's...your mother?" His voice was dry, raspy. He spoke softly, as if each word was an effort.

"She went to get help. She'll be back soon."

"When...?"

"When did she go? This afternoon, about eight hours ago."

"Eight...?"

"She'll be here soon, Dad."

"Water?"

"Here." I grabbed his water bottle and tipped a bit of water into his mouth. His Adam's apple bobbed up and down. His tongue slithered over his cracked lips, probing for every last drop.

"More," he said.

"Mom said we have to save it—"

"More!"

I poured a bit more into his mouth.

"More."

"Mom said—"

His hand moved amazingly fast, snagging my wrist.

"Ow!" I cried.

"Let go," he said.

I obeyed. The bottle toppled onto its side. My dad released my wrist, retrieved the bottle, and finished what was left.

He smacked his lips weakly. "Where's yours?" he said.

"I—It's finished," I lied.

"Show me."

"It's all gone."

He tried to grab me again, but I scuttled out of the way this time.

He maneuvered himself onto his elbows. In the firelight his face was a severe mask of strained muscles and hard angles. Sweat beaded his skin, making it shinier than ever. His dusty eyes swept the area, locking onto my water bottle, which was propped against my backpack a few feet away.

He held a shaking hand toward it. "Give me it, Brian."

"Mom said we have to save what we have."

"Give it!"

I hesitated. Under normal circumstances I would never oppose my dad's wishes like this. But my dad wasn't acting like my dad. He was acting like a stranger.

"Brian," he said more gently, as if realizing he was scaring me. "Please. I'm...de'drated."

I retrieved the water bottle and handed it to him. He finished all the water in two gulps, tossed the bottle aside, and lay back down. He closed his eyes.

"Dad?"

He didn't reply.

"Dad?"

Nothing.

"*Dad?* Are you okay?"

"I'm not your fucking dad, Brian."

I stared at him, confused, waiting for him to explain what he'd meant. But he didn't. He fell back to sleep almost immediately, once again making that slurpy breathing sound.

*I'm not your fucking dad, Brian.*

❈ ❈ ❈

In the nightmare my dad and I were in some kind of treehouse, a big one like in the *Return of the Jedi*, only ours was a lot closer to the ground, and bad people were trying to climb the tree to get in. I could see them huddled together below, conspiring. My dad kept shouting orders at me, getting angrier and angrier because I didn't understand what he wanted me to do. At one point he got so mad he hit me. When he tried to hit me again I knocked aside his arm with mine and realized I was stronger than him. I shoved him to the ground and told him to stop hitting my mom. I was telling him this in a reasonable voice, but I was shouting too. A part of me kept waiting for him to say he wasn't my dad, for him to tell me to go away, but he never did. He just kept yelling at me to stop the invaders—

I woke to blackness, disorientation, my dad hissing dangerously, telling me to wake up.

"I'm awake, Dad," I whispered. "What's wrong? What happened?"

"Bear. There."

His words zapped me like an electrical shock. I looked in the direction he was looking, past the still-burning fire. I didn't see anything but darkness.

"Where...?"

A forceful expulsion of air startled me, louder than that which any human could make. A second later I saw the bear. I had been staring right at it, though it was little more than a black patch against the black night.

*Holy crap!* I thought, sucking back a mouthful of dread.

My mind reeled.

*Why's it just standing there?*

*What's it doing?*

I wanted to ask my dad these questions, but my throat was suddenly too small, my tongue too thick.

*"Brian?"* my dad hissed.

"What?" I managed.

"Scare it away."

*Scare it away?*

"I can't."

"Brian!"

The bear—which had been investigating my mom's backpack, I realized—now swung its huge round head toward me. Its eyes shone silver. It snorted and made deep throaty sounds while pawing the ground with its long claws.

"Go away!" my dad said, waving his arm weakly. "Ga! Go away!"

The bear lumbered into the firelight. Its short glossy hair was a bluish-black, and it was skinny, with disproportionally large shoulder humps. Its ears stood erect and rounded, its muzzle narrow and grizzled brown, ending in a broad black nose.

It roared, flashing yellow canines, which dripped with saliva.

My bladder gave out. I barely noticed.

"Ga!" my dad croaked. "Go! Scat! Brian!"

The bear roared again, shaking its head from side to side.

Instinct screamed at me to run away, but I knew I couldn't. If I ran, the bear would chase me, like dogs do. And bears were fast. Someone once told me they were faster than people. So it would catch me, rip me apart, eat my guts.

"Go away!" I yelled, flapping my hands madly.

The bear reared up on its hind legs and roared a third time, reminding me of a bear I had seen at a circus a few years ago.

This gave me a crazy boost of courage—*it's just a stupid animal*—and before I knew what I was doing I was springing toward the fire. I snatched a burning stick from the flames and threw it at the bear. It bounced off its head.

The bear chuffed, as if surprised.

I flung another stick, then another, shrieking nonsense all the while.

The bear started huffing and clacking its teeth while backing away. Euphoric with anticipated victory, I scooped up a smoking log and heaved it at the monstrous thing. When it struck the ground it exploded in sparks.

The bear fled.

❊ ❊ ❊

"Will it come back?" I asked my dad, who was staring in the direction the bear had gone.

"More wood, fire," he rasped. "Now!"

I chose a big fat log from the stockpile and dumped it onto the bed of smoldering ashes. For a moment I was afraid I had ruined the fire. But then flames appeared, licking up the sides of the log. I added some smaller sticks and dry pine needles and anything else that would burn. As I was doing this I detected an icky, sulfuric smell. A moment later I noticed that my hands and forearms were waxy smooth. I'd burned off all the small dark hairs when I'd stuck my hands in the fire to grab the log.

My dad rolled onto his side and began coughing. It sounded like he had a really bad cold, like he was hawking up phlegm... and then I saw it wasn't phlegm, it was blood.

"Dad!" I rushed to his side, but he shoved me away. Finally he stopped coughing and eased himself onto his back, groaning with the effort. His mouth was smeared bright red, as if he had been pigging out on strawberries. He folded his hands together on top of his chest and closed his eyes, looking eerily how my dead grandma had looked in her coffin at the funeral home.

"Dad? Are you okay?"

He didn't reply, and I wasn't sure whether he was ignoring me or sleeping.

"Dad?"

Silence.

I checked his pulse. It was faint, but beating.

*  *  *

That night seemed to stretch forever. I had never been so frightened or jumpy in my life. Every unexplained sound sent my heart galloping. I knew bears were supposed to be more scared of people than people were of bears, yet the one that had attacked us was awfully skinny, which meant it was probably sick—and desperate. It wouldn't hesitate to eat my dad and me. I was one hundred percent sure of that.

As the minutes inched by, I found myself wondering what I would do if the bear returned and I couldn't scare it away again. I could run. But what about my dad? I couldn't leave him here... could I? Yet what else *could* I do? He couldn't walk. I couldn't carry him. I'd have no choice. I'd have to leave him.

*And he isn't really my dad.*

I frowned. Was this true? After all, my dad had been sick when he'd told me this. He'd had a fever. Maybe he didn't know what he was saying. Maybe he was...what was that word? Delirious? Yeah, he was delirious. Of course he was my father. I looked like him, didn't I? That's what my mom was always telling me. "You're just as handsome as your father, Brian. You're going to break a lot of hearts one day."

I went over to my dad, knelt beside him, and studied his face. My frown deepened, because now that I was looking at him, really *looking* at him, I didn't think I resembled him at all. We both had dark hair, and we both had eyes a comparable shade of gray. But that's where the similarities ended and the differences began. Like his eyebrows, for example. I'd never paid any attention to his eyebrows before. They were thick, tilting upward at the outer ends. Mine were thin, arching in the middle, like upside-down smiles. And his nose was long and straight. I touched mine, which curved slightly, like a ski jump. And his jaw and chin were square. Mine were oval. And his head was proportioned normally to his body, while mine was too big. It's why my friends sometimes called me Bighead, or Humpty Dumpty, or Brian the Brain, even though I wasn't that smart.

"Dad?"

He didn't reply.

"Dad?"

No reply.

I pressed my ear to his parted mouth and heard his wet, raspy breathing, almost like he was gargling mouthwash. I should have been relieved, but I wasn't.

I was angry.

"Why don't I look like you, Dad?"

No reply.

"Why haven't you ever liked me?"

No reply.

"Are you my dad, my *real* dad?"

No reply.

"Why do you hit Mom?"

No reply.

"I've heard you. When I'm in my room, and you think I'm sleeping, I hear you yell at her about Geena dying, and hit her. I hear her cry. She tells me the bruises are from other things, but I know they're from when you hit her."

No reply.

"I don't think you're my dad."

No reply.

"I don't think you are."

I stared at him for a long, silent moment, then went back to the fire to keep watch.

\* \* \*

I must have fallen asleep at some point because when I opened my eyes the sun was high in the sky and it was warm, the way it had been yesterday around lunchtime.

Squinting, I glanced about for the bear, half convinced it would be hanging out somewhere nearby, watching me. It wasn't. However, I was startled to discover about a dozen crows perched in the bare branches of the old, twisted tree. Every one of their beady black eyes seemed to be trained on my dad and me.

When had they arrived? And what did they want?

My dad? Did they know he was dying? Were they after an easy meal?

"Go away," I told them.

They remained, staring greedily.

I tossed a stone at the closest one. It cawed, which almost sounded like a bray of witchy laughter.

I turned my attention to my dad. He was in the same position he'd been in earlier, only his hands were no longer clasped together on his chest; they were sprawled to either side of him, as though he were making lazy snow angels in the dirt. His skin appeared pale, sickly, almost yellow. His face seemed thin and older than usual.

My hands were itching and I scratched them absently, thinking about how hungry and thirsty I was, and how there was no food or water.

And where was my mom? She definitely should have been back already. She'd been gone for almost a full day.

"Mom!" I shouted, my voice cracking and echoing throughout the chasm.

She didn't answer.

"Mom?" I repeated, though more to myself this time.

I picked up the water bottle my dad had tossed aside and upended it to my lips. No water came out. Not a drop.

I looked at the river. My mom had warned me not to go near it. She'd said it could sweep me away. I didn't doubt that. But I didn't have to go in it very deep, did I? I could stop at the edge, just close enough to fill the water bottle...

My ankles began to itch. I snuck my hands beneath my pant cuffs and scratched—and realized the skin there was lumpy. I yanked my hands away as if I had been bitten. I rolled up the cuffs.

Red splotches marred my skin. They resembled puffy red birthmarks.

Poison ivy!

"Shoot!" I said, resisting the temptation to scratch more. "Shoot!"

"Water..."

I snapped my head toward my dad. His eyes were open but hooded.

"You drank it all!" I said.

"Water..."

"There's none."

"River..."

"Mom told me I can't go near it."

"Brian..." He cleared his throat. "I need...we need...water..."

"I promised Mom I wouldn't go near it."

"I'm lying."

I frowned at him. Lying about what? About not being my father?

Something shifted inside me. Hope?

"Water..." he said.

Lying or dying? I wondered. Maybe he said he was dying...

That something inside me vanished.

"Brian..."

"What?" I griped. I felt hot, tired, confused.

But he had closed his eyes again.

The minutes ticked by. The sun beat down on the back of my neck. I worked my jaw to generate saliva, then swallowed with difficulty, as if my throat were clogged with a roll of pennies. I rubbed my hands on a large rock that jutted from the ground, thinking that by doing this I wouldn't spread the poison ivy to other parts of my body. I rubbed my ankles on a different part of the same rock. I tried not to think about my dad who wasn't my dad dying, or the crows, waiting to fight over his corpse. I tried not to think about the long, bleak day ahead of me, or about spending another night here if my mom didn't return.

I tried not to think about any of this, but in the end it was all I could think about.

After a bit, I got up and went to the river.

* * *

My mom had been right. The mossy rocks were slippery and sharp. I kept to the pebbly ground when I could and only stepped on the rocks when I had to. Then I was at the edge of the river. I had become so used to its continuous drone I had stopped hearing it, but now it sounded as loud as a million bees buzzing in unison. And it was moving so fast! I glanced east, then west, searching for a calmer section, but it was swift-moving and frothy for as far as I could see in either direction.

I stood on a large slab of rock that sloped downward into the water at maybe a forty-degree angle. I lowered myself to my bum, then butt-hopped forward. Stretching my right arm as far as I could, I submerged my water bottle into the rushing water, pointing the mouth upriver. The frigid water stung my hand and tried to tear the bottle from my grip. I held onto it tightly until it had filled up. Then I raised it in the air triumphantly.

That wasn't so hard, I thought.

Tucking it in my pocket, I attempted to fill my dad's bottle next. Almost immediately, however, it slipped from my grasp. I cried out in dismay, lunged forward—instinctively, stupidly— and skidded down the rock into the river.

I was waist deep in the freezing water before I knew what

was happening and still sliding on the slick surface of the rock. Then my feet touched flat ground. I tried to stand. The current yanked me along with it, away from land.

"Dad!" I shouted. "Help!"

I was pin-wheeling my arms, trying to keep myself upright.

"Dad!"

I could see him by the fire. He was propped up on his elbows, watching me.

"Dad! Help!"

He didn't move.

I flailed toward shore. Top heavy, my feet shot out from beneath me. My head dunked underwater. I opened my mouth, to cry out, and swallowed icy water. Then I was moving, pushed and dragged by the current. I somersaulted, didn't know up from down. My eyes bulged with fear, but I couldn't see anything...or could I? Yes, the sky! It was rippled and blurry and blue. I reached for it, kicked and kicked.

My head crashed through the surface of the river. I sucked back a mouthful of air and spat it out again in a fit of coughing. My throat burned. My lungs ached inside my chest.

As I struggled to remain afloat, I gagged on more water, gasped for air. My body suddenly felt as if it were made of lead. I was going to sink. I was going to drown—

I smashed into a rock. I tried grabbing hold of it, but it was too slippery, there were no handholds, and then it was behind me.

The river spun me twice, and when I was facing forward again another rock reared up in front of me.

Somehow I managed to clasp onto this one and not let go. Water crashed over my shoulders, roared in my ears.

The rock that had stopped me, I noticed with relief, was the first of several that protruded from the water in a line like well-worn molar teeth.

Moving from one to the next, I made slow but steady progress toward shore until I could stand once again.

Thankfully the riverbank here was not as steep as where I'd

slid in, and I was able to clamber onto dry land, where I collapsed onto my chest and spewed my guts out.

* * *

Back at the campsite my dad was still propped on his elbows, still watching me.

"Water...?" he said.

"I lost our bottles."

Something flitted across his face. It took me a moment to realize it was fear. Then a kind of loathing filled his eyes, a kind of hate. I was convinced he was going to jump up and smack me before I remembered he didn't have the strength to do that, even if it's what he wanted to do.

Instead he slumped onto his back.

"I can go get some," I said. "I can bring it back in my hands?"

He didn't reply, and I didn't persist. I didn't really want to go back to the river anyway.

I turned my attention to my right hand. A half-moon gash split my palm from thumb to pinky finger. I didn't recall when or how it happened, but it must have been when I'd grabbed onto one of the rocks.

I scavenged the first-aid kit from my mom's backpack and tended to the wound. The white cotton bandage bloomed red immediately. I unwrapped it and applied a fresh one, securing it more tightly. It turned just as red just as quickly.

"Dad," I said, "my cut won't stop bleeding."

He didn't reply.

"Dad!"

He mumbled something. I caught "guy" and thought he was saying "Bri-guy."

"Huh?" I said.

"Guy...knocked up your mom..."

"Who?"

"Left..."

"Who?

"Because...you..."

"Me?"

"Didn't want..."

"What—?"

But I understood.

*My real dad didn't want me. That's why he left my mom. Not because of her. Because of me.*

*Because I was born.*

❊ ❊ ❊

Over the course of the day the old twisted tree had become host to at least fifty crows. The black birds had taken up residence on every rotting branch, turning the tree into a living monstrosity, like something out of a dark fairytale, or a haunted forest. Aside from the odd caw, or the leathery beat of wings, however, they remained eerily quiet.

The last of the sunlight had faded to dusk a few minutes ago, and although I could no longer see the ghastly tree or the greedy crows, I knew they were still there, still watching my dad and me with their unreadable black eyes, biding their time until they could feast.

The gash across my palm had stopped bleeding some time ago, so I was no longer worried I was going to bleed to death. But my poison ivy was worse than ever. It had spread everywhere. To my ankles, my stomach, my upper arms, my neck, behind my ears. Even to the dreaded area between my fingers. The itching there was so intense, the small puss bubbles so intolerable, I wanted to chop off my hands.

My mom had yet to return, and I'd resigned myself to the fact that I would be spending another night just me and my dad who wasn't my dad.

*My dad who wasn't my dad.*

I glared at him in the firelight, and for the first time in my life

I felt nothing for him. No love, no fear, no respect. Nothing.

Actually, that wasn't true, I realized. I did feel something. I felt cheated. He was a phony, an impostor, a stranger who'd only pretended to be my dad to make my mom happy. He had been lying to me for my entire life—or, at least, since I was three. I knew this because there was a photograph in my baby book that showed him and my mom and me together at my third birthday party.

So what happened to my real dad? Did he really leave my mom and me because I was born? Where did he go? Why didn't he ever come back to see me grown up? Did he try? Did my fake dad send him away...?

A noise distracted me from these reflections. I glanced about, surprised to find the night had already deepened to an ebony black. I didn't see anything.

It could have been my imagination, or a falling rock, or the crows.

*Or the bear.*

I waited, listened.

Nothing.

Not the bear.

But it would be coming. I was sure of that. It would be coming because it was sick and starving and knew it had an easy meal—an easy *two* meals.

I stood decisively. Maybe I should just go, just start running. But which way? What if I ran straight into the bear? By myself? Without a fire?

I looked at my fake dad. He resembled a corpse. He wasn't one, not yet. Sometimes his breathing would go real quiet, and sometimes it would go real loud. Now it was real loud. It almost sounded as though he were snoring.

Could the bear hear him? I wondered. Was it coming for us this minute? And when it arrived, who would it attack? My dad was helpless, yeah, but the bear didn't know that. Chances were, it would go for me, because I was smaller.

I added another log and more sticks to the fire, feeding the flames. All the while my eyes kept drifting to my dad.

*Maybe if he was farther away from the fire, the bear would go for him first. Maybe it would stuff itself silly, and it would leave me alone...*

"Dad?" I said, stepping quietly toward him.

He didn't reply.

"Dad?"

His hair was drenched with perspiration, plastered to his head like when you get out of a swimming pool. His eye sockets seemed to have grown bigger, while somehow sinking into his face. Black stubble covered his jaw, forming a thick tangle that could almost be called a beard.

I seized one of his ankles in each hand and dragged him away from the fire, toward the river. He was heavy, and it took all my strength. I stopped after twenty feet or so. I didn't want him too far away in case the bear didn't see him and came straight for me.

I dropped his legs and was about to return to the fire when his eyes opened and he said, "Brian...?"

"You're not my dad."

"What, doing...?"

"You're not my dad."

I left him.

\* \* \*

The bear arrived an hour later. I couldn't see it; the night was too black, the shadows outside the reach of the fire too thick. But I heard it grunting and snuffling. I crouched next to the flames, statue-still, hyper alert, praying it ignored me.

A scream. Weak. My dad.

Another one, so high-pitched it sounded like it belonged to a woman.

I plugged my ears with my fingers and kept them plugged long after the screams had stopped.

\* \* \*

It took the bear forever to eat my dad. It kept making strange chuffing sounds, like when you swallow too quickly and the food gets stuck in your throat. Above the constant rush of the river I heard bones breaking, cartilage crackling, like when you tear a wing from a barbecued chicken, only much louder.

Then, finally, the munching sounds stopped.

Later, I tried to sleep. I couldn't. My body was exhausted, but my mind was wired. I rolled from side to side, from back to front. The poison ivy itched maddeningly.

I ended up pacing to keep warm in the dark, frigid morning for what seemed like hours. Then, in the silvered light of breaking dawn, I made out my dad...or what remained of him. For a moment my brain couldn't recognize what it was seeing because my dad no longer conformed to the shape and form of a man. He was more like a pile of clothes tossed haphazardly on the floor.

I went closer.

His red tank-top was split down the middle. His stomach was slit open. White ribs, several snapped in half, jutted into the air, glistening wetly like a mouthful of monster teeth. Everything they used to protect, all his organs and guts, were missing, leaving an empty, sagging cavity. Both his legs were chewed to the bone. Oddly his left forearm and his face were perfectly intact, though covered with blood splatter.

His eyes stared blankly at nothing.

I returned to the dying fire, shrugged my backpack over my shoulder, and went looking for my mom.

\* \* \*

I found her on the other side of the poison ivy patch, a little ways along the steep path we'd followed to reach the canyon floor.

"Mom!" I shouted, waving my hands over my head ecstatically.

She stood there for a moment, as if she didn't recognize me, or thought I was a mirage. Then she called my name—*shrieked* it, actually—and ran toward me.

She scooped me into a mammoth hug. I think she tried to lift me off my feet, but either I was too heavy or she was too weak and we collapsed to the ground. She started laughing and crying and kissing me all over.

* * *

My mom looked as bad as I felt. Her hair was messy and knotted, her face and clothes streaked with dirt and sweat, her hands enflamed with poison ivy. But she was smiling like she'd just won a million bucks.

"Oh baby, oh God, oh baby," she cooed. "I couldn't find the car...then night came...then I got even more lost..." She stiffened. Her smile faltered. "Where's your father, angel? Why'd you leave him by himself? What happened?"

I told her.

* * *

Well, not everything. I told her a bear ate him. But I didn't tell her I dragged him from the fire to use as bait. I said the bear did that, dragged him away.

I wasn't sure how I'd expected her to react to this news, but she surprised me by not reacting at all.

Face impassive, she stood, ordered me to wait where I was, and went to confirm my dad's death for herself.

* * *

When she returned I could tell she was super upset because she didn't say anything to me. In fact, she barely looked at me, just marched past where I was waiting, back up the canyon wall. I fell into line behind her, relieved to be with her again, and even more relieved to be returning to the campsite.

After five or ten minutes we came to an eighty-foot-long iron chain that had been installed in the drainage passage we were ascending.

"Why's this here, Mom?" I asked. "To help people climb?"

She didn't answer me.

"Mom?"

No answer. She was breathing as heavily as I was. Perspiration saturated her white top, making it cling to her shoulder blades and her bare breasts. She drew a hand across her forehead.

"I don't think this is the right way," I went on. "We never saw the chain on our way down—"

"Shut up, Brian! Please! Just…shut up!"

I frowned at her. She was looking at me in a way she had never looked at me before. I didn't know if she was sad or angry or what. Then her legs gave out and she dropped to her knees. She leaned forward and vomited.

I stared, terrified. I had never seen her puke before.

When she finished, I tried to help her—but she pushed me away.

My eyes narrowed. "What's wrong, Mom?"

She glared at me sidelong. "Did you move him?" she asked quietly. A string of saliva dripped from her mouth. She didn't seem to care.

"Huh?" I said.

"Your father. Did you move him?"

"No," I said, telling myself I wasn't lying, because she didn't ask me *when* I moved him. And I didn't move him today. So I wasn't lying, not really.

Besides, how could she know I'd moved him?

"There were footprints," she said, as if reading my mind.

"Footprints?" I said, pretending not to understand. But I thought did. My insides turned to mush.

"Next to...drag marks. He was dragged. You dragged him."

"The bear dragged him."

"They were your footprints, Brian!" she blurted, and I thought she might throw up again. She didn't. She just kept looking at me, but in a pleading way now, as if she wanted me to tell her she was wrong.

But what could I say? How could I explain why my footprints were next to the drag marks?

"Did you do something to Geena, Brian?" she said.

Geena? Why was she asking me about Geena?

"No, Mom, Geena died in her sleep," I said earnestly. "I didn't do anything to her. I swear."

&ast; &ast; &ast;

Geena died one month after her first birthday. My parents had gone to the neighbors who lived four doors down the street. I was only nine then, too young to babysit, but my parents didn't want to pay for a real babysitter so they left me in charge. Geena had already been fed and put to bed. All I had to do was keep an eye on her, and if there was any trouble, to call the Applebee's. Their telephone number was stuck to the fridge with a Budweiser magnet. My parents said they would be home around eight o'clock. They didn't return until midnight or so. I'd fallen asleep on the sofa in the living room, and I was just waking up, clearing the fuzz from my head, when my mom started screaming hysterically from Geena's room. Then she was shouting, and my fake dad was shouting, and I was asking what was wrong, but nobody would tell me.

An ambulance arrived a few minutes later. The serious-looking paramedics took Geena to Craig Hospital. No one there could save her though. She'd been dead for too long.

Over the next couple days specially trained police officers came to our house to comfort my parents and me while Geena's death was investigated. At one point a detective asked me if I had been alone all evening, if anyone had come over, if Geena had been behaving differently, and a bunch of other questions. I told him Geena had been sleeping quietly. I had been watching TV, then I fell asleep. That was all that happened, all I could remember. I think he believed me. *I* believed me.

Since then, however, I've always wondered whether maybe I did do something to Geena after all. Because every once in a while I would have the same memory, sometimes when I was awake, sometimes when I was asleep. I'm standing by Geena's crib, looking down at her, and I hate her. I mean, I really, really hate her, for no reason at all. I hate that she is so small. I hate that she is so unaware. I hate how she looks at me with her big black eyes. I hate how she kicks her pudgy legs and arms. And in the memory I see myself reaching down, into the crib, and pinching her nose between my index finger and thumb. And when Geena begins crying loudly, *squealing*, I cover her mouth with my other hand. And then I begin counting Mississippis to fifty...

✳ ✳ ✳

"Geena died in her sleep, Mom," I said again. "That's what the doctor said—"

"And I believed him!" my mom said, pushing stringy hair from her face. "I believed him, I believed him. You were her older brother, you would never do something to hurt her. Why would you? You wouldn't, so that's what I believed. She just stopped breathing..."

"That's what happened, Mom."

"I don't believe you, Brian! God forgive me, I don't, not anymore..."

Convulsions shook her body.

"Mom..." Her crying made me want to cry too. I patted her head.

"Don't touch me, Brian!" She batted my hand away. "Why did you drag your father away from the fire?"

"I didn't."

"Don't lie to me! Stop lying! Stop it! I saw your footprints!"

"Are you mad at me, Mom?"

"Mad at you? Mad? *You murdered your father*—"

"He's not my dad!" I shouted, tears bursting from my eyes.

Her mouth gaped wide in surprise.

"Not my *real* dad!" I plowed on. "He told me! *You* lied to me! You both lied to me! He's not my real dad, that's why he's never liked me—"

"He stopped liking you, Brian," my mom snapped, almost wearily, "because he thought you killed Geena! Everybody thought that! Don't you remember the police, the family court, the judge? Don't you remember any of that?"

I frowned, because I didn't. Not exactly. It was foggy, dream-like, like the memory of standing at the crib, looking down at Geena.

"I was the only one who believed you, Brian. I've always believed you. But now...not now. You killed Geena. You killed your father. My boy, my baby boy...why...?"

She covered her face with her hands and curled into a ball.

✳ ✳ ✳

I studied my mom coldly, processing what she had told me. Everyone knew I'd killed Geena? Was that really why my dad never liked me? Why we moved to a new neighborhood shortly after Geena died? Why I started going to a different school?

If this was true—everyone knew I'd killed Geena—and my mom told the police I dragged my fake dad away from the fire so the bear would eat him and not me, then they'd probably believe her over me. They might even go to my house to search for clues and stuff. They might check my fort in the backyard. If they did that, they would find the squirrel heads. I got rid of the bodies, tossed them into some bushes in Cushing Park, but I kept the heads in a shoebox so I could look at them now and then. They had dried up and were just bones and teeth and tufts of fur. But if the police found those, they would know I liked to kill things, and they might change their minds and arrest me for killing Geena, and for helping the bear kill my dad.

They might put me in jail and throw away the key.

I didn't want them to do that.

I couldn't let them do that.

* * *

I chose a rock the size of baseball and approached my mom from behind. She was still folded into a ball, still holding her head in her hands, crying. I didn't want to do this. I really didn't. But she had forced me to. She was going to tell on me. And maybe she would be happy being dead. She would be with Geena and my fake dad.

I swung the rock.

* * *

I hit her squarely on the top of the head. The impact jarred my hand and caused me to drop the rock. Instead of dying, though, my mom sat up. Her left hand went to the top of her skull and she stared at me in shock and horror. Then she was pushing herself away from me.

I scanned the ground for the rock, saw it a few feet away. I snatched it up and turned back to my mom. She was still trying to get away from me and trying to stand at the same time. Luckily she didn't have the strength, or the balance, and she kept falling to her side.

I raised the rock.

"Brian!" she said, protecting her head with her arms.

The first blow deflected off one of her forearms. The second struck her in the same spot as before.

"Brian!" she cried.

Furious that she was proving so hard to kill, I swung the rock a third time with all the strength I could muster. This blow was the best yet, cracking open her skull. She collapsed to her chest. Blood gushed down the visible side of her face. One scared eye stared at me, fish-like.

I didn't think I could strike her again, not with her looking at me like that, and she would probably be dead soon enough anyway. She had a hole in her head.

I tossed the rock aside, grabbed her ankles like I had my dad's, and began dragging her.

❊ ❊ ❊

I dragged her all the way to the canyon floor. Moving her was a lot easier than moving my dad had been. One, it was downhill. Two, she was smaller than he was, my size, and just as skinny. Even so, it still took me most of the morning to get her to the river. She was awake for the first bit. She kept trying to talk to me, but she wasn't making any sense. Now she was quiet, her eyes closed. I figured she had finally died.

I rolled her body into the raging river and watched it wash her away.

❊ ❊ ❊

I made it to the original campsite shortly before night descended. Everything was as we'd left it. I'd forgotten to search my mom's pockets for the car keys, so I broke one of the Chevy's windows with a rock to unlock the trunk and get to the food. I was so hungry I wolfed down four Oscar Mayer wieners raw and an entire box of salted crackers. I also drank the three remaining Pepsis, then about a liter of tap water. Later that evening, I nibbled on Oreo cookies and read an *Archie* until I fell asleep in my tent.

When Ranger Ernie found me two days later I was filthy but in otherwise fine shape. Nevertheless, I pretended I was worse off than I was and made myself cry while I explained how a bear had killed my parents. I'd tried to help them, I insisted—that's why I'd gotten blood all over me—but my mom told me to run away, so I ran away.

I spoke to a lot of police officers after that. I even had to speak to the same detective who'd questioned me about Geena's death. I really didn't like him, especially now that I knew he thought I'd killed her. I stuck to my story, however, and he soon gave up badgering me. After all, my dad had clearly been eaten by a bear—I couldn't fake that—and my mom's body, discovered far downriver, had been too bashed up and decayed to determine the cause of death.

The police never searched my home as I'd feared they would, never found the squirrel heads, which I packed with all my other stuff when I moved into foster care, where I lived with other kids who didn't have parents.

I missed my mom at first, but gradually I forgot what she sounded like, then what she looked like. After about a year I didn't miss her at all.

I never gave my fake dad a second thought—except when I replayed in my head the bear eating him, and when I did that, I always made it daytime, so I could watch it all happen again.

# THE PRESENT

When I had first approached the young Swedish couple thirty minutes earlier, they had been friendly and chatty. I told them I was camping in the lot one over from theirs, and they told me to join them for a beer. Their accented English was close to fluent but sometimes difficult to understand. From what I gathered they had both been hired as ski instructors at Aspen for the winter season, and they had decided to camp in Black Canyon to save money on their accommodation until they had to report to the ski resort. The man had introduced himself as Raoul. He was handsome and blond, the hair on one side of his head cropped short, the hair on the other side wavy and chin length. The woman, Anna, was an impish brunette with a thin yet voluptuous body. In fact, she reminded me of my old flame Stephanie. I'd never had a chance to see Steph again before I was shipped off to foster care, but I'd tracked her down through Facebook a couple years back. She was married, a stay-at-home mom with two young boys. She didn't remember me when I knocked on her door late on a Tuesday morning. But she remembered when I mentioned our elementary school. It had been nice to hear her say my name again, which she did over and over as she begged unsuccessfully for her life.

The once-chatty Swedes, who had been so eager to hear my Black Canyon story, had become fidgety during the last quarter of it, and now, after its conclusion, seemed downright uncomfortable.

"So you see," I told them, opening my hands expansively. "I really had no choice. I had to kill my parents. It was either me or them."

Silence ensued, pleasantly uncomfortable.

"You know, that is a good story," Raoul said finally, clearing his throat. He was sitting across the campfire from me, next to Anna. He ran a hand over the side of his head that had hair. "But, well, it is late. I think we will go to bed soon."

"Yeah, sure. Bed, sure." Never one to overstay my welcome, I stood and smiled, to show there were no hard feelings for the not-so-discreet send off. "Well, thanks for listening, guys. It really is a good story, isn't it? I like to tell it. You can psychoanalyze me tomorrow. Nature or nurture, right?" I tipped him a wink, Anna a smile. She returned the smile nervously, looked at her feet.

"Right," Raoul said, though I don't think he understood what I was talking about.

I strolled east, cutting through the forest. When I had gone fifty feet, I stopped and faced the way I had come. Although Raoul and Anna would not be able to see me in the thick shadows, I could see them in the firelight. They were leaning close to one another in conversation. Raoul was gesturing quickly. The next moment they got up and ducked inside their tent.

Still watching them, I undid my shoelaces, slipped off my shoes, then my socks.

Raoul and Anna emerged from the tent carrying their backpacks. Raoul opened the backdoor of the old station wagon they were driving and tossed both bags onto the backseat.

I shrugged out of my jacket, then pulled off my T-shirt.

Raoul and Anna returned to the tent and began dismantling it.

I retrieved the twelve-inch hunting knife from where it had been secured snug against the small of my back and clenched it between my teeth. I unbuttoned my jeans, unzipped the zipper, then stepped out of the legs. I shoved my boxers down my hips, stepped out of them too.

Naked, I started forward, transferring the knife to my right hand.

Raoul and Anna were making too much noise with the tent to hear me approach. When I was fifteen feet away, however, Anna looked up from the stake she had pried from the ground and saw me. She froze, like a hare that had just spotted a predator.

She said something in Swedish to Raoul, who jerked around.

I went for him first, closing the distance between us in a burst of speed. He sprang to his feet and bumbled backward into the tent as I plunged the blade into his heart and tugged down.

People don't die easily. My mom taught me this. But if you don't mind the mess, slitting open the heart will always get the job done.

Blood fountained from Raoul's chest and struck my shoulder with wonderful force.

Anna wasn't screaming, not exactly. I don't know how to explain the sound she was making, because it wasn't really human. Warbling? Yowling?

She ran.

I gave chase. For thirty-six I was in great shape. I went to the gym five days a week and was lean as a barracuda.

I caught Anna before she had even decided which way she wanted to flee.

I sank the knife into her back, into her heart, and twisted the blade sharply, blending the vital muscle into puree.

She expelled a jet of blood from her mouth and belly-flopped to the ground.

I gripped a fistful of her hair, tilted her impish head back, and slit her throat from ear to ear. Then I returned my attention to the boyfriend. He was still on his feet, his hands trying to stem the fountain spurting from his chest as he tottered back and forth on legs that would never ski again.

I finished him off.

\* \* \*

I know all about famous serial killers. I've read about them in books and on the internet. I've watched documentaries on *A Current Affair* and *60 Minutes*. I've rented biopics on Netflix. I don't look up to the Gacys and the Bundys of the world. I don't idolize them, or want to imitate them. I simply relate to them. They're my kin. Yet as similar as they and I may be, we are all equally unique in regard to what tickles our fancies. Dean Corll, for instance, only tortured and murdered young boys. Bruno Ludke was into young women, and necrophilia. Gerald Stano strangled and shot hitchhikers of both sexes, provided they were Anglo Saxon. Personally, I didn't care much for the demographics of my victims; I just liked feeding them to bears.

\* \* \*

After Raoul bled out, I rinsed the blood from my skin using the campground tap, then collected my clothes from where I'd shed them in the woods. Back at my car I dressed, then drove to the Swede's campsite. I parked fifty feet from their bodies, cut the engine, but kept the high beams on.

The bear arrived thirty minutes later. It never took bears long to show. They were always hanging around campsites, even in the off-season before they went into hibernation, in the hopes of scrounging a last-minute meal. They had amazing noses too. They were like bloodhounds and could zero in on a fresh kill from miles away.

This one came from the west. It stood at the perimeter of the campsite, on all fours, sniffing the air as if searching for a trap. It looked directly at me, but I knew it couldn't see or smell me in the darkened cab.

Eventually it waddled toward the dead ski instructors, into the throw of the headlights. It sniffed the hunks of meat, then made a loud mewling sound, calling its two cubs from their hiding spot among the nearby vegetation.

I leaned forward with anticipation as the mama bear and her kids got ready to chow down.

# REWIND

# CHAPTER 1

When I opened my eyes, the slab of ceiling above me skated back and forth. I blinked repeatedly until the ceiling stopped moving. More blinks brought it into focus—or what I could see of it that wasn't lost in inky shadows. It was off-white, the paint blistered and cracking in places.

Light came from the left. I squinted at the glow that was bright as the sun. The spangles faded. I made out a single-watt light bulb screwed into a fixture. No shade or anything. Just the bulb, naked, a phosphorescent pear surrounded by darkness.

My mouth, I realized, was hanging ajar. I closed it. My lips felt scratchy. I worked my mouth to generate saliva, but I couldn't muster any.

Where had I gone last night? I wondered groggily. How much had I drunk? Whose bed was I in?

No, no bed. Some sort of reclining chair. As I pushed myself to my elbows something tugged at my head. In the next moment I discovered a dozen multi-colored wires extending from my skull to a machine on a nearby table. The machine was about the size of a home printer and bristling with knobs and dials. Next to it stood a giant flat-screen monitor, the screen blank, and a laptop, the screen also blank.

My first instinct was to tear the wires free, but I didn't. I wasn't sure of their purpose.

Suddenly wide awake, I glanced about the room: sallow

yellow walls dirtied with age, scuffed and chipped hardwood floor, a single door, closed.

"Hello?" I called—and almost jerked about to see who had spoken. But it had been me, only I didn't recognize my voice. It wasn't coarse from a hangover; wasn't nasally from a cold; wasn't high-pitched from fear. It was just...different. *Not mine* were the two words that came to mind. "Hello?" I repeated. Then, to hear more: "Where am I? What's going on?" Gruff, deep, generic.

*Not mine.*

A trick? A gag? A candid camera thing?

I gripped a blue wire, hesitated, then tugged it free, consequences be damned. The printer-sized machine didn't whirl and click in alarm. My brain didn't explode.

Nothing happened.

I studied the end of the wire. It didn't squirm madly in my grip with a life of its own. It didn't have devil-red eyes and a wormy orifice bristling with razor teeth. In fact, it appeared to be nothing more sinister than some sort of electrode pad.

Still, it filled me with fear.

*What the fuck was going on?*

I removed the dozen or so other wires, swung my feet to the floor, and pushed myself free of what I now recognized to be an old-fashioned dentist chair. A wave of dizziness washed through me, though it passed quickly enough. I went to the door, gripped the brass doorknob, but hesitated, wondering whether I might be walking into some sort of trap. Yet why would someone bother with that? I had just been out cold in that chair. They could have done to me whatever they pleased then.

I opened the door and peered into the adjoining room. A dozen feet from me a grotesquely fat bearded man lay on his back on the floor, bovine eyes staring sightlessly at the ceiling.

The skin over my skull tightened and tingled, as if it had shrunk a size. But I wasn't all that surprised to discover the body, was I? Because I was in some sort of waking nightmare, and this is what happened in nightmares.

I forced myself forward. The new room was bigger than the previous one and featured boarded up windows. To my left was a closed door, which I guessed led to a bathroom. Adjacent to the door, in a shadowed corner, sat a cardboard box spewing reams of printouts and manila folders and other miscellaneous stationary. A refrigerator hummed in a dingy kitchenette. An open can of SpaghettiOs and a spoon encrusted with tomato sauce rested on the table.

When I reached the body, I tried to avoid looking at the bloated face and the glassy eyes. The guy must have been close to four-hundred pounds. He wore jeans and an enormous shirt. The mass that was his belly strained at the buttons and hung over his groin like an apron. I crouched and felt his doughy neck. The skin was cool. There was no pulse. I had known this would be the case, of course, yet at least now I could tell the police I had checked—

I stiffened as a bolt of fear iced my spine.

The police? Yes, the police—I didn't want anything to do them. I didn't know why. But I didn't.

*Get out of there. Now.*

Obeying the warning, I hurried down a short hallway. I took the steps to the ground level two at a time. At the bottom I unlocked and opened a black-painted door and squinted at daylight so bright it seared my gloom-rotted eyes.

I stumbled onto a quiet commercial street lined with dilapidated buildings and started away from the second-floor apartment, my hands jammed into my pockets, my head bowed. I didn't look back.

# CHAPTER 2

My name is Harry Parker. I live at 3225 Turtle Creek Boulevard in Dallas. I'm forty-eight years old, five foot eleven inches tall. I have a full head of black hair tapered into a widow's peak. My eyes are brown, set into a handsomely rugged face that could have belonged to a washed-out boxer, or a world-weary traveler.

This was all according to my Texas-issued driver's license, which had been in my wallet, which had been in the inside pocket of my sports coat.

Sitting on a park bench several blocks from the apartment containing the *Doctor Who* machine and the dead body, I examined the other pieces of identification inside my wallet. Two credit cards, a Visa and an American Express, both issued by Citibank. A debit card, also with Citibank. A birth certificate. A social insurance card. And a scrap of paper with a seven-digit telephone number scrawled on it.

I didn't know if the number was written in my handwriting or not.

I put the wallet away and stared at the playground in the middle of the park. A Hispanic mother sat on the grass next to a stroller, watching her daughter play on the colorful equipment while sipping from a bottle in a paper bag.

I watched the girl too, wondering what the fuck I'd gotten myself into.

Why had I been in that chair, in that apartment, hooked up to that machine? Had I been a guinea pig in some madcap experiment, and something went terribly wrong, something along the lines of accidentally pressing the delete key in a word-processing document, or formatting a computer hard drive? Then again, maybe I had known something important, perhaps some government or industrial secret, and someone had wanted it badly enough to take it from my head with all the finesse and compassion that one uses when removing a hook from a fish that had swallowed the hook to the gills?

I grimaced, drawing my thumb and forefinger over my eyes. Now was not the time for fanciful speculation. A couple minutes ago the park had seemed like a safe, inviting spot to gather my thoughts. Yet sitting here, in the open, I was becoming increasingly paranoid. After all, I had walked away from a dead body without reporting it. I felt like a fugitive. And more, I thought maybe I *was* a fugitive. I didn't believe I'd murdered Moby Dick. There had been no indication of a struggle, no physical signs of trauma to his body. Nevertheless, any thought of the police still sent a shock of anxiety through me, which led me to believe my unconscious self knew something my conscious self didn't. In fact, the cops could very well be cruising the neighborhood looking for me at that very moment.

So I needed to put as much distance between myself and that twisted apartment as I could. That was priority one. Yet where could I bunker down? Not the Turtle Creek address. No hotels either. Because if I was indeed wanted for some crime or another, hanging out in my home or using my credit card to check into a Holiday Inn would likely land me on an episode of *America's Dumbest Criminals*.

There was the debit card, of course, but I wasn't sure I wanted to risk making a bank withdrawal in person, and I didn't know the pin number—

7-4-9-9.

Jesus Christ! I thought, sitting straight. *7-4-9-9.* That was it. That was the pin number. I was positive of it.

I sprang off the park bench and went searching for an ATM.

* * *

I wasn't in Dallas as I'd initially believed. I was in Brooklyn, New York. I discovered this when, through a break in the buildings, I glimpsed the Manhattan skyline to the north. On the heels of this realization came another one: I was familiar with Manhattan. I couldn't muster any specific memories of myself there, but I could see the streets and neighborhoods in my mind's eye, knew their layouts, knew what buildings and landmarks were where.

I cut through a sprawling cemetery and found a street-facing ATM on the other side of a busy overpass. I stuck the debit card in the slot and punched in 7-4-9-9. I held my breath, waiting to be informed that the pin was incorrect, or that the card was being retained by my financial institution. A second later, however, a prompt asked me how much money I would like to withdrawal. I entered fifty dollars. The guts of the machine churned. The mouth spat out two twenties and a ten. I requested a printed receipt to check the balance.

$749,950.

I had to read the figure one digit at a time until I was certain I was not mistaken. Then, with a trembling hand, I requested another withdrawal. This time I punched in five hundred dollars, hesitated, then added another zero, hoping I didn't bankrupt the machine.

It spat out the money just as dutifully as before.

I continued toward downtown Brooklyn, a pinball of emotions banging around inside me. I mean, on the one hand, waking up to discover you had lost your memory and might be wanted by the police was a pretty lousy way to begin your morning. On the other hand, discovering you had three quarters of a million bucks in the bank was a pretty damn good feeling—especially when only moments before you didn't know whether you had a penny to your name.

I zigzagged through a number of streets, passing the Barclay's Center, Long Island University, and the Brooklyn Academy of Music. I caught glimpses of my reflection in storefront windows, but I didn't want to stop and gawk at myself in public. Instead I popped into a Burger King restroom. Standing in front of the grubby mirror—"Things I hate: vandalism, irony, lists" was scribbled on it in black marker—I was relieved to find the driver's license photo had not been deceptively flattering. I was indeed a ruggedly handsome man.

I leaned closer to the mirror, to examine my eyes, my hairline, the pores on my nose, when the door opened and an old guy with a cane entered. I cleared my throat, rinsed my hands, and left.

Back outside I wandered about in a daze, glancing at the people I passed as if expecting one of them to offer me a nod or a wink, to let me know they were in on the gag. But as I'd already surmised, this was no gag, no candid camera show, none of that. This was real. Fucked up, but real.

I stopped in the middle of the sidewalk, next to a blue postal box, realizing I was famished. I looked back over my shoulder at the Burger King I had recently departed. But I didn't return. Because I didn't like Burger King, did I? No, I didn't. In fact, as hungry as I was, the thought of one of their greasy bacon-and-egg breakfast muffins turned my stomach.

"I don't like Burger King," I said in the voice that wasn't my voice—and felt inspired. This newfound disdain for fast food might not be a memory; more like a feeling, something on the instinctual level that informs thought and memory. Still, it was something, wasn't it? Some echo of my past identity?

Across the street I spotted a sushi restaurant—and *that* got my stomach growling. I entered the shop, which turned out to feature one of those rotating conveyor belts moving dishes around in a big loop. I took a seat on a padded stool and snatched one color-coded plate after the other—salmon, tuna, octopus, mackerel, miso soup, tempura—and washed it all down with countless cups of green tea. By the time the waitress came by to tally up my bill, I had more than twenty plates stacked high beside me.

She was cute, the waitress. Maybe twenty, almond eyes, pouty lips. I felt a need to speak to someone and made small talk. She told me she was Japanese, though I guessed Korean or Chinese. I'm not sure how I knew this; it was just a feeling, like how I knew I didn't like Burger King. Maybe I'd dated a Japanese woman before. Hell, maybe I'd been married to one.

I left her a generous tip—told her *arigatou gozaimasu*, which turned out to be all the Japanese I knew, killing the Japanese-wife theory—and left the restaurant, feeling semi-human for the first time that morning.

The sky was clear and blue. The sun warmed my skin. And for a moment—and only for a moment—I considered going to the police and telling them everything, letting them figure out the quagmire I'd woken in. Nevertheless, as tempting as this seemed, it was not an option—at least not until I had learned enough on my own to know I wasn't going to be cuffed and booked on sight.

I decided to make my way to Manhattan on foot. The walk would do me good, give me time to get my thoughts together, figure out my next move.

I crossed the Brooklyn Bridge via the pedestrian walkway suspended above the road. As traffic roared below me I repeatedly glanced at the World Trade Center soaring to the east. I knew the original two buildings had been destroyed in a terrorist attack on September 11, 2001. I knew there had been subsequent wars in Iraq and Afghanistan as pseudo retaliation. I knew these wars had been the equivalent of kicking a hornet's nest, and now terrorist cells were popping up all over the globe.

So if I knew all this, why couldn't I recall what my house looked like, or what I did for a living, or whether I was married with children?

Or why I'd been hooked up to that fucking machine with a dead guy decomposing in the next room?

I cut north through Chinatown, then followed Second Avenue through the East Village toward Midtown, soaking up the sights and smells and sounds of the dirty Big Apple—all of which remained frustratingly familiar yet unfamiliar.

While waiting at an intersection for a red light to change, I noticed a walk-in medical clinic on the ground floor of a mint-colored building. It hadn't struck me to see a doctor—even now that seemed like an all too ordinary solution to an extraordinary predicament—but perhaps a doctor would know something about memory loss? I couldn't tell him about the machine and the body, of course, but I could tell him I woke knowing fuck all.

What was the worst that could happen anyway? He prescribes me some anti-psychotic meds and tells me to check into Bellevue?

The clinic was air-conditioned to the point of being chilly. The receptionist gave me a patient questionnaire to fill out and told me to take a seat. I completed the form quickly, using the alias "Bart Mulroney" and checking the "no" box next to each question, given I had no clue as to whether I had allergies or existing medical conditions. Then I flicked through the same hotrod magazine three times before my name was called by a female GP in a white coat and a pink hijab.

I followed the doctor down a corridor to a sterile office that smelled of latex. I took a seat on the examination bed, while the doc sat in front of a tidy desk featuring a large-screen Mac.

"I'm sorry to keep you waiting," she said with a faint Indian accent. "My name is Avni Singh." She shook my hand with a cool, dry grip. She was in her fifties, short, her pale skin more white than brown. Beady eyes peered at me over the top of gold-rimmed bifocals.

"I'm Bart," I said, using the alias.

"So how can I help, Bart?"

"My memory's gone," I told her bluntly.

She seemed unimpressed with this declaration and said, "You can't recall what you've done earlier today?"

"I can't recall what I've done before today." I hesitated. "Ever."

Now her thin eyebrows came up—slightly. "What you had for dinner last night?"

"No idea."

"Whether you went to work yesterday?"

"I don't even know what I do."

"You don't know what you do?"

"That's the thing, Doc. I know it's July. I know I'm in New York. But everything about me before this morning—autobiographical information, I'd guess you'd call it—is gone."

She considered that. "But you know your name?" she said, indicating the questionnaire attached to the clipboard in her hand.

I shook my head. "My name was on my driver's license, which was in my wallet when I woke up, which was in my pocket. At first I thought I had someone else's wallet, because I didn't recognize my photo or my name. But then, well, I just sort of had a feeling it was me."

"A feeling?"

"I don't know, Doc. Like being hungry. Just a feeling, an instinct. It was like that, sort of. I don't know how to explain it better."

She took a pen from the desk and scribbled something on the clipboard. I couldn't see what she was writing, but given the conversation thus far I imagined it might be something along the lines of: *Patient equates his ego to hunger, believes he is a cheeseburger.*

I waited for Avni Singh to continue. She did so a moment later.

"When you look in a mirror," she said, "who do you see?"

"Me," I said.

"So you recognize your reflection?"

"No—what I mean is, I know it's me, you know, the way a monkey would know its own reflection, even if it's never seen itself before. So I recognize it's me. I just don't recognize *me.*"

She scribbled more notes. *Patient now believes himself to be a monkey.*

I clenched my jaw in frustration at my inability to articulate my situation. "Look, Dr. Singh," I said, keeping my voice neutral. "I know how this sounds. But it's the truth."

"Yes, I see," she said in a distracted, almost indifferent way. She peered at me again over the bifocals. "Do you have any history of seizures, anxiety, depression?"

I stared at her. "Are you listening to what I'm saying?"

"Excuse me?"

"I don't know my goddamn name, Doc! So how would I know whether I have a history of goddamn seizures?" I stood to leave. "You made your forty bucks. Thanks for your time."

Dr. Singh stood as well. "Where are you going?"

"To be alone."

"Please," she said, indicating for me to sit again.

I hesitated.

"I'm happy to try to help you," she said. Then, sensing my skepticism, added, "Look...Bart...my next patient is going to tell me about chronic back pain, or irritable bowels, or a skin rash, or what they've diagnosed on their own to be a broken hip. You, on the other hand... I've been doing this job for many years now, but I've yet to come across a case like yours before."

"That's supposed to be confidence inspiring?"

"I've treated patients with memory loss before, yes," she amended. "Just not to the extent you're describing."

She indicated again that I sit. I studied her, and decided maybe I'd read her wrong. Maybe she hadn't been distracted earlier because she was uninterested; maybe she'd been distracted because she was trying to figure out what had happened to me.

I sat.

"Thank you," she said, though she remained standing. She set the clipboard on the desk and folded her arms across her chest. "Bart...can you tell me, do you remember what you did today?"

"Yeah," I replied. "Everything."

"How do you feel at the moment? Dizzy? Nauseous? Hangover?"

"I don't think my memory going AWOL is the result of having a few too many last night, Doc."

"I'm not saying you're merely hungover," she said. "I asked because a hangover can be an indication of alcohol abuse, which, over time, can lead to a thiamine deficiency, which can lead to a fugue state."

"Fugue state?" I repeated.

"It's a rare psychiatric disorder characterized by amnesia—including memories and other identifying characteristics of individuality."

I perked up. "Is it reversible?"

She nodded. "And usually short-lived, ranging from a few hours to a few days."

A delicate hope swept through me—delicate because I knew my memory loss didn't have anything to do with a thiamine deficiency; it had to do with that fucking machine I'd been hooked up to. However, the fact people can lose their memory and get it back was welcomed news, regardless.

Avni Singh said, "I'm going to ask you a couple simple questions, if that is all right?"

"Shoot," I said.

"Can you describe your mother or father?"

"What they look like? No."

"Can you recall their names?"

"No."

"Do you know what month it is?"

"I told you that. July."

"What is the capital of the United States?"

"For real?"

"Please?"

"Washington, DC."

"What is the world's most populous country?"

"China. Unless India's caught up."

"Do you know what you're going to do tomorrow?"

I frowned. "Haven't thought about it."

"Any idea?"

"No, none."

Avni Singh said, "May I examine your head?"

"I haven't hit it, if that's what you're thinking."

"How would you know this if you can't remember anything before this morning?"

"Because it doesn't hurt."

"Pain recedes."

I shrugged. "Be my guest."

She tilted my head this way and that, parting my hair, prodding my skull. I sat patiently, feeling like an ape getting groomed by its kin for parasites.

Avni Singh said, "There doesn't appear to be any signs of trauma." She stepped away from me and assumed a thoughtful expression. "I suppose a blood test might—"

I frowned. "A blood test?"

She nodded. "Trauma to head is the most likely candidate for memory loss, but an epileptic seizure or a viral infection can also produce similar effects. A blood test could reveal low thyroid functions, or low vitamin B12—"

"I didn't lose my memory from not eating enough goddamn fish, Doc!" I said, thinking once again of the microwave I'd been hooked up to. "Listen," I added. "You mentioned that a fugue state can be a result of alcohol abuse. Can it also be a result of something else?"

"Certainly," she replied. "A tumor, a stroke—but without running diagnostic tests I can't tell you anything for certain."

"No tests. Not right now. I just want to know what you know about memory loss."

"I'm not a neurosurgeon—"

"Humor me, would you?"

Dr. Singh hesitated, then shrugged. "There are two main types of amnesia I'm familiar with. The more common is called anterograde amnesia. Patients can't remember new information, like what they had for breakfast, or where they left their car."

"My short-term memory is no problem," I reminded her.

"Yes, so we've established. The other type of amnesia is called retrograde amnesia, 'retro' meaning it happened before the injury. In this case patients can't remember information or events that occurred before the trauma."

"Like their name or where they live?"

"Their name, facts about their life—everything you've described."

"So why can I recall who the president is and other shit—stuff—I must have learned before today—those are long-term memories, right?—but nothing about *me*?"

"Like I said, Bart, I'm not a specialist. Nevertheless, I believe that the memories you're describing—the name of the president and such—are stored in a different part of your brain than your autobiographical memories, just as your motor memories such as walking and speaking are stored in a different part of your brain. This is why you know what a bicycle is, you can likely ride one if you tried, but you can't remember the first time your rode one—can you?"

I shook my head. "So you're saying only a specific part of my brain has been affected?"

"That would be my guess. But again, because there are no physical signs of trauma, I would recommend—"

"Thanks, Doc," I said, hopping off the bed and going to the door. "If I change my mind about any of those tests, you'll be the first to know."

I left before she could say anything more.

* * *

As I continued down Second Avenue, I replayed everything Dr. Singh had told me and wondered if maybe I should have gotten a blood test after all. But really, what would have been the point? I didn't, as she suspected, have thyroid or vitamin B12 deficiencies. I had a case of someone screwing around inside my head. So what I needed was a CT scan, or an MRI, something that would show what was going on in my brain, show how badly that machine had scrambled it. Those options, however, were out of the question. I'd need to see a neurosurgeon. I'd need to fill out forms that couldn't be falsified. I'd need to provide my insurance card, proof of identity. Which meant I'd be in the system for anybody looking for me to find. So it seemed I was back to square one. I knew a bit more about memory loss and amnesia, thanks to the good doctor, but I was still in the dark about what happened to me—or how to reverse it.

What I needed to do was figure out what that *Doctor Who* machine was, but the only way to accomplish this would be to return to the apartment, which was also out of the question. I'd seen *Pulp Fiction* (at least I believe I had, because I could recall the plot), and I wasn't prepared to deal with a Vincent Vega taking a shit in the bathroom with a MAC-11 within easy reach.

Remembering that scrap of paper with the telephone number on it, I stopped and dug it from my wallet. Seven digits, no area code—or country code for that matter.

Local? Dallas? Tokyo?

I started walking again, keeping an eye out for a payphone. If I got lucky, really lucky, the number might put me in touch with someone who could tell me what the fuck was going on. But nothing was ever that easy, and I wasn't going to get my hopes up. Still, even if the number was for my favorite pizza restaurant, that would be something, wouldn't it? Because the guy who ran the joint would likely know me and might be able to tell me something about myself other than my name.

At East Forty-second Street I turned west and walked the two blocks to Grand Central Terminal. I passed through the chaos of Vanderbilt Hall and found a bank of public payphones in the main concourse. I accessed Skype on the thirty-two-inch touch-screen display and dialed the unknown number.

Local after all because it rang.

And rang.

And rang.

Cursing, I hung up after a dozen rings.

Back amongst the hustle and bustle of East Forty-second, I paused out front a Kenneth Cole retail store. I was tired and sweaty and fed up with walking, and all I wanted to do was find a hotel—now that I had cash, renting a room anonymously wasn't going to be an issue—where I could make a stiff drink and drown myself in blissful oblivion. Yet before I did this I figured I should purchase some new clothes. Because I would have to wake up at some point, I would have to start another day, and I couldn't continue wearing the same smelly duds until my memory returned and reminded me where I kept my New York wardrobe. So I entered the store, ignored the snooty-looking salespeople, and picked out several pairs of socks and underwear, a pair of white-soled oxfords, five dress shirts, and two suits. I paid for everything with crisp hundred-dollar notes.

Burdened with shopping bags, I stopped at the first hotel I came to—The Roosevelt Hotel—but it was booked out. So was the Crown Plaza Times, and The Manhattan. I got lucky at The Plaza and splurged on a six-hundred-square-foot room that featured high ceilings, a comfortable sitting area, and a mosaic bathroom with gold fixtures and a marble vanity.

"Not too shabby, Harry," I said to myself as I kicked off my shoes and hung the suits in the closet. I snapped on the flat-screen TV for company, dimmed the lighting with the iPad on the writing table, and poured myself a triple Scotch from the stocked bar tucked discretely inside a large armoire.

The news anchor on the tube was rambling on about the latest mission to the newly built lunar base. I couldn't have cared less and went to the bank of tall windows, where I sipped my drink and watched as dusk stole over the harried city, blanketing it in layer of dark and anonymity.

# CHAPTER 3

An hour later, riding a sluggish whiskey buzz, I sat at the room's writing table, staring at the list I'd made. It was divided into two columns. The left read: "Know/like." The right read: "Don't know."

Beneath "Know/like" was: name, address, age, bank, face, PIN, Scotch, Manhattan, Japanese food. After contemplating the pathetically short list I added "a good suit" because I suspected I liked—or was used to—wearing well-tailored suits of fine quality. This might seem like a trivial detail to add to the list, but right then anything and everything was significant. The fact I appreciated a good suit could mean I was some sort of business-man.

This led me to the first point in the "Don't know" column. Occupation. And if there was one sliver of personal information I didn't know about myself that I wanted to most it was what my job had been. Because in a way your job equaled your iden-tity more than anything else. It defined you, explained you. An artist was not an accountant. A sales clerk was not a chief execu-tive. Some Willy Loman might say he was a door-to-door sales-man because times were tough and there hadn't been much else in the classifieds. I didn't buy that. Because Loman was ignoring the thousands of choices he'd made that led to his shitty lot in life. The subjects he'd pursued in school, the time he'd put into studying for tests, the people he'd socialized with. The way he treated others. Sacrifice. Punctuality. Integrity. Honesty. *Every-thing*. Every single choice, good or bad or neutral. These were what composed your identity. What made you President of the United States or a door-to-door salesman. Not the fact there were no other fucking jobs available the day you checked the paper.

So me? My occupation?

No idea. I began jotting down adjectives I felt applied to me. Then, in the next instant, I scribbled across the page so violently the tip of the pen tore the paper. I scrunched the list into a ball and threw it against the wall.

*What the fuck was I doing?* A list! It was bullshit. It wasn't getting me anywhere.

My mind was a tabula rasa, a blank slate, and maybe I was just going to have to live with that.

Tears burned in my eyes. I got up and paced the room before stopping in front of the gilded mirror on the wall. I stared at my reflection, stared hard, and told myself to get a grip.

*Look, you ungrateful bastard, you're a good-looking guy, and you have nearly a million dollars banked. Things could have been a lot worse. You could have looked like Steve Buscemi and been dirt broke.*

*Besides, maybe there's an upside to having no knowledge of the past. It means no baggage. Fine, you don't know what you do for a living, whether you have kids somewhere, what you did last Christmas. But you don't have any bad memories either, do you? No heartbreak, no shame, no guilt, no regrets.*

*Tabula rasa? Good. Great. Fan-fucking-tastic. You get to start over however you please. How many people get that opportunity? How many people get a second chance like that?*

Holding onto these positive thoughts, I decided I needed to get out of the room, do something, anything. Sitting around getting drunk by myself wasn't proving to be the solace I'd hoped for. So I showered in the walk-in waterfall shower, dressed in a new suit, and left the hotel.

The humidity of the afternoon had been replaced by a dry evening heat, and West Fifty-seventh Street buzzed with smartly dressed people and an electric energy. I didn't mind the lights and noise, but the touts trying to hawk me tickets to comedy shows pissed me off, so I veered north into Central Park. I passed couples strolling under romantic pools of lamplight, dog-walkers trying to keep up with their eager canines, cyclists and joggers. The desultory clop of carriage horses echoed in the distance, accompanied by the occasional honk of a car horn.

Eventually I left the park and strolled through the 60s and 70s east of Park Avenue. The side streets were studded with nineteenth-century brownstones, most carved up into apartments. Madison, on the other hand, was thick with bars, restaurants, boutiques, and retail shops.

I found myself in the mood for something quiet and classy and entered an elegant-looking cigar bar. The crowd was predominantly male, white, and upscale—and I immediately felt at home. Also, one whiff of the pungent aroma of cigars and I knew I was a cigar smoker myself.

Something else to add to the list, I thought dryly.

I took a seat at one of two bars. A waitress dressed in tight black pants, a white tuxedo shirt with rolled-up sleeves, a black bowtie, and suspenders greeted me with, "What can I get you?"

"Chivas, neat," I said.

"Won't be a sec."

I watched her as she made the drink. She was blonde, late thirties, tall and thin. Her lashes were long and full, her nose straight, her cheekbones prominent. The lashes were fake, the makeup heavy under the buttery light from the barrel-shaped light fixtures, but she was attractive nonetheless.

And her eyes—they captivated me immediately. They were blue, intelligent...and sad.

How could someone so beautiful be so sad, or at least cynical?

She set the Scotch in front of me. "Would you care to see the cigar menu?"

"I think I'd like something mild," I said, pleased to discover several cigar brands pop into my mind. "A Gran Habano Connecticut would do fine, thank you."

While she disappeared into the humidor room, I sipped my drink and tried to puzzle out for the hundredth time the paradox of how I could know I liked something without any recollection of ever having tried it before. Dr. Singh had mentioned that different memories were stored in different parts of the brain, and I guess I bought that. It was just so bizarre to discover in the span of seconds that you possessed a preference, such as an appreciation for certain cigars, which would have taken you months or years to acquire.

This led me back to that stupid Know/Don't Know list, and I ruminated over what other preferences or qualities or skills I possessed. Was I a wine connoisseur, for instance? Could I downhill ski? Hell, maybe I had a black belt in karate?

*Maybe I'm a raging alcoholic?* I thought as a quiet voice reminded me I was on my fifth or sixth drink of the evening and had no interest in slowing down.

I executed a swift karate chop through the air with my right hand. The gesture didn't feel natural or instinctual. I tried again, this time striking the polished mahogany bar.

"Do you have a grudge against wood?"

I glanced at the waitress, who had returned and was fixing me with an amused expression.

"I'm Harry," I said.

She snipped the cap off the Gran Habano with a guillotine, handed the cigar to me, and lit the foot with a butane torch. I puffed, drawing smoke into my mouth. The sweet tobacco flavor was immediately familiar and pleasant.

"Satisfactory, Harry?" the waitress asked.

"I can't remember having a better one."

"I don't think I've seen you here before?"

"I don't think I've been."

"Don't think?"

"I—no, I haven't. Have you worked here long?"

"Too long," she said as a tourist who'd been perusing the one hundred-plus bottles on display behind the bar waved her over.

"But, hey," she added over her shoulder as she left me, "don't tell my boss that."

* * *

Her name, I learned a short while later, was Beth, and I think she found me attractive. She kept pausing in her duties to talk to me at any rate. Maybe she was simply bored. There weren't many customers at the bar. But I didn't think this was the case. She didn't bat her long eyelashes or anything melodramatic like that, but she seemed genuinely interested in sharing my company.

Nevertheless, whatever the reason for her decision to chat me up, she managed the impossible and made what was likely the shittiest day of my life a little less shitty. In fact, in her company, I was almost enjoying myself.

While I rested my cigar in the ashtray—it had burned itself out—Beth finished telling me a story about a German tourist who'd incorrectly believed a long, stiff ash was the sign of a cigar aficionado and accidentally tipped his two-inch ash down the cleavage of his date.

I took a swig of Scotch and said, "What are you doing later, Beth?"

Beth looked at my coyly. "Later?"

"What time do you get off work?" I asked. It was nuts, bloody nuts. My memory had more holes than Swiss cheese, I might be wanted by the police, and all I could think about right then was what sweet, flirtatious Beth had on beneath her tight black pants and tuxedo shirt.

Beth polished a spot on the counter with her rag that didn't need polishing. "Ten," she said without looking at me.

"Would you care to join me for a drink?"

"I don't know anything about you, Harry."

I almost laughed at the irony of that. "You know my name."

"You could be a total scumbag." And her deadpan delivery

told me she'd likely had her fair share of scumbags walk through her life.

"Did I make that good of a first impression?" I asked, to lighten the mood.

She smiled.

"Give me a chance, Beth," I said. "One drink, that's all. Maybe two, when you realize what a fun guy I am."

"Are you even from New York?"

I hesitated, thought about lying, then realized I'd hesitated too long to pull off the lie. "No," I said.

She frowned. "Well, see, that could be a problem for me, Harry. I don't do one-night stands."

"Hey, I don't either," I said. "I'm in New York for a while."

"A while?"

I nodded, deciding this was true, given I had no immediate plans to return to Dallas. "And like I said, a drink, nothing more. I'm just looking for some company."

"Harry, you seem like a nice guy—"

"Look, Beth, when you get off at ten come by The Plaza. It's only a few blocks south of here. I'll be in the Rose Club. If you decide not to come, no hard feelings."

"Is that where you're staying?" she asked.

"Rest assured. I haven't seen any cockroaches yet."

"What did you say you do again?"

"I didn't." I stood and left a hundred on the bar for the cigar and the drinks. "So I'll see you there?"

"I'll think about it," she said.

\* \* \*

The Rose Club was dimly lit and opulent, though I found the rose neon garish. I settled into an oversized velvet chair at a table overlooking the lobby and ordered a Chivas. I wasn't smashed, but I was definitely getting there. My thoughts felt slow and loose, my body heavy, and I decided I liked this feeling very much.

The white-jacketed Bangladeshi waiter brought my drink, along with complimentary popcorn, dried fruit, nuts, and pretzels. I ignored the snacks, finished the whiskey in two minutes, and waved Bangladesh over again. He was a strange-looking fellow. Too big ears, too small chin that almost melted into his neck. A pencil mustache and thick, black-rimmed glasses added character to an otherwise unfortunate face.

"'nother," I said, raising the empty tumbler.

"Of course, sir," he said.

"Is there a problem?"

"Sir?"

"The way you're looking at me. I don't like it."

"Sir?"

He was still looking at me the same way. How you looked at a drunk relative at Christmas dinner: wary, wondering if he might topple over at any moment. A rage warmed inside me. Because this guy, this meaningless waiter making minimum wage, was judging me?

"Is that all you can say?" I said. "Sir? *Sir?* You know, maybe had you tried a little harder in high school, you wouldn't be pouring drinks to pay the rent. Or did you just get off a boat?"

His nonexistent chin quivered.

"Go get my bloody drink."

He went to the U-shaped bar, where a guy in a suit and a guy in a military uniform were sitting by themselves, and proceeded to make my drink. Watching him, I felt like total shit.

For most of the day I'd believed myself—or at least believed whoever I had once been—to be an admirable person. I seemed polite and cultured. I spoke with an educated inflection. I had what I believed to be an above-average vocabulary. I felt I commanded a certain amount of respect. I'd even go so far to say I was charming. After all, I talked the receptionist at The Plaza into letting me pay upfront in cash, and I got Beautiful Beth to meet me for a drink.

But was this the real me? Or was it a civilized front masking a depraved asshole?

*Go get my bloody drink.*

Because, really, nobody was the person they presented to others, were they? Everyone had a private persona and a public one. In many cases these two identities meshed closely enough to lump them together as one. Off the top of my head I'd say roughly fifty percent of the population fit that bill. But then there was the other half. The smiling kindergarten teacher by day, the pedophile by night. The bubbly coworker with a fifty grand gambling debt. The successful doctor with a safe full of snuff videos. The handsome Ted Bundy next door.

Humans were masters of deceit and disguise. It's what allowed them to live together in relative harmony in such large numbers.

Deceit and disguise.

My, Mrs. Harrison, you look lovely today. *When are you going to get that growth burned off your eyebrow?*

Great seeing you again, Steve. Give the wife my best. *Or don't, because I'll tell her myself while fucking her in a Motel 6 tomorrow evening.*

Your children are rambunctious little angels, aren't they? *Maybe if you learned some parenting responsibilities and showed a little tough love they wouldn't be such snot-nosed brats.*

"Your drink, sir," Bangladesh said. He set the Chivas on a coaster before me. He was smiling. Not smug. Worried, like he feared I was going to lash out at him again.

"What's your name?" I asked him.

"Sir?" he said, then seemed to think better of that response and added, "Sumon, sir."

"Listen, Sumon. I want to apologize for my behavior. I've been having a bad day."

"No need, sir."

I took a hundred from my wallet and pinched it between my fingers. "No hard feelings?" I said.

His face lit up. The bill disappeared into his tux pocket with a magician's flourish. "None at all, sir."

He returned to the bar, where alternating colors of light played behind the crystal glasses. My eyes drifted to the other patrons for the first time. No families or whining kids thankfully. Mostly couples and a splattering of business people racking up their company tabs with the twenty-five-dollar cocktails.

I glanced at my wristwatch. It was a Rolex, an Oyster perpetual model, steel, as unassuming as a Rolex could get. I'd noticed Beautiful Beth peek at it a few times earlier.

The hands read 10:42 p.m. Beth was already close to three-quarters of an hour late. Was she coming or had she stood me up?

Well, screw her if she had, I thought tiredly. It was getting late. The anxiety and depression gnawing in my gut like a nest of rats was stronger than ever, and Beth standing me up was the last thing I needed—especially when I had been so looking forward to seeing her.

Maybe I'd go find myself a prostitute and bring her back to the suite? Then again, The Plaza wasn't the type of place to which you invited streetwalkers.

An escort? One of those classy ones that cost a grand an hour?

I raised my hand, to catch Bangladesh's attention and signal the bill. Then I changed my mind. As much as I wanted to get my rocks off—who knew the last time I'd had sex?—I figured maybe I wanted company even more. Real company. Beautiful Beth company. We had clicked. I had enjoyed her conversation, her stories, her humor.

And if we ended up in bed? Well, that would be a very pleasant bonus.

I'd give her another twenty minutes.

I picked up the Chivas, swished the amber liquid around in the tumbler. God, I wanted it. In fact, I do believe I actually craved it. But I was walking a very thin line. I'd held my composure together pretty well thus far. Yet the last couple drinks had hit me hard. Beth would take one look at me, see a bumbling drunk who couldn't slur together two words, and turn right back around.

I set the Scotch aside and went to the bar, happy to find myself surefooted. If I was indeed an alcoholic, at least I was an accomplished one.

I tipped the guy in military fatigues a brief nod. He tipped one back. I might be a sleaze. I might be a drunk. I might be a murderer for all I knew—but I respected the kids who put their lives on the line for this country, and that was something I knew as innately as I'd known anything all day.

Bangladesh flashed me a smile as big as the guilt-fuelled gratuity I'd given him. "Help you, sir?"

"Bathroom?"

"Right that way." He pointed.

The bathroom turned out to be a mishmash of marble and sophistication, a place where Marie Antoinette wouldn't have minded taking a royal dump. I leaned close to the mirror and studied my reflection. My eyes were lidded, but the whites weren't bloodshot.

I ran cold water and splashed my face repeatedly. The frigid water helped wake me up. I checked my reflection again, which was now dripping wet, and saw the same droopy face.

Once again I considered returning to the suite, calling an escort. I could tell Beth I'd waited for her for over an hour—which would be true—and when she failed to appear, I left to take an important business call. Tomorrow when I got myself together, I could return to the cigar bar, apologize, and ask for a second chance.

Hell, maybe I would wake up in the morning with my memory fully intact. Wouldn't that be something!

*Or maybe you'll wake up like you did this morning with your memory wiped clean all over again?*

Not wanting to contemplate that, I turned off the tap and heard a swine-like snort originate from one of the stalls. I patted my face dry with paper towel for a good twenty seconds until the stall door opened and a yuppie in a fitted navy suit, open collar, silver cufflinks, and coifed hair emerged, running a finger beneath his nose. He went to the door.

"Got any more?" I asked him.

He glanced over his shoulder, barely slowing. "Don't know what you're talking about, brother."

"A gram."

"Sorry—"

"Two hundred bucks."

He stopped, hand on the door handle. "For a gram?" He shrugged, sniffed. "Show me the money."

I presented him two Franklins. He glanced left and right, like a SWAT team might bust out of the ventilation system, then pressed a baggie into my palm.

He left the restroom.

I went to the same stall he'd used, closed the door, and examined the baggie. Half a gram at most. He'd vacuumed up the other half a minute ago. But I didn't care. Half a gram would do fine.

I tapped three lines onto the top of the ceramic toilet tank, rolled a hundred, and snorted the lines consecutively. I flushed the empty baggie down the toilet and inhaled deeply. The high hit me right away, and just like that the drunk was gone. I exited the stall and studied myself in the mirror to make sure there wasn't any residual powder on my nose.

All good.

I left the restroom and retook my seat in the velvet chair and sipped the Scotch. I checked the Rolex, discovered the time to be a bit past eleven, and cursed myself for not asking Beth for her number. At least that way I could have called her to find out whether she was coming or not.

Nevertheless, I didn't dwell on this. My thoughts were wickedly alert and euphoric, and for the first time all day I actually wanted to think about that *Doctor Who* machine and the fat bastard who'd died on the floor in the next room. They were no longer mysteries to be feared, but mysteries to be solved.

So what was that half-baked theory I'd come up with in the park the day before? Not the secret spy shit... Right-o, someone hitting the delete key of my mind. That was at least plausible. But why were they in my mind in the first place? Was I a guinea pig like I'd speculated? I didn't think so. It simply didn't ring true, because why, with all my wealth, would I participate in something so sketchy? And sketchy it was, given that apartment was of the variety where you sold your organs and woke up in a bathtub full of ice.

The police, Harry. The goddamn police.

Right. I'd messed up somehow.

I was on the run.

But why the apartment?

Why the chair and the machine?

*The fat guy*, I thought. He was the key—or had been the key.

Bangladesh appeared at the table. My drink, I realized, was nearly empty. The guy had eyes like a hawk.

"Another, sir?"

"Please," I said.

When he left, I checked my wristwatch again. 11:08. Beautiful Beth's time was up. Nevertheless, given I had another drink coming, and was still wired from the blow, I wasn't going anywhere.

So what had I been thinking about? Right. Moby Dick. So had that been his apartment? Unlikely. There were only two rooms. The one I had been in, and the one his body had been in. No bed anywhere, no shoes by the front door, no photos, no personal artifacts of any sort.

So it wasn't his residence. It was his shop or laboratory or whatever you wanted to call the place where he...

Where he what?

Performed underground medical procedures?

I swallowed, feeling momentarily ill.

Was that true? And did that mean I had a brain tumor? Dementia? Some other malign disease that doctors—legit doctors—told me was inoperable?

But why would his death, whatever caused it, leave me in identity limbo? And why did I have a fear of the police? Surely not because I'd volunteered for some experimental operation? Moreover, where were the scalpels he would need to cut me open? The IV drip? All the other medical equipment…?

*Fuck it*, I thought decisively, draining my drink. Enough of this. Enough speculating. I needed to return to that ratty apartment, I needed to find out more about that machine and the dead guy. Not now. Not pissed out of my gourd. I'd do it first thing tomorrow morning—Vincent Vega on the can be damned.

* * *

Beth arrived at exactly 11:26 p.m. From my table overlooking the glitzy lobby I watched her sweep across the marble floor and glide up the palatial staircase to the Rose Club like Cinderella on the eve of the king's ball. This wasn't hyperbole. She really did look like a princess right then. She'd changed into a shapely off-the-shoulder red dress that accentuated her thin waist, decent bust, and delicate arms. She'd also pulled her blonde hair into a bun which sat atop her head like a bird's nest, lifting her sharp cheekbones and swan-like neck.

All for me?

I stood when she spotted me. I offered her a smile and a wave. When she reached the table I pecked her cheek. "You look absolutely stunning," I told her. It might have been the coke, or it might have been the adrenaline pumping through me at the sight of her, but right then I didn't feel the effects of the ten or whatever drinks I'd guzzled. Warm and fuzzy inside, sure, but definitely clear-headed. "And you smell just as lovely," I added.

Beth smiled, though it was the smile of someone not yet comfortable in another's company. An elevator smile, I guess you could call it. "I'm sure you say that to all the girls you pick up at cigar bars," she said.

"Issey Miyake?" I said, surprising myself with the knowledge of the fragrance she wore.

"My, my, Harry," she said. "You continue to impress."

I pulled out her chair and said, "Please, sit."

She sat and glanced about the sultry atmosphere.

"I'm not a fan of the neon," I told her.

"You should come on a Wednesday night for the jazz."

"You've been here before?" I said, surprised.

"A few times."

Bangladesh came by and, after consulting with Beth, I ordered oysters, a cheese platter, and a bottle of one hundred fifty dollar champagne.

If Beth was impressed, she didn't let on.

"You said you've been here?" I said.

She had crossed her legs and was sitting rather stiffly. "That surprises you?"

"No—"

"Please, Harry. I'm a waitress. I know what you're thinking. Don't patronize me." She smiled and touched a finger to her forehead, almost the way people do when they've realized they've made a mistake.

"What?" I asked.

"Nothing. Nothing at all. Really. It's just…I can't believe I'm here with you. No offense. It has nothing to do with you. It's me. I—I just don't do things like this."

"Like what?" I asked.

"Accept invitations for drinks with strange men."

"I may be a little eccentric, but strange is a bit harsh."

"Maybe that's it. Your sense of humor—it's…corny."

"Corny?" I said, raising an amused eyebrow.

"So corny it's disarming. Please, take what I'm saying as a compliment."

"I've never been more flattered." I leaned forward on my seat. "Listen, Beth, I'm very happy you decided to join me."

"I think I am too."

"Just loosen up. We'll have some fun."

"This is the thing, Harry—and I know I must sound like such a nag—but I don't know anything about you. You don't know anything about me. I'll loosen up, don't worry. It might just take some time." She glanced at the bar, as if wondering where the waiter was with the champagne.

Bangladesh arrived a moment later carrying the bottle of bubbly wrapped in a linen cloth. He showed us the label, then removed the cork expertly so it didn't pop but rather sighed. He poured me a taster. I nodded. He filled Beth's flute, then mine, then left the bottle in an ice bucket.

I raised my glass. "To strangers."

Beth clinked. "To strangers."

We sipped.

"Look," I said, "I get it. You have this thing for not dating strange men—"

"I don't have a 'thing.' I simply stopped going out with men I don't know."

"So let's break the ice then," I said. "Get to know each other."

"Truth or dare?" she said sarcastically.

"Three questions," I said. "Anything you want to ask, ask away, and I will tell."

"You sound like a genie in a bottle." She crossed her legs again, this time placing the left thigh over the right. The dress was long enough I only caught a glimpse of her bare ankle, but I nevertheless felt myself get aroused. "What do you do, Harry? You never answered me at the bar."

"Used to do," I said, winging it. "I was a financial advisor. Started a brokerage firm in Dallas, then built a rental real estate portfolio. Sold it off last year and retired." I offered a disarming grin. "I know, not the most interesting of professions. But I never had the 20/20 eyesight to become an astronaut."

"Do you miss it, not working?"

"Sure."

Bangladesh arrived with the oysters and the cheese platter. We nibbled and I refilled our champagne flutes. We spoke a bit about travel, hobbies, all that usual get-to-know-you jive. I did a fair job improvising. Mostly, however, I did the listening. I thought I could listen to Beth all night and not get bored.

At one point Beth asked, "So you're not in New York for

work?"

"Didn't we agree on three questions?" I said. "I think this is something like your twentieth."

"The ice is broken, Harry. I'm trying to see what's lying beneath."

"Fair enough." I sat back, sipped the champagne, shrugged. "So what am I doing in New York?" *Good question, Beth—and one I should have anticipated and planned for.* "I'm doing what all retired men do," I said, buying time.

"And what's that?"

"Working—through my bucket list."

"Last night you told me you've been to New York before for business."

"For business," I said, nodding. "But all I remember are the inside of conference rooms and hotels and airports. I wanted to do the touristy stuff."

Beth sipped her champagne. She had applied red lipstick that added a fullness to her lips. She tucked an errand strand of blonde hair behind her left ear. She wore diamond or zirconia studs in each lobe. They matched the simple necklace looped around her slender neck. "Have you been to the Statue of Liberty yet?" she asked.

"Nope," I said. "Would you care to join me?"

"You said you're only in New York for a couple weeks."

"That's what I said. But that's another great thing about being retired. You can sit on a tree stump in a forest for a month, if it suits your fancy."

She glanced shyly at her champagne flute. "It might be nice if you stuck around for a while."

"Goodness gracious, Beth! I think that might be the nicest thing you've said to me yet."

She looked at me now—really looked. Her eyes pierced mine. I almost had to look away. "You're not married, are you, Harry?"

I laughed out loud, relieved. I hadn't known what was coming, but this was manageable. "Wow," I said.

"I'm sorry. But some men..."

I held up my left hand, wiggled my ring finger.

"It could be by your bathroom sink."

"Would you like to come upstairs and check?"

"You are, aren't you?"

"Married?" I took her hand across the table. "Beth, I'm not married. I'm not that type of guy."

"Girlfriend?"

"Are you offering?"

"Harry, you're an attractive middle-aged man. Most attractive middle-aged men are either married or lecherous bachelors. I'm being cautious, that's all. I told you—"

"I'm not married, Beth, and I don't have a girlfriend." I released her hand. I was starting to feel as though I was being interrogated and decided I needed to take control of the conversation. "Now it's my turn, Beth," I said. "Tell me something about yourself."

"I used to be a singer," she said simply.

"Like an opera singer?"

She laughed, a wonderfully sweet sound. "No, I was in a punk rock band. We were called the Pink Gypsies. I shaved half my head and dyed the rest purple. Don't laugh. We were good. I'm not just saying that. We almost signed with a major record label. But they pulled out literally on the day we were to sign the contract so they could sign some other band."

"Anyone I've heard of?"

"Their first album flopped. The singer lived out of his van for a year before killing himself."

"Jesus."

"I didn't know him."

"You weren't picked up by a different label?"

"We broke up—the band, I mean."

"Why would you do that if you were talented enough to nearly sign with a major label?"

"This was like fifteen years ago, Harry. I was still a kid. We all were. We thought we had the world by the tail, you know. Then this happened—our manager calling us one morning to tell us we were dumped. Johnny—he was the bassist—he was shooting heroin. Everyone else in the band was doing everything from acid to ecstasy on a daily basis. We all had Mick Jagger egos. We started hating each other. It got to a point we couldn't even get together for rehearsals, let alone put out a new demo tape. In other words, we were a mess. The record deal—had we scored it…who knows? It might have given us the motivation to get our shit together. Pardon my French. On the other hand, getting so close, then getting a 'thanks but no thanks'…it just sort of tore us apart. Johnny got an offer from another band and left us. Then the drummer died."

"Died?"

"Well, he came back to life. Speedball overdose. His heart stopped before he got an adrenaline shot. He went to rehab and we didn't keep in touch. Then it was just Jamie and me. Jamie was the lead guitarist. We were best friends. Went to this all-girl's school together, founded the band. We decided to give LA a shot, just the two of us. We went there knowing nobody, maybe a hundred bucks between us. But this wasn't the eighties. You couldn't just chat up someone and get a gig at The Troubadour, or The Roxy. We put together a new band, played a few no-name clubs, but…it was just over. That's how it is with bands. You either have that fire, or you don't. There's no in-between. Then Jamie was in a motorbike accident. Broke a bunch of bones. She was okay…eventually. Anyway, like I said, it was over. Us, the band. Jamie met a guy with a painting business. She stayed in LA. I returned to New York. I was thirty. I needed a job. I started working at the cigar bar." She shrugged. "And I've been there ever since. Eight lovely years." She glanced at her champagne flute with those sad, sexy eyes—and now I thought I understood where the pain came from.

It wasn't the not-making-it bit. A lot of people didn't achieve their dreams. It was the getting-so-close. That's what would keep you up at nights. A single record executive's decision, some dickhead who probably played the demo tapes to his kids for their opinions, and you're either Madonna or a cigar-bar waitress.

I said, "I'd love to hear you sing."

"My voice ain't what it used to be, honey," she said in a mock trashy accent.

"I'd still like to."

"Thanks, Harry. Maybe one day."

All this talking of squashed dreams was killing my high, and I could tell Beth wasn't thrilled to be reliving it all, so I said to her, "Would you like to dance?"

"This isn't exactly a disco. And I don't table-dance in public."

"Then let's go find somewhere." I stood and took her hand. "Come on, Beth. I promised you some fun, and we're going to have it."

# CHAPTER 4

My nightmares were the stuff of nightmares—really bad ones. I don't remember them all, but the one right before I woke had me without a face. I mean, I had a nose, and eyes, and ears—but they were all smoothed over, like I'd been plastered in paper machete. I couldn't see, couldn't smell. But I could hear. I was in a room with a woman. She had me tied to a chair and she kept snipping off parts of me: fingers, toes, nipples. She threatened my penis a few times, but thankfully I woke before that happened.

I didn't jerk awake bathed in sweat. Didn't cry out like they do in movies. I simply opened my eyes and thanked God I'd only been dreaming.

A moment later, however, the dream was forgotten, replaced by memories of the previous day. They hit me with the force of a sledgehammer to the chest, a kaleidoscope of images: the machine with the wires, the dead guy, seeing my reflection in the Burger King mirror for the first time, Dr. Singh, shopping at Kenneth Cole—Beth!

Now I did sit up in the king bed abruptly. The white cotton linens to my left were a tangled mess, intertwined with the faux fur runner. On one pillow lay a long strand of blonde hair. I lifted the pillow to my nose and inhaled the faint trace of her fragrance.

So it had been real. Thank God for that.

"Beth?" I said, wondering whether she was in the bathroom. The sound of my gruff voice jarred me. I had gotten used to it the day before, but now it was almost as unfamiliar as the first time I'd heard it.

Beth didn't reply.

"Harry Parker," I said, hoping for some epiphany to my identity, some recollection of my past, anything. Nevertheless, the name still meant nothing. My memory didn't magically return overnight.

*But at least it didn't disappear again either.*

I swung my legs off the bed and rubbed my eyes. Given how much I'd drank the night before, I felt surprisingly fresh. Physically at least. Mentally—well, shit, I was almost prepared to go straight to the minibar and start the day with a bottle of Scotch.

Beth. Where had she gone? Why hadn't she woken me? Had she tried? Had I been too passed out?

I rubbed my eyes, remembering the sex. It had been pretty goddamn amazing, if I do say so myself. And it seemed Dr. Singh was right in regard to all that mumbo jumbo about different memories being stored in different parts of the brain. Because although Beth was the only woman I could recall ever having sex with, I definitely had not forgotten the tricks of the trade. I had her moaning, squirming, scratching, whispering all night long—or at least for a couple hours until she fell asleep in my arms.

After the Rose Club we'd taken a taxi to a disco Beth had recommended. She knew the bouncer, we skipped the queue, and danced for a good hour or so. The place was packed, the music loud, everyone sweaty, everyone grinding. Beth's wall of caution came crumbling down, and when I invited her back to The Plaza around 1 a.m., she agreed without hesitation.

I looked around the empty suite.

So where the hell was she?

I stood, naked, and went to one of the windows. West Fifty-seventh was already filled with people marching about like ants in search of food.

I turned, stretching my arms above my head—and saw my wallet on the writing table.

"Aw, no," I said, going to it. I opened the sleeve and practically swooned with relief. The money was all there. Had it been gone, I wouldn't have cared I was out the cash. I would have cared that Beth had taken it.

Right now she was the only real thing in my life, and I needed her.

I went to the bathroom, to relieve my bladder, and found a note on the marble vanity. Black pen on the beige hotel stationary: "You looked too adorable to wake. Tonight—my place?" And below this, an Upper East Side address.

"You bet, Beth," I said, and ran the shower.

\* \* \*

I put on a fresh suit, studied my reflection in the mirror— I still had trouble believing the stranger staring back was me— then called the concierge to arrange a taxi.

"The hotel's Rolls Royce Ghost is currently available, Mr. Parker, if you would prefer," he said.

"Just a taxi, please."

"It's complimentary for our guests."

"A taxi, thanks."

"Of course. For what time?"

"I'll be down in ten."

"Certainly. A taxi will be waiting for you, Mr. Parker."

I hung up. A Rolls? Yeah, that would be discrete for what I was about to do.

I finished fixing myself up, collected *The New York Times* left in front of my door, then rode the elevator cab to the lobby.

The concierge—his nametag read "Ron"—was a young man with a smile as fake as a fresh-faced politician's. He led me to the taxi waiting out front by the curb, I palmed him a ten, and he said, "Anything else you need, Mr. Parker, just let me know. Are you a Knicks fan?"

"Nope."

Ron nodded agreeably. "Well, just let me know. That's what I'm here for."

"How about sending a couple bottles of Chivas Regal to my room?"

"Of course. Anything else?"

"How about a past?"

He frowned. "Excuse me, sir?"

I slid into the backseat of the taxi, closed the door on Ron, and told the driver to take me to Brooklyn.

* * *

Although I had no clue what the shitty apartment building that I woke up in the day before looked like, I recognized a dry-cleaning shop in which I had glimpsed some eastern European woman toiling behind a sewing machine. Only then did I pick out the building a little further down the street, and its black door.

"Do a loop around the block," I told the driver. "I know it's around here somewhere."

The driver was Thai, spoke broken English, and had kept to himself for the last fifteen minutes. I wanted him to circle the block so I could make sure there were no cops or hit men staked out, waiting for me to return to the scene of whatever the crime might be.

All the cars parked along the curbs appeared to be empty.

When we were approaching the dry-cleaning shop for the second time, the driver said, "You see yet?"

"I think it's that place there with the black door." I pointed. "Can you pull up out front?"

He rolled to a stop directly in front of the building.

"I'm not going to be long," I told him. "Two minutes at most. Can you wait right here for me?"

"I wait, no problem."

I gave him a twenty as a deposit, got out of the taxi, and ducked into the building, where I paused at the bottom of the staircase to listen.

I didn't hear anything.

I started up the steep, narrow steps. They creaked loudly. Anyone lying in wait for me would surely hear me coming, and I almost considered turning around and leaving. Almost. Because I needed answers. Were they worth my life? No. But I was being paranoid. Nobody was here. And it was just two minutes, in and out.

I continued up the steps and soon caught the first whiff of decay—a strange sweet scent, almost like cheap perfume, or a moldy apple.

When I reached the second floor I found Moby Dick in the same spot he'd been the day before, only now gravity had dragged the heavier red blood cells to the lowest parts of his body, leaving his face a ghostly white, and ugly purple splotches on the back of his neck and arms. The cloying stench emanating from the billions of bacterium eating him from the inside out nearly made me gag, but I steeled my stomach, covered my nose with the crook of my arm, and knelt next to him. Flies buzzed everywhere, searching for prime real estate to lay their adorable little maggots. Shooing them away, I patted down his pockets and retrieved a wallet and a smartphone, which I stuffed into my own pockets.

I went to the room with the *Dr. Who* machine. The machine was too large to take with me, so I flipped it over, searching for a label, a product number, something to give me a clue to its purpose or identity. Finding nothing except unremarkable black plastic and a series of heat vents, I committed the placement of every knob, every dial, every detail to memory. Then I collected the laptop and returned to the main room. I dumped the laptop into the cardboard box in the corner, burying it beneath manila folders and other stationary so the taxi driver didn't think I was looting the place. I scooped the box into my arms and was about to leave when I hesitated. I glanced at the door that led to what I suspected was the bathroom.

I had to know.

Going to it, I shifted the box to one arm, twisted the bronze handle with my free hand, and toed open the door. No Vincent Vega on the shitter aiming a MAC-11 at my head. Just a white porcelain toilet with dried piss on the seat and a crusty sink affixed to the wall below a cracked mirror. On the dirty tile floor a cockroach almost the size of a small mouse lay on its back, its hair-thin legs and antennae twitching as it died a slow death.

Releasing the breath I hadn't even realized I'd been holding, I got the hell out of there.

* * *

Back in my suite at The Plaza I set the box on the bed and went through Moby Dick's wallet first. His name was Charles McCarthy. The wallet was filled with receipts, grubby five and ten dollar notes, worn business cards, and, sheathed in plastic inserts, a photo of a woman who was likely his wife, and a photo of a child who was likely his son. Aside from half a dozen bank cards, there was a Macy's voucher, a coffee shop card with one hole-punch short of a free coffee, and a dozen other miscellaneous items. This made me reflect on my wallet, which now seemed sterile in comparison. Where was all the miscellaneous junk that people kept that they didn't need?

Nevertheless, this thought came and went without further contemplation because I was too anxious to examine the other stuff in the box. I went through the reams of paper first, but was soon disheartened. The pages were crammed with nothing but mathematical equations and symbols that were as alien to me as a foreign language. Inside the manila folders were more pages, these covered in messy handwriting. They didn't compose a journal. Just notes, scribbles, none of which I could make sense of. Whoever had written them had done so in a broken stream of consciousness, mentioning a string of scientific nonsense in one sentence, then a reflection on life in the next. At the bottom of one page, underlined twice, was, "Knowing is knowing that you don't know." The fat guy was either a genius, a nutjob, or a philosopher—or perhaps all three.

I whipped the manila folder I'd been flipping through across the room in frustration. Loose leaf fluttered to the bed and the floor.

I didn't know what I had been expecting to find—a tell-all confession written by me and addressed to myself—but there was nothing of the sort.

I powered on the laptop—the battery held a full charge—though my initial optimism on the ride back in the taxi had already curdled into dark pessimism.

I scanned the desktop. There were the usual programs you find with any operating system, and a few I didn't recognize. I opened the latter ones. The information that popped up was as meaningless as all the crap in the box.

Still, I wasn't about to give up. I would search through every file and folder on the computer until my fingers bled. First, however, I needed a stiff drink—badly. Ron the concierge was true to his word, and two bottles of Chivas Regal had been sitting on the writing table when I'd returned. I opened one, took a belt, went to the window—and contemplated smashing the glass with a chair and leaping to my death.

The thought was so startling I took an involuntary step backward.

*Fuck, Harry, what's wrong with you?* So you don't have a past. So you may never recover it. So what? That's worth ending your life over? People have it a lot worse than you, you cowardly son of a bitch. A lot worse. People have lost their legs in car accidents. People have had their faces burned off with acid by jealous exes. People have had their families murdered in front of their eyes maybe for no reason other than the fact the perpetrator was a sick bastard. People have been chewed in half by sharks and brain-zapped by lightning. And what's your problem? You can't remember the first girl you kissed, or whether you've ever been to Hawaii. Poor you. Poor Harry.

And by the way, have you already forgotten about that $750,000 in your bank account? Go buy yourself a first-class ticket to the Philippines, buy a luxury hut on some tropical island, and spend your days and nights drinking all the whiskey you want, and fucking all the twenty-year-old girls you can get your dick up for.

I tipped the bottle to my mouth, ruminating on the island fantasy, when my eyes fell on the dead guy's smartphone. It rested on the bed, next to his wallet.

"Shit," I said, crossing the room quickly. I'd been so focused on the box and the laptop I hadn't considered checking the phone.

I snatched it up and shook it awake. However, it turned out to be brand new, or at least factory reset: no photographs, no videos, nothing in the calendar or other apps. No contacts. It was as though he'd bought it to use a few times before disposing of it.

*And why would he do that, Harry?* I thought, navigating to the call log. *To make calls that couldn't be traced back to him. Calls to the kind of people I would very much like to have a word with.*

According to the log, he had one missed call yesterday afternoon at 2:43 p.m.—or right about the time I'd rung the mystery number in my wallet from Grand Central.

"Jesus," I mumbled.

I scrolled through the other calls. Twenty-six in total over a three-day period. Thirteen incoming, thirteen outgoing.

And all to and from the same number.

# CHAPTER 5

After several minutes of deliberation, I dialed the number. It was answered halfway through the second ring. "Charlie?" the voice on the other end of the line said. Male, hushed, the way you might speak while standing on a train and not wanting to disturb others. "Charlie?" the man repeated, louder. "Hey, Charlie, you there?"

"This isn't Charlie," I said.

"Barney!" the voice exclaimed.

I didn't say anything. My heart spiked in my chest. My stomach seesawed.

*He knew me.*

Or did he? Because why was he calling me Barney?

"Goddamn, man," he went on, "what the hell is going on? Where's Charlie? Why haven't you done it yet?"

"We need to talk," I said.

"Did something happen? Something happened, right? What happened? Where's Charlie? You know I can't be talking to you. Why are you calling me from Charlie's phone? What the hell is up, Barn? I'm at work. I can't talk now—"

"Meet me in Central Park in thirty minutes."

"Central Park? What are you talking about?"

"Thirty minutes. Out front the zoo. Wear a baseball cap."

"I'm not meeting you in Central Park, Barn! I can't be seen with you! And what the heck are you talking about baseball caps? I don't even own a baseball cap."

"Then I'll be at your work in fifteen minutes," I said, bluffing. I had no idea where he worked.

"Are you crazy?" He was no longer speaking in a hushed voice. He was close to shouting. Maybe he'd stepped outside, or into his office and shut the door. "Don't you dare. You hear me, Barn? You show up here—that's the craziest idea I've ever heard. How do you think you'd even get in? One retina scan, there'll be a dozen guns pointed at your head in seconds. What's wrong with you? Calling here, calling *me*. Is Charlie there? Let me speak to him."

"Charlie's dead."

Silence.

"Dead?" the man repeated.

I said, "Central Park in thirty, or I come to you."

A long pause. "Damn you, Barn." Another pause, even longer. "Central Park. The zoo. But I'm not wearing any stupid hat."

* * *

It was midafternoon, barely a cloud in the blue sky. The zoo was brimming with tourists and families and children. A safe enough meeting spot as any, I thought. I didn't believe the guy on the phone was going to slit my throat. He didn't sound threatening. Scared, confused—but not threatening. Still, better to meet somewhere public.

I waited a hundred yards from the zoo entrance, partly obscured by a tree. I'd been lurking in the same spot for twenty minutes now, as it had only taken me ten to reach the zoo from The Plaza.

At five to noon—forty-five minutes since the phone call, fifteen minutes later than agreed upon—I thought I spotted the man I had spoken with. For starters, unlike the dads and boyfriends and out-of-towners, he was dressed in a gray business suit and blue necktie. Secondly, he checked his wristwatch a half dozen times in under two minutes, all the while looking this way and that.

He was relatively young, thirty-five or about, freshly shaven, cropped hair, a tanned complexion. He wore dark sunglasses and had the arrogant, impatient air of a Hollywood talent agent.

I left the tree and approached him. He noticed me when I was twenty feet away. He pushed himself off the zoo's low wrought-iron perimeter fence. When I stopped before him, he extended his hand, surprising me. I made myself shake it. Then, to my greater astonishment, he pulled me into an embrace and patted my back. "Sorry about Charlie, Barn." He released me and stepped back. "So what happened? Heart attack? Am I right?"

"I have no idea."

"Had to be," the man said, shaking his head. "What else, right? Right?"

"I have no idea."

"No idea? Goddamn it, Barn—you know the risks I'm taking seeing you. You gotta do better than 'no idea.' Tell me what the hell's going on."

I stared at him. *Me* tell *him* what was going on? I didn't even know his name.

He snapped his fingers. "Hey, Barn, you there? You're looking —"

"We need to talk."

"You bet we do. Does anyone else know about Charlie? I haven't heard a thing. All anyone knows, far as I'm aware, he's still on sick leave."

Was the man stalling? Waiting for backup—the cops?

I glanced about, half expecting to spot an undercover agent whispering into a wrist mike, or a steely eyed assassin watching us from behind a newspaper.

"Walk with me," I said.

I started toward the zoo entrance. I had already purchased two adult tickets. The man hesitated, then followed. We passed through the gate and continued to the sea lions in the central garden area. I stopped in the middle of a bustling crowd of people, feeling less exposed.

"You still have Charlie's phone, right?" the man said.

I nodded.

"You gotta get rid of it. Trash it."

"Why?"

"Because my bloody number's on it, that's why!" He shook his head, rubbed his face. "Sorry, Barn. No disrespect—none at all. This is just all too much. I thought it was a done deal... But Charlie dead... Jesus Christ. Heart attack, had to be. He still at the apartment?"

I nodded.

"I guess we can take care of that. Moving him. It's going to take a goddamn forklift, but we can get it done." He hesitated, thinking. "Okay, Barn, listen up. We can fix this. We go back to the apartment. We take a cab. I'll call Skip. He'll finish the procedure. We'll get Charlie out of there, make it look like—well, hell, we don't have to make it look like anything if it was a heart attack. We just got to figure out some place to leave him where he wouldn't have been discovered for a few days. But don't worry. Don't worry about a thing. We'll get it done. Three days you'll be in Dallas, and none of this will have ever happened."

*None of this will have ever happened?* I began walking again, my mind reeling. *None of this will have ever happened?* It was almost as if I were in some horror movie in which the director was snipping and cutting scenes, gluing them back together however he pleased. I stopped in front a penguin exhibit. Two dozen of the birds stood on the rock surrounding their dipping pool, their wings either tucked against their sides or flapping ineffectively. The man was still next to me, still talking. I barely heard him. My thoughts were too loud. The kids around us were too loud. Everything was too fucking loud.

I closed my eyes, searching for an inner anchor.

"Barn, hey, Barn—"

I snapped my eyes open again and seized the man by the lapels of his tailored suit, yanking him toward me so our faces were inches apart.

"Who the fuck am I?" I said.

"Barn...?" His mouth dropped open, but he didn't seem to know what to say. "Dammit, let go of me!"

"Why do you keep calling me Barney?"

"Barn, what's— Oh God no."

"Answer me!" I shook him for emphasis.

"Listen, Barn," he said in a low voice, barely more than a whisper. "I get it. I think. What happened. I think I get it now. But Barn, let go, you're making a scene."

His sunglasses had slid down the bridge of his nose so I could see his eyes for the first time. They were brown, wide, frightened. I didn't see anything in them that hinted at deception.

I released him.

"Goddamn, man," he said, straightening his blazer, then looking about, offering a shit-happens grin to anyone who'd been watching us. He fingered his sunglasses back into place.

"Why do you keep calling me Barney?" I asked again.

"Because that's your name, Barn," he said, still using that hush-hush voice. He hooked an arm around my shoulder and led me along the path. "Your real name anyway. Now, look, you have to tell me everything that happened. Everything. Then I'll explain what I can. But I have to know what's happened."

"How can I trust you?"

"Me?" He seemed surprised. "Barn, we've known each other for five years..." His face fell. "But you don't have any memories of me, do you?"

"I don't even know your name."

"Stan, Barn. My name's Stan."

"Let me see your ID."

"Are you kidding me?"

"Now."

Chuckling to himself, the man slipped his wallet from the inside pocket of his blazer, passed me his driver's license. Stanley Phillip Williams. The ID looked real enough. I handed it back.

"Now listen, Barn," he said, tucking the wallet away, "you don't have any memories of me—of anything about your past.

Am I right?"

I nodded.

"You just woke up in a crappy old apartment?"

I nodded again.

"And Charlie?"

"On the floor. Dead."

Stan shook his head sadly. Then, like a switch flipping, the pity left his voice. He became all business. "Okay, listen up, Barn. This is no big deal." I could almost see his mind clicking, whirling, searching for solutions. "Like I said," he went on, "Charlie dying, it's a shame, a real goddamn shame, but we'll deal with it. You want to know what's going on—you're going to have to trust me. I know I seem like a total stranger to you. But I'm not. You have to trust what I'm going to tell you. It's going to blow your mind, but every word of it's true. And afterward, we go back to the apartment, you and me. That's the deal. You and me. We get this mess fixed up."

"I'm all ears, Stan," I said, and suddenly I wished I'd chosen a whiskey bar as our meeting spot instead of the zoo. We passed a grizzly bear enclosure without stopping and continued along the meandering path.

"What it seems like to me, Barn," the man named Stan said, "what it seems like, it seems like Charlie died before or just after he finished cleaning."

I frowned. "Cleaning?"

"The...erasing part."

"Of my memory."

"Your episodic memory."

"Why?"

"I'm not really sure how to tell you this, Barn..."

I squeezed his biceps, yanking him to a halt. "Listen to me, you son of a bitch. Stop dicking me around and tell me what the fuck is going on. I woke up in a chair yesterday morning with no memories of my life. *None.* I don't know my mother's name, or whether she's alive. *I don't know shit.* So you tell me why I was in that chair, and if you're lying—"

Stan tugged his arm free, almost indignantly. "We were saving your life, Barn."

I blinked in surprise.

"Saving my life?" I repeated. And a door deep inside me inched open, letting loose the fears of those inoperable diseases I'd imagined earlier. "What's wrong with me?"

Stan shook his head. "Nothing—not physically, I mean."

My relief lasted only a moment before the confusion and frustration returned in full force. "Who am I?" I demanded. "Who the hell am I?"

Stan gave me an ironic smile. He tucked his sunglasses into the breast pocket of his blazer and held my eyes, as if seeing me, the real me. He said, "Your name is Barney Hunter, my friend. You're a drunk and a part-time asshole, and you're probably the most influential man of the twenty-first century."

\* \* \*

I stared at Stan, searching for a sign that what he was saying was a joke. But it wasn't. I knew that. I *felt* that. For a moment the world canted. My knees wobbled. Stan slipped his arm around my waist to support my weight and led me to a bench next to a water fountain. I collapsed onto the wooden plank seat. He sat beside me. Across from us a snow leopard padded back and forth anxiously in its artificial environment.

"What are you talking about?" I said, and now I was the one speaking in little more than a whisper.

Stan produced a pack of Marlboros and lit up. He didn't offer me one. I didn't want one. I only smoked cigars. But he would know this, wouldn't he, if he really was who he said he was?

"I'm still not sure where to begin," Stan said, turning his head away from me as he blew smoke from his mouth.

"From the beginning," I said.

"You and Charlie—"

"Dead Charlie?"

"Yeah, dead Charlie." He glanced at me sadly. "Dead Charlie. That's all he is to you, isn't he? Dead Charlie?"

"I don't know him from fly shit."

"No, you don't," Stan said matter-of-factly, and perhaps with a touch of anger. "Not anymore. But you two were as close as close got. You met at Stanford. Neuroscience students. Geniuses, the both of you. I know how that sounds, but I'm not using the word lightly. Before you finished your degrees, you were publishing research in *Nature* and other scientific journals."

"Bullshit" was on the tip of my tongue. But my vanity and curiosity caused me to ask, "What kind of research?"

"The memory kind, to put it simply." Stan inhaled a final drag, then crushed the cigarette out beneath the toe of his expensive monk-strap loafer. "Look, Barn," he said. "Given what's happened, I don't know how to do this, so I'm just going to talk. You're just going to listen. Then you decide for yourself if you believe me or not. Okay?"

I nodded.

Stan nodded also, as if satisfied with his decision about how to proceed. He shot another Marlboro from his pack and lit up. He took a long, pensive drag, then continued. "Ever since the beginning of rational thought—the ancient Greeks, whenever—people have been trying to figure out what exactly memories are. Plato compared them to impressions in a wax tablet. A decade ago scientists compared them to a biological hard drive. The metaphors changed over time obviously, but they've always had one thing in common: persistence. A memory is a recollection of something that happened, and once that something happened, once that recollection is formed, it stays that way, always. It's why we trust our memories. They feel like snapshots of the past. At least, this is what we've believed for thousands of years—until you and Charlie proved that none of it was true."

\* \* \*

"Not true?" I repeated. The craving for a drink was almost all-consuming. My hands, I noticed, were trembling. I clasped them together and pressed them onto my lap.

Stan took a drag, blew the smoke away from me, and said, "Memories *feel* persistent, Barn, but they're not. They're malleable, always changing." He shook his head. "You've won a Nobel Prize, and here I am telling you about... You know, if you did an internet search of yourself—" He cut himself off, looked away again.

"What?" I said.

"Nothing," he said. The cigarette had nearly burned to the filter. Stan had it pinched between his thumb and forefinger. "I've just—I think I'm just starting to realize how hard this is going to be for you to take in."

There was something about the way he'd cut himself off that didn't sit right with me. It was almost as if he'd slipped up. But he was talking, I didn't want him to stop, so I pressed on and said, "So memories change. How?"

Stan waited until a mother pushing a baby carriage continued past us, then he flicked the butt of his smoke across the path. "Because," he said, "the act of remembering changes the memory itself. Each time you recall an event, the cells in your brain are being triggered and fired. They build new connections and links—literally rewiring the circuitry of your mind. In other words, when you recall and reflect upon memories, you're physically changing that memory. The entire structure of it is being altered in relation to the present moment, specifically the way you feel and what you're thinking at that moment."

"And you're saying I'm the most influential person of the twenty-first century because of this?" I said skeptically.

"Look, Barn, I'm not going to get into some molecular explanation. What would it matter anyway? It would make about as much sense to you as how the inside of a computer works. But in a nutshell you and Charlie discovered that the change in memories are facilitated by proteins in the brain. If those proteins don't exist, neither do the memories. And so you guys developed protein-inhibiting drugs that targeted specific proteins across the brain and, well, literally created the ability to erase specific memories. Still, it was mostly theory, all in the experimental stage. Mice, animals. Practical implications for humans were a ways off. But then the army got interested. They've been trying to block negative connections to the brain's emotional nexus for decades, to help soldiers deal with post-traumatic stress disorders. See, even though PTSD is created by trauma, it's really a disease of the memory. The problem isn't the trauma. Often the soldier's not even hurt. It's that the trauma can't be forgotten. Most memories, and the traumas associated with them, fade with time. Spot the family dog gets run over by a car, you cry for a week as a kid, but then you forget, or at least the memory of Spot doesn't hurt as much. You can thank evolution for that. A coping mechanism. But PTSD has always been different. The memories are too intense to fade."

"So…what…I work for the army?"

"Hell no," Stan said. "That was ten years ago or so. You and Charlie were only contracted to them for three years. And with a blank check from the Pentagon, along with a team of the best scientists in the country, you perfected your work. The FDA gave the drugs you created the stamp of approval. And overnight you made PTSD as redundant as the measles." He paused. "And in the bigger picture, you made the act of remembering a choice."

❋ ❋ ❋

A long silence followed that statement. My head felt ready to explode. How could this be possible? How could I be this man Stan was talking about? How could I be responsible for all this… this progress…and barely know what a neutron was?

I asked.

"After the success with the army," Stan said, "you were getting grants up the gazoo from every investment firm imaginable. Charlie was a simple guy, content with the scientific recognition of his peers, academia. He wanted to keep working on PTSD and other mental illnesses. But you were always different. I don't know how to put it. You were the Jobs to the Wozniak, I guess. You were the visionary. You had this idea of changing the world. And you did."

"By figuring out how to erase bad memories?"

"Hardly," Stan said. "You did much more than that. You founded a company which, within a year, was working on ways not only to erase bad memories but *enhance* them. And then... well...everything snowballed from there. Soon Rewind was developing methods to add *new* memories all together."

"Rewind...?"

"First company in history to be valued at more than a trillion dollars, my friend."

"Rewind," I said, repeating the name, but it meant nothing. Thinking about wandering around the city without a memory for the last forty-eight hours, the hell it had caused me, I said, "Why? Why would anyone want to erase their memories?"

"Because life's ugly, brutish, and short. Isn't that what they used to say? And it's true. Most people are unhappy. They screw up all the time. Accidents happen. Loved ones die. You do bad stuff. This all causes guilt, regret, pain, unhappiness, suffering. Scientists are convinced that the first person who will live to one thousand years old is already alive today. Imagine one thousand years of unhappiness and suffering." He hesitated. "Or imagine no suffering at all." Two young children ran past us, followed by their father. Stan waited until they were out of earshot before adding, "Thanks to you, Barn, the conscious mind is no longer ruled by the unconscious, by memories that cause negative emotions such as fear and, as a byproduct, anxiety."

I was staring at the pacing snow leopard but not seeing it. A thumping had started behind my eyes. My body felt light, almost as though it didn't weigh anything. "It's fake," I said. "It's all...fake. These memories, they're not real..."

"Fake?" Stan seemed amused. "A memory is something that happened in the past, Barn. But the past no longer exists. All memories are fake. I'm going to paraphrase you here. The mind's greatest magic trick is making us believe memories are real. They're as insubstantial as thoughts of the future are. All that matters is the present. Rewind not only lets people choose what they want to remember in the present, but it lets them become whoever they want to be in the present. You've allowed people to start their lives over."

I heard the click of his lighter, smelled burning tobacco. I rubbed my forehead where the thumping continued in tune with the beat of my pulse.

"Look, I'm not going to get philosophical on you, Barn," Stan said, exhaling a jet of smoke. "The ethics of your achievements have been debated for the last several years now. Sure, there are detractors. But the majority of people believe you've made life better for the human race."

*For the human race.* A laugh bubbled inside my chest, followed by another, and another. Soon I was in fits, wiping my eyes. Tears of pride, confusion, horror—I didn't know. I rested my elbows on my knees and covered my face with my hands. All the while I was wondering whether I was mad, whether this was all some schizophrenic delusion.

Stan was patting me on the shoulder, buddy-buddy, telling me words of reassurance.

Finally I got myself together and asked, "So how does it work?"

Stan flicked the butt of his cigarette to the same spot as the previous one. He shrugged. "There are more Rewind clinics than Starbucks around the country. You just walk in, you don't even need an appointment. You want a single memory cleaned—something embarrassing at school or work—no problem. You want an enhancement—turn your deadbeat dad who abandoned you into a man who loved you dearly—no problem either. You want a completely new identity, you got that too. That, however, is a bit more complicated, and only for those who can afford it."

So here we were, full circle, I thought, recalling how this conversation had started. "That's what I was undergoing," I said, more of a statement than a question. "I was getting a new identity."

Stan nodded.

"But why? If I'm this...this...genius or whatever you're making me out to be, why would I want to...rewind, flush my mind, my identity, my achievements, all down the toilet?"

Stan looked everywhere but at me. "Listen, Barn. I've told you all you need to know. The rest, it doesn't matter. Now what we have to do, we have go back to the apartment. Skip's one of our best techs, and more importantly, you can trust him. He won't speak a word of your new identity. He'll finish what Charlie started. You'll wake up in Dallas, but wake up right this time. You'll have a complete past, present, an entire life. You'll know everything from your favorite porn site to the codes for your overseas bank accounts—"

"I have overseas bank accounts?"

"What we've put in your Citibank account is spare change, my friend. Your new life, you're going to love it."

"Tell me why I would want a new life, Stan."

"You don't need to know that. You don't want to."

"Yes, I do."

"No, you don't."

I stood. "See ya."

Stan shot to his feet a second later. "Wait!" He gripped my arm. "Jesus Christ, Barn, you've always been a stubborn bastard." Sweat beaded his forehead. "Why you're doing this?" He shrugged. "For the same reason why everyone else does it."

"I have traumatic memories. Sorry, Stan. I don't buy that."

"It's true. But for you, Barn, there's more to it." He swallowed. "You're in trouble. Big trouble. With the law."

I wasn't surprised by this revelation. In fact, it's what I'd been waiting to hear. "What did I do?" I asked simply.

"I told you, Barn, you don't need to—"

"Tell me!"

"Barn, I'm one of your best friends. Trust me when I tell you that you don't want to know. It's why you agreed to the procedure in the first place."

"What if I don't want to go through with 'the procedure' anymore?"

Stan was shaking his head. "Don't you get it, my friend? Behind door number one is a life of pleasure. Behind door number two is a life in prison—haunted by memories that will cannibalize you from the inside out until you die an old, forgotten man."

\* \* \*

"Murder?" I stated. "That's it, isn't it? I murdered someone?"

Stan didn't reply, but the look on his face told me it was true.

"Who?" I said. "My wife? Was I married? Did I murder my wife?"

"Barn..."

I shook my head, causing the headache behind my eyes to flare. I rubbed my forehead. "I've been strolling around the city for the last day, Stan. I'm supposedly one of the most influential people of the twenty-first century, I'm a murderer to boot, and no one recognizes me?"

"Because you've already got your new face," he said.

I started. "My new face?"

"Face transplant," he said. He must have mistaken my expression of horror for one of surprise because he added, "It's no big deal, Barn. Doctors have been doing head transplants for quadriplegics for years now. Charlie, it's why he let himself go the way he did. Said he'd just get a head transplant one day, place his on a new young body. But he always had some excuse or another why he wouldn't go through with it. Anyway, face transplants are routine. Once you secure a donor, you're in and out in a few hours, and the lasers don't leave any scars. Same with your voice box. Easy-peasy. We could have given you a voice like Sinatra, but you insisted on...well, what you got."

I touched my face, plied the skin with my fingers, yanked my hands away in disgust.

It wasn't mine. I was wearing something else's face.

"I know, Barn," Stan said, "it's a lot to take in. Let's just go back to the apartment, finish the rewind—"

I stumbled backward, away from him.

Stan frowned. "What are you doing?"

"I'm going to look myself up on the internet."

"Barn—"

"Why not?" I said. "If I'm getting my memory wiped again, why not know what I've done—everything?"

"Because..." Stan hesitated. "Because you might do something to yourself. After what happened...we had to watch you until you got into that chair. You were suicidal. You tried to kill yourself. Twice. I was the one who found you the second time. You'd slit your wrists."

I glanced at them. Smooth as a baby's bottom.

"Same guy who did your face," Stan said.

I shook my head. "I don't think I want this anymore."

"Barn, you've already made the choice. It's why you were in that chair in the first place."

"I need time—"

"You've had time!" he snapped. "Eight months, to be exact. This was your best option. This or prison. No, there's a third option now, I guess. Doing nothing. Remaining just like you are. And I don't think that's something you want, is it, Barn?"

"Why Dallas?" I said. "Why can't I stay here in New York?"

"Our technology is near perfect. Near perfect. Ninety-ninety percent perfect. But sometimes a client's memories come back. Impressions usually, nothing more. Maybe you read about your brother's obituary in the paper, and something just...clicks. You think you know him, so you ring up his wife to pay your condolences, and things get a bit messy. It's why we've started offering to relocate the clients who opt for a complete new identity. It's a precaution so they don't go through, well, what I suppose you went through these past couple days. You chose Dallas yourself. Good climate, big place, easy to be anonymous."

"I took the laptop."

"What?"

"From the apartment," I said. "I was trying to figure out who the hell I was. I took it, and a box of papers—"

"Sure, sure, no problem. Skip will bring everything he needs, don't worry, don't worry about any of that, Barn. It'll be sorted. Now come on, we'll grab a cab—"

"I'll meet you there."

"Where?"

"At the apartment."

Stan frowned. "We had a deal, Barn. You agreed, you and me —"

He stepped forward; I stepped backward.

"I'll be there," I said. "Six tomorrow morning. I just—I need some time on my own."

"Barn—"

"Six. End of discussion."

I turned and walked away.

When I reached a branching path, I glanced behind me. Stan remained by the bench twenty yards back, though now he was speaking on his phone.

I turned left down the new path until I was out of sight, then I ran.

# CHAPTER 6

I n the suite at The Plaza I grabbed a bottle of Chivas with one hand and flipped open the laptop with the other. I took a long, burning drink, then stared at the desktop. I must have remained standing there for at least a few minutes, because the androgynous face of the operating system's personal assistant appeared and asked me how it could be of help.

"I need information on a person," I said.

"What is the person's name?"

"Barney—" I bit my lip.

"Can you provide a surname?"

"Forget it."

"Is there anything else I can assist you with—?"

I slapped the screen shut, then fell backward onto the bed, arms spread eagle, still gripping the Chivas in one hand. My mind replayed everything Stanley Williams had told me. All the while I took swigs from the bottle and debated with myself the pros and cons of verifying the information for myself. On the one hand, of course, I would learn the truth about my past and my influence in history—and who I murdered and why. On the other hand, I might find what I did so horrific I would... what? Kill myself?

Maybe. Because I was suicidal, wasn't I? Stan had said I'd tried to kill myself twice already, and the temptation to jump through the window over yonder had indeed crossed my mind just this afternoon…

These were the last thoughts before I fell into an exhausted, drunken sleep. I didn't remember closing my eyes, but when I opened them it was dark outside, and the room lights had dimmed themselves.

The bottle of Scotch lay on the bed next to me, empty. I glanced at the clock on the night table. It was eight thirty in the evening. I would have kept lying there, kept feeling sorry for myself, had my bladder not ached so badly. I got up and went to the bathroom. I avoided my reflection in the mirror—I didn't want to see the face that wasn't the one I was born with—and by doing so noticed the note Beth had left on the vanity.

I picked it up and read what she'd written in her quick, slanted script. Then I read it again. And again. The third time an emptiness filled me. Because I was going to go through with it, wasn't I? I was going to be at the decrepit apartment at 6 a.m. tomorrow. I was going to wipe my memory. Beautiful Beth with the sad eyes would become nothing but a… The word that came to me was "memory," but she wouldn't even be that, would she? She'd be nothing. As if she'd never existed.

Same went for me. Barney Hunter. I might not remember my life, but I still had a sense of self. And regardless of whether or not I knew or liked that self, wiping my memory felt a bit like agreeing to be taken off life support, because everything this poor shmuck had been, and currently was, would be gone, cleaned, erased, forever.

As if I'd never existed.

\* \* \*

I knocked on Beth's door an hour later. I had showered, dressed in a new suit, purchased two bottles of wine from a liquor store a short walk from The Plaza, and took a taxi to the address she'd left me. I knocked again, then stepped back on the small stoop, looking up at the two-story Victorian brownstone.

All the lights were on inside.

A moment later Beth opened the front door. She was dressed casual-chic in tight jeans and a gray turtleneck over a white dress shirt, putting it up for debate whether she had just stepped out of a supermarket, or off a catwalk. She greeted me with a dazzling smile. "I wasn't sure you were going to come," she said.

"Sorry I'm late," I said. "I—"

"You're fine. Come in, please."

Beth stepped aside and I entered a small foyer. I had expected the house to be carved up into individual units, but it appeared she owned or rented the entire place. She led me through a cozy living room and a pink-walled dining room—both with twelve-foot ceilings and decorative crown moldings—to a spacious, modern chef's kitchen.

I handed her the gift bag that contained the two bottles of wine. "I wasn't sure what was on the menu," I said. "So I came prepared."

"Just a salad and lasagna, I'm afraid. My mother's recipe though. I hope you'll like it."

"Smells delicious," I said, and it did. When was the last time I'd eaten something substantial?

Beth read the labels on both bottles, then set them on the center island. "Would you care for a glass? It'll still be another half hour until the lasagna is ready."

"Love one," I said. "White, please."

I would have preferred a Scotch, but who brought a bottle of Scotch to a romantic dinner date? I wasn't going to ask Beth if she had anything harder than wine in the liquor cabinet either. The shower had sobered me up a fair bit. I'd also drunk about a liter of water before leaving the suite at the hotel. Consequently, I felt in control and didn't need to make a mess of myself.

Not on the last night Beth and I would ever see each other.

This thought hammered me with regret, and I shoved it promptly from my mind.

Beth retrieved a corkscrew from a drawer, opened the Chardonnay, and poured two glasses, filling each a finger more than a standard drink.

"Cheers," she said, raising her glass.

"Cheers," I said, clinking.

"Umm... Should we go to the living room?" she asked.

"You're the boss."

She led me back the way we'd come and sat on a two-seat Queen Anne sofa with white leather and black wood trim. I hesitated a moment, wondering if I should choose the armchair. I sat next to her.

"You have a beautiful home," I said.

"Thanks, Harry."

*Harry.* The name rattled me. I had already begun thinking of myself as Barney.

*What other lies had I told her?*

"Are you okay?" Beth was looking at me, a frown touching the corners of her mouth.

"Sorry," I said, giving her a reassuring smile. "Just wondering if I'd remembered to bring the keycard to my room. Not that it matters. I can get another from the front desk." I sipped the wine to stop babbling.

"See any interesting sites today?"

"Central Park Zoo."

"You know, I've lived in this city my entire life, and I've only been there once."

"The sea lions were great. Had beach balls and everything."

"The best zoo I've ever been to was in San Diego. It's—" She shook her head. "I apologize. This is silly."

"What's silly?" I asked.

"We're talking about zoos, Harry."

"They make the best small talk."

"I'm just a bit...you know..." She stared into her wine.

Yes, I knew. She was nervous. She had a thing against dating strangers, and here I was, in her home, seeing her for the second time in as many days.

"You have roommates?" I asked, to change the topic.

"Roommates? Oh, you mean because of the house?"

"It's a big place for one person."

She smiled. "Thanks for being tactful, Harry, but I know you mean an *expensive* place for one person."

"I was thinking that too."

"It was a gift from my ex-husband."

I raised my eyebrows. "You were married?"

"For three years. Signed a prenup, so the house is all I got in the divorce. It was a gift."

"Nice gift."

"He traveled a lot. Where we lived together, it always felt like his place. Fine when we were together, but when I was alone I wanted something more...homey, I guess the word is. So he bought this townhouse for me as a birthday present."

"What did he do for a living?"

"He had his own business." She pushed a loose strand of hair behind her ear. "Anyway—"

"He must have done pretty well for himself."

"He did very well."

"What was he into—?"

"He's dead, Harry."

I blinked. "Jesus, Beth. I'm sorry."

"No, I'm sorry. I don't even know how we got onto him."

"My fault," I said quickly. "We should have stuck to zoos."

She laughed at that, breaking the tension that had stolen over the conversation.

"How about you?" I said, eager to move on. "Do anything fun today?"

"I went to the supermarket to buy the ingredients for dinner."

"That's fun?"

"I enjoy grocery shopping. I really do. There's something about a supermarket that's calming." She glanced at me sideways. "You think I'm an idiot, don't you?"

"Beth, you're one of the most beautiful, kindest women I

know," I said. And this wasn't a wisecrack because of my lack of memory. I was being one-hundred percent sincere. "To be truthful," I went on, "I really wouldn't care if we talked about cows all night."

Beth leaned close and kissed my cheek. "You're a very sweet man, Harry." She stood. "I'm going to check on the lasagna. Be right back."

I watched her pass through the dining room, skirt the large spruce table, and disappear around the corner into the kitchen —all the while wondering to myself what the hell I was doing. I'd decided to see Beth a final time because I had been alone and scared in the suite and wanted to be with someone for my final night as "me." I enjoyed her company the previous evening, and I knew if anybody could take my mind off what awaited me tomorrow morning, it would be her. And, yes, somewhere in the back of this depraved, selfish mind of mine, I thought maybe I could get her to sleep with me again.

*And then what? Sneak out of her bed in the middle of the night. No note. No nothing. Just—gone.*

I swished the wine around in my glass, then finished it off with one gulp.

Shit, I wasn't a part-time asshole. I was a fulltime one.

I got up and made my way to the kitchen. Beth wasn't there.

I went to the fridge, to retrieve the bottle of Chardonnay, and noticed a photograph stuck to the door with a magnet. It was of a little boy, no older than six or seven. I plucked it free and examined it more closely.

"He was my son."

I turned. Beth stood several feet behind me, at the mouth to the hallway. She'd likely been in the bathroom.

"Adorable," I said, sticking the photograph back onto the fridge. I opened the stainless steel door and withdrew the Chardonnay. "Just looking for this. Top-up?"

"Please."

I refilled both our glasses and we returned to the living room.

"Lasagna is nearly done," she said. "Fifteen minutes." She sat on the sofa.

"Wonderful," I said. This time, however, I chose the arm-chair.

"So what's the plan for tomorrow?"

"Tomorrow?" I said, poker-faced.

*How could she know?*

"Statue of Liberty? Empire State Building?"

"Right." I swallowed. "I...um..."

"I don't start work until five. If you'd care for a tour guide, I'd be happy to show you around. And I promise, no boardrooms or airports."

I smiled at her joke—and felt my heart break. Seeing her so bright, innocent, lovely, *caring* made me feel like scum, and I knew I couldn't do this, couldn't go through with the evening, lead her on, leave her in the middle of the night without an explanation.

"Harry?" she said, concerned.

I cleared my throat. "There's something I have to tell you, Beth. I know I said I was going to be around New York for a while. But the truth is something has come up." I hesitated. "I have to leave tomorrow."

Her face remained stoic. Nevertheless, her eyes said it all. Surprise, confusion—and anger, lots of it. "For how long?" she said tightly.

"I'm not sure."

"That means a long time?"

I hesitated, then nodded.

"I'm sorry, Beth, I—"

She shook her head. "I knew it. I *knew* it."

"Beth..."

"I open up, I let myself feel again, trust again, and...and... Damn you, Harry!" Tears spilled from her eyes. She wiped them irritably and stood. "Excuse me."

She vanished into the kitchen.

I stood. "Beth?"

She didn't reply.

"Stupid," I mumbled to myself. "Stupid, stupid, stupid."

I paced back and forth, wondering whether Beth was coming back, whether I should just leave, when I noticed for the first time the five framed photographs lining the fireplace mantle. They were all of the boy on the refrigerator door, her son. Smiling wildly while on a swing in autumn. Standing in front of a Christmas tree holding a present almost as big as he was. Sitting at a table with what might have been chocolate cake on his face.

I picked up the largest photograph. The boy was plopped on a carpeted floor, still a toddler in this one, gripping a rubber He-Man figurine in his hand—

*Bailey.*

I almost dropped the photograph. I spun around, convinced Beth had returned and said the boy's name. The room was empty.

I looked again at the toddler.

*Bailey.*

Why did I know his name? Why did I feel like I knew him?

Suddenly, bizarrely, I was nauseous to the point I might be sick. I leaned forward against the mantle and took several deep breaths.

"Harry, I think maybe it's best if you left, if we just called it a night."

I turned my head slightly, saw Beth in my peripheral vision. She was standing in the threshold to the dining room.

"Harry?"

I shook my head, no longer merely nauseous; I was woozy, disoriented, as if I'd been drugged.

"Your son," I said, raising the photo of the toddler. "What happened to him?"

"Harry, please, you should just leave."

I forced myself to stand straight and face her. "His name was Bailey."

Beth blanched. "How do you know his name?"

"What happened to him?"

*"How do you know his name?"*

"He's dead. How did he die?"

"Harry, I want you to leave. Now."

"I need to know, Beth."

"*You* need to know?" she said. "*You* need to know about *my* son? How he died? Are you sick? What kind of question—?"

But the rest of her words were drowned out in white noise. Beth's living room disappeared, and I was in the nursery ward of a hospital, cradling a wrinkled, pink Bailey in my arms. Then I was pushing him from behind as he peddled his new Big Wheel along a sidewalk. Tobogganing with him down Pilgrim Hill in Central Park. Reading him bedtime stories with a flashlight in the dark. A dozen other memories.

"Tonka truck," I said, exchanging the toddler photo for the Christmas one. "That's what was in the present. A Tonka dump truck. He loved it—until he left it in the snow one winter and it rusted."

Beth was backing away from me. She clapped her hands over her mouth and said something I couldn't understand.

"What?" I said.

"You."

"What the hell are you talking about?"

"Barney?" she whispered. "Oh my God. *Barney…*"

I threw the photograph across the room into a wall. The glass shattered. The silver frame clattered to the floor. Beth yelped.

"What happened to Bailey, Beth?" I said, stepping toward her.

"You're dead," she said.

"I seem to be very much not."

Beth ran. I caught her in the kitchen and slammed her against the refrigerator. "What happened to Bailey, Beth?"

"Barney, please—"

I pressed my right forearm against her throat, choking her.

"What did you do to him, you fucking bitch?"

"You did!" she cried, her face turning a beat red. "You killed him, Barney! *You killed our son!*"

A new tsunami of memories stormed through me, these of

Beth. Meeting her at the cigar bar for the first time, the real first time, while I was there with colleagues from Rewind. Dinners with her at expensive restaurants, often Japanese, because that was her favorite cuisine. Talking about having children one evening while strolling down Fifth Avenue. Entertaining friends at our Park Avenue penthouse.

*Returning from an overseas business trip two days early, stepping from the elevator into the triplex. Going first to the wine room and selecting a fine champagne to share with Beth, to celebrate the latest deal I'd inked. Calling her name but receiving no answer. Checking the master bedroom, then the sitting room, then the gym and the spa. Taking the gallery stairs to the second floor. Hearing music coming from the library. Pushing open the door to find a fire glowing warmly in the fireplace. Beth naked on the bearskin rug in front of the fire, sleeping in the arms of a man half her age. Walking to them calmly and bashing the man's head open with the bottle of wine. Beth waking and screaming and telling me to stop. Chasing her through the ballroom, through the dining room, catching her in the foyer as she attempted to flee either to the upper or lower floors. Pummeling her with the bloody, broken bottle until Bailey appeared, crying, telling me to stop. Gripping the boy by his pajama top and shoving him away. Bailey flipping backward over the bannister and falling to the marble floor twenty feet below, breaking his neck, dying instantly.*

Beth was yelling at me now, clawing at my face, trying to free herself. I leaned against her with all my strength.

"You made me do it," I spat, seeing red.

She kept yelling, clawing.

I rammed my forearm harder into her throat.

She made a noise like she might retch.

"You did!" I repeated "You!"

"You—" she croaked.

"You!" I shouted. "You made me do it! You ruined my life!"

Breathing hard, like I'd just run a mile, I released her. She doubled over coughing, gagging. I seized the bottle of Merlot by the neck, which was still on the kitchen's island, and smashed it against the back of her skull. She dropped to her knees. I bashed her again and again, wine and blood painting the kitchen red.

\* \* \*

I cleaned myself up in Beth's bathroom the best I could and walked back to The Plaza. In my suite I opened the laptop, requested the personal assistant, and spent the rest of the night and early hours of the morning learning about Barney Hunter. Everything Stanley Williams had told me turned out to be true. I was a genius. I revolutionized life in the twenty-first century. And I was also a coldblooded murderer. I'd killed the guy Beth had been sleeping with. I'd been charged and convicted with first-degree murder in absentia. Same with Beth and Bailey, convicted in absentia, though in Beth's case it had been attempted murder, and in Bailey's, second-degree murder.

Beth had dismissed the staff the night before the double homicide, no doubt so they wouldn't witness her affair. The first maid to arrive the following morning found the three bodies. Beth remained on life-support for two days before making a full recovery. She had also been villainized in the media. According to a "close source" in one story, this was the reason she'd ended up back at the cigar bar; she was friends with the owner, and he was the only person in town who would hire her.

Most photographs of Barney Hunter were of a middle-aged man with gray hair, eyeglasses, and unremarkable features. In one photo I noticed he had brown eyes while I—Harry Parker, at least—had blue eyes.

It had been eight months since I'd returned from Tokyo early to find Beth and her lover in the library. A week to the day, the police speculated I'd committed suicide. Security video footage showed me—wearing a rudimentary disguise—renting a power boat from the Chelsea Piers Maritime Center. The boat was later discovered abandoned in the middle of the Hudson River. Because my body was never recovered there has been an ongoing debate as to whether I was still alive or not.

Most believed the latter. After all, I'd killed my own god-damn son, accident though it may have been.

At five in the morning I closed the laptop and took a long hot shower. I dressed in a fresh suit and tossed the bloodied one, along with all the other clothes I had purchased, into the plastic bags they had come in. Then I rang the concierge to order me a taxi. The bellhop loaded the waiting cab with my belongings—including the cardboard box and laptop—while I settled my bill in cash.

I arrived at the derelict Brooklyn apartment at 5.46 a.m. I opened the black door and stepped inside. Stan was sitting on the third step. He jumped to his feet when he saw me, an expression of immeasurable relief on his face.

"Thank God, Barn!" he exclaimed. "You came!"

"It's Harry—Harry Parker," I said. "Let's get this over with."

# RUN

# PROLOGUE

They had set up camp in the foothills of the Catskill Mountains earlier in the day. Located in the southeastern part of New York State, the area was a wilderness of mixed hardwood forests carved up by narrow valleys, rushing rivers, and a plethora of hiking trails. Now it was a little past midnight. The nippy autumn air was redolent with the smell of dead leaves. Overhead, the black expanse of night sky glowed with stars.

Sitting with her knees pulled into her chest, close enough to the fire to warm her hands, Charlotte recalled the time she'd come to a park somewhere in these parts as a kid. She'd spent much of the morning at a swimming hole, catching tadpoles and fishing with an eggbeater rod. Her grandfather showed her how to decapitate and gut a trout. He loved fishing, and he must have told her the story how he caught the twenty-one-inch largemouth bass mounted above the fireplace in his study a dozen times.

Her grandparents had raised Charlotte since she was eight. That's how old she was when her parents were murdered in a home robbery. They'd been shot with a sawed-off shotgun. Charlotte had been the one to find them. She'd heard the shots but remained at her bedroom door, too scared to do anything except call out for them. When they didn't reply, she eventually crept down the stairs to the ground floor. She saw the bloody footprints first. They zigzagged all over the marble foyer floor. She followed the bloodiest set to the kitchen, where her father had been on his back, his brains spilling from his skull, her mother on her stomach, her blouse frayed, the skin beneath shredded and wet with blood.

Charlotte didn't remember any details after that. The memories of the rest of the night had faded to some dark corner of her mind. All she knew was that the neighbors had called the police. She was taken to the hospital. She talked to a lot of people, detectives and doctors probably. Then her grandparents arrived and told her she would be living with them.

The thieves, she'd learned a couple years later when she was deemed mature enough to be told how and why her parents were slaughtered, had stolen most of her mother's jewelry, which had been valued at roughly two hundred thousand dollars. They were never caught.

Charlotte always found it strange how she had only known her parents for eight years of her life—really, only known *known* them on a cognitive level for half that time—but they remained more real and important to her than anybody else she'd met to date, her grandparents included. She could still recall their faces, their expressions, their voices, their laughter. How her mother would let her cook and bake with her at the stove. How her father would give her scratchy chin kisses when he didn't shave.

Charlotte had organized the present camping trip because she had hoped the solitude and fresh air and raw nature would do her boyfriend Luke some good. And for a while it had worked. He'd seemed to be somewhat at peace with himself—until fifteen minutes ago anyway.

Emma said, "What do you think they're doing?" She was sitting across the fire from Charlotte, dressed in an over-sized Icelandic sweater, black tights, and Timberland boots. Her glossy black hair fell past her shoulders, in stark contrast to her porcelain skin, which seemed timeless in the firelight. Her father was the CEO of an aviation-aerospace company, her mother a successful real estate agent, and she'd grown up likely believing credit cards only came in platinum. That being said, she was smart, a good listener, and one of Charlotte's best friends.

Charlotte shrugged. "I guess they're talking." She was twisting the engagement ring on her finger unconsciously.

"I feel bad," Emma said. "It was my fault."

"It wasn't your fault."

"I can't believe he got so mad at me."

Ten minutes earlier Emma had been telling a ghost story about a girl who was burned to death at an orphanage and kept coming back to haunt the kids who had teased her. When she began explaining in detail what the burned girl looked like, blistering skin and all, Luke snapped. He went from being so quiet you almost forgot he was there to raging at Emma so viciously she shrank back in fear. Charlotte tried to placate him. He waved her away and stormed off. She explained to Emma and Emma's boyfriend Tom what Luke had been through in Afghanistan, how small things could set him off. He wasn't really mad at Emma, she'd insisted, he just needed some time to cool off. Eventually Tom went to check up on him while Charlotte remained with Emma.

"Like, he was normal one minute," Emma went on, "and the next..."

"He's still adjusting," Charlotte said. "It takes time."

"You said he was just quiet. You didn't say anything about a temper."

"He never had a temper before. This is all new for me too."

"This happened before?"

"He hasn't snapped like that. But like I said...he's different." Charlotte hesitated, wondering where to begin. Emma had never met Luke. Charlotte and Emma were friends from their time at NYU where they'd been neighbors in Third North, a residency on the Washington Square Campus. Luke had been in the army all that time.

"Different?" Emma said.

"Different—like, *different*. He doesn't like talking. Not much anyway. We don't sleep together. We did the first couple nights he was back. But now I usually find him on the sofa in the basement, with all the lights on."

"Usually?"

"Sometimes he's in the kitchen when I wake up."

"What? Sleeping on the table?" Emma started to laugh, but seemed to think better of it.

"Awake," Charlotte said. "Drinking whatever booze is around."

"In the *morning*?"

"I think all night."

"You never told me this."

"It's tough to talk about. You don't know him."

"So does he drink, like, all the time? I mean, every day?"

Charlotte nodded. "He's…I don't know what you call it. Self-medicating? Sometimes I wonder if he still thinks he's in Afghanistan. He never leaves the house. And when he does, he's all agitated. He hates crowds. They make him nervous. That's why I thought this camping trip would be good."

"A lot of army guys go through this when they come back, don't they? Like that guy in *Forest Gump*. Not Tom Hanks. You know, the guy without the legs?"

"Yeah, but Luke's injury is in his head. Think about it, Em. The army spends months training you to kill people, right? You go to war and see some horrible stuff, right? You probably do some horrible stuff too. Then you come back on a Thursday and everyone expects you to get a job on Monday. There's no decompressing."

"Can't he go to VA, Veteran Affairs, whatever it's called?"

"Don't get me started on them."

"What do you mean?"

"After what happened—you know, with Luke's unit, the ambush—he began having a lot of problems with the guys above him. I don't know the details, Luke won't talk about it. But he did something and they wanted him gone. They ended up making him sign this thing called a Chapter 10. Pretty much it means you don't get thrown in the brig, but you get a less than honorable discharge, which means you're not eligible for medical benefits."

"What did he do that got him in so much trouble?"

"Not following orders? Getting into fights? I don't know. But what really gets me mad is that whatever got him kicked out was a direct result of the ambush. It doesn't take a rocket scientist to realize that seeing your whole unit get wiped out is going to give you more than a few nightmares. Who's not going to flip out a bit? The army should have tried some counseling with him or something, or gave him some time off. Instead, they just gave him a bunch of meds and kept sending him back out to shoot people, which made him worse and worse until he did whatever he did. What the fuck is that?"

"I don't get it," Emma said, her long-lashed, green eyes flashing with anger. She tucked a lock of hair behind her ear. "Why wouldn't they just help him?"

"It's too expensive. It would cost them billions to give ongoing treatment to soldiers with psychological conditions. It's true. It's all over the internet. It's been going on for years. At first the army was misdiagnosing soldiers with something called a personality disorder, which they said was a preexisting condition to service, which again means no benefits. This is garbage because every soldier is screened before boot camp for stuff like personality disorders. They all have to pass psych tests and be deemed fit for duty to get into the military. So five or six years ago, when the media started getting wise to all this, there was this big backlash. So now instead of the army wrongfully diagnosing soldiers and screwing them out of their benefits, they're just not diagnosing them at all. They're pretending there's nothing wrong with them. And when these guys, guys like Luke, start breaking down and getting in trouble while still enlisted, the army makes it look like it's their fault, and they kick them out when it's the army that made them that way."

"There has to be someone you can talk to about this, Char."

"Maybe if it was only Luke. Maybe someone would cut him

a break. But it's the system right now. You can't fight it. At least one person can't fight it."

They sat in silence for several long seconds. The flames of the fire licked and spit. Crickets chirruped. The breeze changed direction and blew smoke in Charlotte's direction. She covered her nose with her hand but didn't move from the heat.

"So, what's wrong with Luke then?" Emma asked. "Is he, like, depressed or something?"

"That, plus anxiety, nightmares. He's even been having hallucinations and flashbacks." She shrugged. "Post-traumatic stress kind of stuff—which, I should mention, the army does acknowledge can be a result of combat trauma, and which his disability benefits would have covered."

"Can't you take him to a normal doctor or something?"

"A civilian doctor?" Charlotte said. "I've mentioned it to Luke. I'm hoping I can convince him to go when we get back to the city." She put on a brave face. "But who knows? Luke, he's tough. He's only been back for a few weeks. This all might pass. He might get better on his own."

"Or he might get worse." Emma fiddled with one of her nails. "Have you ever thought of...well...like, leaving him? Just listen," she added quickly. "I don't want to sound indifferent to what he's going through, but to be honest, I was a bit freaked out when I met him this morning. He was so aloof, shifty. And now, knowing this..."

"It's not his fault, Em."

"No, maybe not. But it's not your fault either, or your responsibility, I guess I should say. You guys really only dated way back in high school. Okay, so you saw him a few times over the years when he was on leave. But that's a long time not to be with someone on a regular basis. Like you said, he's changed."

"What do you expect me to do, Em? Dump him when he needs me the most? He just spent the last six months in a warzone trying to kill people and having them trying to kill him. He needs time to readjust to normal life. Imagine if you were dropped in Afghanistan tomorrow—"

"I'm just saying—"

"I know what you're saying. And would you be telling me to dump him if he had cancer or something like that?"

"It's not the same."

"Why not?"

"Because he's scary, Char. I mean, I might not know him well, and he might be getting better, I don't know. But right now I'm worried about you."

Charlotte shook her head. She didn't want to talk about Luke anymore. She shouldn't have bothered in the first place. Emma didn't understand. She couldn't understand. Charlotte stood. "Come on," she said. "Let's see if Tom found him."

✳ ✳ ✳

As they started down the path toward the lake Charlotte played the flashlight beam among the hemlock, sugar maple, and birch trees crowding the beaten path. It didn't reveal much except the shadowy outlines of tree trunks and the canopy of spindly branches overhead.

Abruptly Tom's voice cut through the night. He sounded panicked.

Charlotte glanced at Emma, who shook her head. Then they broke into a run. The trees thinned, tapering off to smaller shrubs and scrub. Slabs of rock angled down into the three-mile-wide lake that spread away from them like a vast oil spill. The waxing moon cast a silvery reflection over the mirror-smooth surface.

Tom and Luke stood twenty feet away, facing one another. Tom was holding up his hands, palms outward, as if trying to calm Luke. His family was filthy rich, and everyone knew him as a spoiled brat womanizer who'd gotten accepted to Columbia's MBA program because his father was a Wall Street big shot. Physically, he was a muscular jock type, with a brown mop of hair and an unkempt beard. His shirtless upper body was lean and tanned in the moonlight. Right then, however, backing away from Luke, who stood six four, he looked small and unimpressive.

Luke's hair was still cut military high and tight. His features, always straight and handsome, now seemed sharper, carved out by black shadows, his eyes lost in the dark recess below his brow. He wore board shorts and a white T-shirt. Sleeve tattoos covered his biceps and forearms, running the gamut from machine guns enshrined in roses to demon drill sergeants to skulls and snakes, a fury of green ink. "You wanna know?" Luke was saying. "You really wanna fucking know?"

"Dude," Tom said, "I was just chatting."

Charlotte stopped a few feet from them. "Luke, what's going on?" she demanded.

"This motherfucker asked me if I'd shot anyone."

Tom shrugged. "I didn't know it was such a big deal."

"Shooting someone's no big deal? You ever shoot someone, dickhead?"

"It's all right, Luke," Charlotte said.

"He's fucking crazy—" Tom said.

Luke head butted Tom in the face. The sound was like someone snapping their finger and thumb together, and that might have been Tom's nose breaking.

Tom collapsed to his knees, then to his side, where he rocked back and forth moaning and cupping his face in his hands.

"Luke!" Charlotte cried, seizing his arm and yanking him away from Tom. He shoved her hard, sending her flying through the air. She landed on her tailbone. The flashlight clattered away from her.

Yelling, Emma attacked Luke, batting him with her hands, but she might have been a butterfly attacking a bear for all the good she was doing. He swung a sideways closed fist at her, striking her temple. She collapsed to the rocky ground, unmoving.

Luke kicked her in the head with his bare foot. The impact made little noise but snapped her head sideways.

Leaping to her feet, Charlotte felt ill, and all she could think was: *This can't be happening! This isn't happening! He's going to kill them!*

Luke raised his foot over Emma's head, as if to stomp it like an egg.

Charlotte crashed into him, pleading with him to stop.

One of his hands clamped her around her throat. His eyes shone like an animal's, intense, emotionless, unrecognizable.

She raked her nails down his cheek, drawing blood.

Cursing, he let her go.

She ran.

\* \* \*

Dead leaves and moss and lichen scattered beneath her feet. The scent of rot and evergreen seared her nostrils. Her heart was pounding. Her breathing came in gasping sobs. Everything whipped past her in a blur of darkness.

She risked a glance over her shoulder to gauge Luke's pursuit.

He was a dozen feet back, gaining on her.

She reached the campsite moments later and blew past the two dome-shaped tents, knowing there was no time to search them for the car keys. She ducked the clothesline they'd strung up and leapt over the orange ice box. She landed awkwardly, touched a knee to the ground, then barreled through waist-high grass and cattails. Trees closed around her once more.

She didn't need to risk another glance over her shoulder to know Luke had followed her into the thicket. She heard the racket of his pursuit.

She thought she was running parallel to the road they'd driven in on, which meant if she continued in a straight line she would end up at the main camping area, where there would be others.

Yet would this matter? Would Luke get hold of himself and calm down? Or would he continue his insane rampage and attack everyone? Was she putting others in danger by leading him to them?

But what else could she do?

The trees became denser. Branches tore her dress and skin, scraping and cutting her bare arms and legs.

She had never been this terrified in her life. She wanted to scream, to tell Luke to leave her the fuck alone. But she was too scared, too winded, to do so.

Luke barked something at her, something vicious, and just as she was thinking he was going to catch her, and beat her to a pulp, and maybe kill her in his madness, she burst into a clearing —a clearing filled with a handful of cabins. She veered toward one which had light seeping from a window.

Luke tackled her from behind. The impact with the ground blasted the air from her lungs. She skinned the palms of her hands and bit her lower lip. She tried to yell for help but choked on blood.

She rolled onto her back, gasping, struggling to free herself from beneath his bulk. He raised a fist. She shoved her hands into his face, pushing with all her strength. One of her thumbs found an eye socket. She dug it into his eyeball.

Luke cried out. Charlotte wormed out from beneath him and scrambled to her feet. Before she could flee, however, he snagged her hair and yanked hard. Her feet flew out from beneath her and the back of her head struck the ground with blinding force.

Blackness washed over her like a monster wave.

# CHAPTER 1

*ONE YEAR LATER*

**T**hey were learning how to make Neapolitan-style pizza that evening.

The kitchen was warm and homely with brick walls and wood furniture and blue countertops. The seven students, including Charlotte, sat around a long rectangular table with their ingredients placed before them. The teacher wasn't a personable Paula Dean or Jamie Oliver type. Her name was Lucinda, a robust Scottish woman with a perm that resembled a helmet and a front tooth that had decayed and turned a rotten gray. She was loud and crass and ran the workshop like a gastronomic boot camp, browbeating anyone who dared make a mistake. Having said that, she was funny too, and Charlotte was laughing with everyone else when she told one of the students that her pizza looked like it had been set on fire and put out with a golf shoe.

This was Charlotte's third workshop since she'd arrived in Asheville, North Carolina, last month. Her plan was to take one a week until she knew Italian cuisine inside-out.

When Lucinda dismissed the class at eight thirty, Charlotte said goodbye to the other students and stepped outside into the pleasantly cool autumn night. Asheville has been called everything from a New Age mecca, to one of the most beautiful places in America, to the "New Freak Capital of the US," courtesy of *Rolling Stone* magazine. Primarily known for its relaxed artistic community and panoramic mountain views, it was nevertheless gaining recognition for its burgeoning culinary scene, which was the reason Charlotte had chosen to do her masters of hospitality management at the University of North Carolina Asheville campus.

While heading down Broadway, trying to remember what time her first class at the university began tomorrow, a pair of hands clapped over her eyes. She froze mid-step.

"Guess who?"

She turned around. "God, Tony," she said, touching a hand to her heart. "You scared me half to death."

He grinned. "Who did you think it was?"

"What are you doing here?" she asked.

"Stalking you."

"I thought you had something with your friends?"

"Dan's birthday. We're going to Off the Wagon. Your cooking school was on the way, so I thought I'd pop by."

Tony was also enrolled in hospitality management. They'd met in one of their classes. He came late and sat beside her, then asked her out for a drink afterward. He had a dark, mysterious look with long black hair, brown eyes, and mocha skin. Thinking it wouldn't hurt to get to know some people in her course, maybe start a study group, she accepted his invitation. After a few drinks, however, one thing led to another and she ended up back at his place. Fast forward three weeks and they were unofficially dating—unofficially because neither of them had brought up the topic of dating. They were friends who had sex every now and then, no strings attached. So far Charlotte was fine with that arrangement. She wasn't ready for anything more serious.

"Dan..." she said, trying to put a face to the name. She'd only met Tony's friends a few times.

"You don't like him, remember?" Tony said.

"Was he the one who puked everywhere Monday?"

"And wiped his mouth on your shirt."

"It was my jacket."

"Yeah, I know, and sorry about that. He can be a prick sometimes. You want to come for a drink or two now?"

"So Dan can wipe his puke on me again? No thanks."

"It's early. He won't be smashed for a good couple hours."

"Sounds riveting, Tony. But I haven't even looked at the readings I have for my classes tomorrow."

"I haven't opened a textbook all week."

"I plan to graduate."

"I'll graduate. Don't worry about that. I'm more of a crammer than a planner."

They stopped at the corner to her street. "Give Dan my best wishes on his birthday," she said.

"You free tomorrow night?"

She pretended to think about it. "I have this speed dating thing between six and nine. But after that…"

"Speed dating? Just get on Tinder." He shrugged. "So how about dinner?"

"Sure. There's a place called Eddie Spaghetti I want to try."

"You and your Italian."

"That's the kind of restaurant I'm going to open."

"Hey, I'm in on that too. We just need to round up a million bucks somewhere first. By the way, I'm going to be away this weekend. I gotta go to Charleston. My sister's in the theatre company there. Her new play's opening."

Charlotte raised her eyebrows. "She's an actor?"

"She prefers performer. She sings and stuff."

"When are you coming back?"

"Sunday. Classes on Monday, right?"

"Well, enjoy," she said, stepping close to him. "I'll miss you."

"Me too. You—I mean. I'll miss you."

They kissed for a good five seconds, and just as it was heating up Charlotte pulled away. She wasn't going to make out in the middle of the street.

Tony said, "You sure you don't want to come for a drink?"

"I really do have work to do. Tomorrow."

"I'll call you."

Charlotte watched Tony cross Broadway, a pang of regret building in her chest. She knew Off the Wagon would be filled with attractive girls, and she almost changed her mind and joined him after all. But then he reached the far sidewalk, a bus grumbled to a halt in front of her, and the moment passed.

\* \* \*

Charlotte was renting a room in a two-story, mauve-painted townhouse on a gently sloping street lush with greenery. She'd chosen it because it was close to both the university and the cozy downtown center of Asheville. Also, it was clean, well-maintained, and her bedroom window overlooked a small wooded area. She shared the house with three roommates, all students. The two girls stayed at their boyfriends a lot, and the guy was always out at the bars, so she usually only saw them in the mornings getting ready for school. Thankfully, there were two full bathrooms, one on each floor, so there was never a queue to take a shower.

Standing in the kitchen, waiting for the water to boil in the kettle, Charlotte found herself once again thinking about Tony, wondering what he was doing right then. Knocking back beers and chatting up girls? Did he do that—chat up girls—when she wasn't around? After all, they weren't a couple. She'd been careful not to open up too much, get too close. She liked his company, but she needed her space too. So if the opportunity presented itself for him to take home some floozy tonight, would he oblige? She didn't think so. At least, she hoped not.

Maybe she should stop being so aloof, she thought. Maybe it was finally time to move on from Luke. On one level she had. She'd never visited him in prison, and she'd returned her engagement ring. That had been six months ago. She'd mailed it to him in a padded envelope with nothing else.

So on that level—on severing ties—she had moved on. Yet emotionally she hadn't. She still thought about him too much. She still hated the way she'd abandoned him. She still blamed herself for not doing more to help him.

She still wouldn't allow herself to get close to someone else.

The kettle whistled. Charlotte poured the steaming water into her mug, stirred the peppermint tea bag with a spoon, then left the kitchen. She was crossing the living room, on the way to the stairs, when the front door opened and Rashid entered.

"Oh, hey, Charlotte," he said, smiling at her. He was an Arab from Syria with fair hair and Nordic features. The navy three-quarter-length pea coat he always wore was draped over one arm. A beat up leather attaché case hung from his shoulder. "What are you doing home?"

"I live here," she said.

"Right. I mean, you know, I haven't seen you around much since you moved in."

"I was at a cooking class."

"What were you cooking?"

"Pizza. Learned how to make my own mozzarella cheese to boot."

"You should make it around here one night."

"Cheese?"

"Pizza. We'll have a house dinner or something."

"Definitely." She continued to the stairway.

"Oh, hey," Rashid said. "What're you up to tonight?"

She touched the railing, looked back. "A bath, then school-work."

"All right, sure." He was scratching his head. "I'll see you around."

Charlotte climbed the stairs to the second floor, wondering whether Rashid had just asked her out in a roundabout way. It wasn't so much what he said; it was the flow of the conversation. It had felt awkward, forced, like he'd been thinking about it before it happened.

She flicked on the light in her bedroom, grabbed a towel,

then her bathrobe from the closet. In the bathroom she drew hot water for a bath, stripped out of her clothes, and lowered herself into the tub. She sighed half in pleasure and half in discomfort at the scorching heat and closed her eyes.

Someone knocked on the door.

Charlotte jerked upright, splashing water over the lip of the tub.

"I'm in the bath!" she said, hoping she'd remembered to depress the button lock.

"Uh, someone's here to see you," Rashid said.

Charlotte frowned. She'd made a few friends so far, but nobody who'd drop by without forewarning. Not even Tony had been by yet. She always went to his place. She said, "What's his name?"

"Didn't ask. You want me to tell him to go?"

"No, I'll be down in a sec."

She climbed out of the tub and toweled herself dry. She left the water as it was, figuring she'd be back soon. Then she tugged on the clothes she'd worn earlier, glanced at her reflection in the mirror, and left the bathroom.

Halfway down the stairway to the first floor she hit an invisible wall.

*No!*

# CHAPTER 2

C harlotte's mind reeled. She was thinking this couldn't be real, Luke couldn't be standing in the foyer, looking up at her. Someone was playing a trick on her—only she knew it was real, he was standing there, it was no trick.

"Hey, Char," Luke said in his deep, gruff voice. He was dressed in black jeans and a black pullover that covered his sleeve tattoos. His hair was longer than it had been before, scruffy. His skin was pale, but he was as lean and muscular as ever, and she had to admit he looked good, healthy. Nevertheless, that was a clinical observation. Charlotte didn't feel nostalgia for him, nor attraction. She didn't feel anything right then except a cold lump of fear in her throat.

*What the fuck was he doing here?*

"Luke?" she said.

"Surprise." He opened his arms in a ta-da type of way.

Rashid, who was standing in the foyer next to Luke, frowned.

"Rashid?" she said, clearing her throat. "Can you give us a few minutes alone?"

"You sure?" But he was already heading to his bedroom, which was off the living room. "You need anything, I'm here." He closed the door.

"Luke?" Charlotte said again, forcing a smile.

"I would have called," he said. "But your number wasn't working."

"I lost my old phone." That wasn't true. She'd gotten a new number precisely so Luke wouldn't be able to get in touch with her when he got out of prison. "How'd you know I left New York?"

"It's not a secret, is it?"

"I'm just curious."

"Your friends told me you were accepted to UNC. Congrats, by the way."

Charlotte was livid. Which of her friends would tell Luke this? They all knew what happened on the Catskills trip. However, she kept her expression neutral. She had no idea of Luke's state of mind, whether he was still a ticking time bomb, what might set him off.

"How did you—when did you get here?" she asked.

"To Asheville? This afternoon."

"How—?" Her nice-to-see-you act crumbled. Her forehead creased. This was all too bizarre. "How'd you get this address?"

"The university gave it to me." He took a step forward, and she resisted the urge to back up a step. "Look, Char," he said, "we have some things to talk about. Can we sit down somewhere?"

*Sit? I want you to leave. Go home! You're not supposed to be here.*

She said, "I'm heading out in a bit, to a friend's birthday."

"It won't take long."

Charlotte hesitated, then decided she didn't have much of a choice in the matter short of throwing him out. "This way," she said, descending the rest of the stairs. She led him to the kitchen and gestured at the table. He sat in one of the metal folding chairs. Charlotte couldn't bring herself to sit across from him. It was too close. In fact, the entire kitchen seemed suddenly too small for two people. "Do you want a glass of water or anything?" she asked, an excuse to keep on her feet.

"Sure," he said.

She took two glasses from the cupboard and filled them with water from a Brita jug in the fridge. She passed one to Luke, then leaned against the counter with the other.

"You don't want to sit?" he said.

"I'm okay." She sipped the water. "Luke—why are you here?"

He rolled his glass between his palms without looking at her. "You remember when we met?"

"Of course," she said. They had been seniors in high school. She and her best friend had gone to a house party of an acquaintance. Halfway through the evening her friend abandoned her for a guy with a mouthful of braces. Alone, Charlotte was hit on by a few different guys before Luke gave it a shot. He went to a different school. Still, she knew who he was. She'd seen him around at dances and events. They ended up chatting all night, then for an hour the next day on the phone. By Monday afternoon they were dating.

"Jay's party," he said.

She nodded.

"We were a good couple," he added. "Everyone thought so."

"That was a long time ago."

"Look, Char," he said, lifting his eyes to meet hers. "I never should have enlisted. I should have listened to you. I should have stayed with you."

"It's what you wanted," she said.

"It's what my dad wanted."

"You could have told him no."

"He's a three-star general, Char. You don't say no to him. I had to give the army a shot. Four years. It didn't seem like so long back in high school."

"What's done is done."

"I've changed," he said. "I want to prove that to you."

She was shaking her head. "Luke—"

"Hear me out," he said. "When I came back, I was fucked, I know that. I wasn't myself. And your friends—I can't even remember doing what I did to them. It's like I blacked out, or someone else had taken over."

"You almost killed Emma."

"And I turned myself in. I did the time. Ten fucking months in prison, two in the box. You know what solitary confinement's like?"

"Why were you in solitary confinement?"

"Some bullshit reason," he said dismissively. "Everything in prison's bullshit. You look at a screw the wrong way, you're fucked."

"I'm sorry, Luke," she said.

"I sent you letters," he said.

"I got them."

"Did you read them?"

"Yes," she lied.

"You didn't write back."

"Luke—"

"But whatever. I understood," he went on. "I fucked up. I scared you. You needed a break."

"No, not a break, Luke," she said, edging her words with something between frustration and anger. "It's not a break. We're done. I'm sorry, but I've moved on, and you need to too. I don't know what else to say."

Luke sat back in his seat. The metal groaned beneath his weight. "You're not listening to me, Char."

She glared at him. "You're not listening to *me.*"

Something shifted in his eyes. It was there one second, then gone the next, like a blip on a radar.

She said, "I have to go, Luke."

He stood. "I haven't had a drink since that night."

"Last I checked they didn't have bars in prison." She regretted the quip immediately. "I didn't mean that..."

"I've been out for two weeks," he said, "and I haven't had a drop. I don't need booze anymore. I'm different. You need to believe that."

"I do," she said, though she wasn't sure she did. He might have learned to cope with his anxiety and depression and paranoia while in prison. But he wasn't the Luke she had fallen in love with in high school, the Luke who had proposed to her at the top of Diamond Head in Hawaii. There was still that hardness to him he'd brought back from Afghanistan, that simmering anger, like he could snap at any moment. He was doing a good job masking it, but it was there. It's what she'd seen in his eyes.

She glanced at her wristwatch. "I really have to go."

"Nearly five years, Char," he said, moving around the table toward her. "That's longer than most people stay married for nowadays. You can't throw it away. I want another chance. Just a few weeks, you'll see." He stopped before her, slipped his hand down the throat of his pullover, and produced a necklace. He snapped it free from around his neck with a quick tug and held it for her to take.

Looped on the silver chain was the engagement ring she'd sent back to him.

She stared at it with dread and sadness—and mounting anger. Did he really think he would just show up on her doorstep, give her back her ring, and everything would be hunky dory between them. She'd cut off communication, moved to a different city. She wanted nothing to do with him. Couldn't he take the hint?

"Take it," he insisted. "You don't have to wear it. But you didn't need to send it back. It's yours."

She stepped away from him. "No, Luke."

"Take it."

"Listen to me, Luke!" she said. "*No, okay?* No to everything. I'm sorry you came all this way, but we're not getting back together. We're just not."

She tried brushing past him. He gripped her left biceps, hard.

He said, "Where's this birthday party of yours?"

"Let go of me."

"I'll come. Meet some of your friends."

"Let go!"

She jerked her arm but couldn't free it.

"You seeing someone?" he asked.

"No," she said.

"Who is he?"

"I'm not seeing anyone! Now let me fucking go!" She jerked her arm again, this time with all her strength, and stumbled free. She dashed from the kitchen.

Rashid's bedroom door was ajar. He stood half in his room, half out, apparently eavesdropping on her and Luke.

Something loud crashed in the kitchen. It sounded like one of the metal chairs being launched into the wall.

Another crash, glass shattering.

"Jesus!" Rashid said.

Charlotte pushed him into his room and slammed the door closed behind them.

*　*　*

Two long minutes later Rashid whispered, "Should we go check?"

"He might be waiting in there," Charlotte said.

"We can't stay in here all night."

"You don't know what he's like."

"Do you want me to call the cops?"

She shook her head, then eased open the door.

"Hold on." Rashid grabbed a bronze bookend in the shape of a bear, presumably to use as a weapon.

Charlotte peeked her head inside the kitchen first.

The table lay on its side. The glass bowl that had served as its centerpiece was shattered into a thousand pieces on the floor. Both metal chairs were overturned. A couple of the legs were bent at different angles. The door that led to the backyard was wide open.

Charlotte circumvented the mess and stuck her head outside.

Luke was gone.

*　*　*

Later that night Charlotte lay in bed, unable to sleep, the surreal scene that had played out in the kitchen turning over and over in her head, a hundred questions racing through her mind. Luke obviously hadn't gotten better in prison, like he'd said he had. He'd been acting, the way practiced alcoholics could pass off being sober, only he was passing off being sane. So how bad had his mental state deteriorated? And where had he gone after trashing the kitchen? To a bar, to get drunk? Would he come back tonight, or tomorrow, or the next day? What if he decided to stick around Asheville? Jesus, he wouldn't do that—would he? No. Once he calmed down, slept on what she'd told him, the reality that they were finished as a couple would settle in, he'd realize there was nothing to gain from harassing her. He'd leave, go back to New York. It would be over—

Charlotte sat up quickly in the dark. She'd heard a creak. The house settling, or a footstep? She tilted her head, listening. She heard it again. Floorboards. Someone was coming down the hallway.

*It's just Sarah*, she told herself. *Getting home from her boyfriend's late.*

Only the footsteps didn't continue past Charlotte's room; they stopped on the other side of her door.

Luke!

Charlotte threw off the covers and jumped out of bed. For a crazy moment she considered escaping through the window, but it was a straight drop to the ground.

Instead she pressed her back against the wall that was flush with the door, which was about four feet to her right.

The doorknob jiggled, rotated. The door inched open. Light spilled into the room, creating a triangular wedge on the floor.

Luke appeared in the crack between the door and doorframe, silhouetted against the bright hallway light.

Charlotte's heart was galloping inside her chest.

What the fuck was he thinking? What was he planning on doing?

*Screw it*, she decided.

She reached blindly along the wall and flicked the light switch.

Luke spun toward her, squinting—only it wasn't Luke. It was Rashid.

"Rashid!" she said, dizzy with relief.

"Oh, hey, you're up."

His eyes went to her legs. She was wearing a cotton camisole, panties, and nothing else.

"Don't look!" She grabbed a pair of track pants from the hamper next to her and yanked them on, almost toppling over in her embarrassment. "Jesus, Rashid," she said, folding her arms across her chest. "What the hell are you doing?"

"I just wanted to check on you, see if you were all right."

She smelled alcohol on him.

"You're drunk."

"Naw, I'm good."

"Haven't you heard of knocking?"

"I was about to say something."

"Well, I'm fine," she said. "Thanks."

"You sure?"

"I'm fine, Rashid! Now get out!"

"Okay, okay. Jeez."

He left, pulling the door closed behind him.

She listened to him retreat down the hall, then down the stairs. She shook her head, thinking this night couldn't possibly get any creepier.

Leaving the light on, Charlotte got back in bed, but she didn't fall asleep for a long time.

# CHAPTER 3

Charlotte got up as soon as dawn broke. She sat on the edge of the bed and stared at the gray sky outside the window. Raindrops pattered the windowpane, foretelling a gloomy, overcast day. She'd slept lightly, waking every hour or so, and now she felt somehow both exhausted and wide awake.

By the time she showered, dressed, and made herself up, it was six thirty, though no one else in the house had stirred. In the kitchen, which she and Rashid had cleaned up the night before, she grabbed an apple for breakfast and ate it during the twenty-minute walk along Broadway to the university. The campus was dead at the early hour. There was a scattering of cars in the parking lots she passed, and an odd person walking their dog or riding their bike through the forested grounds, but the organized chaos of academia wouldn't kick in for another hour or so.

As she approached Rhoades-Robinson Hall she noticed a girl sitting on a bench, bent over, her head in her hands. Charlotte had seen her a few times downtown before, usually sitting outside restaurants and bars begging for change. She couldn't have been any older than eighteen or nineteen, and Charlotte could never understand how her life had gone downhill so quickly, so one evening she sat next to her and tried to start a dialogue. The girl smelled like she hadn't had a bath for a week. She was also incoherent and strung out, likely on heroin, which explained a lot. Charlotte left a couple dollars in the Bob Marley crochet cap the girl was using as a collection tin and went on her way.

Now she stopped before the girl and said, "Hi."

The girl looked up at her with glazed, suspicious eyes.

"Are you okay?" Charlotte asked.

The girl looked away. "Get lost."

"I've seen you around."

"So?"

"Listen, I don't want to sound like a charity case, but I'm friends with the owner of the Lexington Avenue Brewery. You know it?"

"So?"

"It's just that, if you want, I'll talk to him, and if you stop in on a Friday night, every Friday night if you want, I'll let him know your meal's on me."

The girl studied her dirty shoes in silence.

"What's your name?"

"Krista."

"I'm Charlotte. You tell the waiter that. Tell them Charlotte is paying for the meal. Okay?"

No reply.

Charlotte hesitated a moment, not sure if she'd gotten through to the girl, then decided there was nothing more she could do. She started away. She wasn't actually friends with the owner of the LAB. She had met him. He'd come up to Tony and her table one night while they were dining there to introduce himself and inquire how their evening was progressing. They chatted for a good five minutes, and Charlotte believed him to be a kind, generous man who'd have no objection to Charlotte starting a tab to cover Krista's meals each Friday—no booze permitted.

Buoyed by the good deed, Charlotte found a dry spot beneath a tree out front Ramsey Library and caught up on her reading, which she hadn't gotten to the night before. At quarter to eight she made her way to Hospitality Financial Accounting. She had five classes in total today, but for once she was glad for the heavy load. They would distract her from thinking too much about Luke, and his state of mind.

* * *

She spotted Luke shortly past noon. She was rushing from Marketing to Food Safety—the classes were located in buildings on opposite corners of the campus—and she had to do a double take. He stood twenty feet away, a hood pulled over his head, staring directly at her. He turned and began walking away.

Charlotte chased after him, her incredulity that he was stalking her trumping her fear that he might have another melt-down.

"Luke!" she said.

He ignored her.

"Luke!" She gripped his shoulder. "Stop!"

He turned around—only it wasn't Luke. He was the same size and build, had the same purposeful walk, but he had a bony brow, a birdish nose, and wide-spaced eyes. In fact, he didn't look anything like Luke.

"You talking to me?" he said, taking ear buds from his ears.

"Sorry, thought you were someone else."

She hurried away, her cheeks burning.

"Get a grip, Char," she mumbled to herself. "He's gone."

* * *

Her final class was Food Production and Service Management. It was the only one she had with Tony that day. She sat at the back of the lecture hall and listened distractedly as the professor rambled on about time management skills. Tony arrived late as usual—ironic, she thought, given the subject matter of the lecture. He tried to ease the auditorium door closed, but it nevertheless made a loud clank, which earned him a few dozen glances. He sat next to Charlotte and doodled stick men and women having sex in different positions. He showed each to her, giving her a thumbs up or thumbs down. She ignored him for the most part and focused on copying all the bullet points on the video projector screen

Afterward, while she and Tony made their way across the campus to Broadway, he filled her in on all the happenings she'd missed the night before. He showed her a photo he had taken with his phone of Dan, passed out next to a public toilet, a striped party hat clapped on his head, a mustache and surprised eyebrows drawn on his face with permanent black marker.

Given it was only five o'clock by the time they reached the city's downtown area, and the reservation Charlotte made at Eddy Spaghetti wasn't until six thirty, they decided to kill some time at Lexington Avenue Brewery, which was where Tony took her when they'd first met. It was busy, the crowd a mix of locals, hippies, and students. Nevertheless, they found two seats on the patio at a long counter-like table that faced the street. The waiter brought a giant basket of onion rings to three guys a few seats down from theirs. The deep-fried smell would usually get Charlotte's stomach growling, but right then she wasn't hungry at all.

"Do you want anything to eat?" Tony asked her. "Or do you want to wait till we get to the restaurant?"

"I can wait."

Tony ordered an Imperial Rye pale ale, while she asked for one of the five-dollar margaritas.

"So what's up, Gilby?" Tony said when the waiter left.

"Huh?" she said.

"What's eating Gilbert Grape? You've been a hundred miles away the entire walk here."

Charlotte had planned on telling Tony about Luke—at some point—and she decided now was as good a time as any. "You're going to think it's nuts," she said.

"I love nuts—crazy nuts, I mean. Not balls, obviously."

"My ex showed up at my house last night," she said.

Tony's eyebrows jumped. "Your ex?"

"He drove here from New York."

"Just to see you?"

"Told you it was nuts."

"Are you still seeing him?"

"No! He's...he's not well. I never mentioned him because I thought it was all behind me. I guess it's not." She shrugged. "Do you still want to hear?"

"Yeah, I wanna hear. This guy sounds psycho."

"He just got out of prison."

"You're bullshitting me. What'd he do?"

"Beat up some of my friends."

"And he went to prison for that?"

"He nearly killed one of them. She had serious head wounds and was in a coma for nearly three days. She's okay now."

The waiter returned with their drinks, and an uncomfortable silence ensued until he left.

"He beat up a girl?" Tony said, ignoring his beer.

"And a guy," Charlotte replied. "And me. Well, he chased me. I bashed my head on the ground and blacked out for a few seconds. When I came round a bunch of guys staying in a nearby cabin—we were camping—were pulling Luke off me. That's his name. Luke. It took four of them to pin him down until the police came."

Tony blew out some air. "What a fucking tool monkey. Sorry, Char. I know he's your ex. But going after girls? What the fuck's wrong with him?"

"He was a solider, a gunner—you know, the guy who sits behind the turret in a Humvee. A bit over a year ago his unit was escorting a convoy of fuel tankers to a forward operating base. They stopped to examine a dead dog on the side of the road. Apparently terrorists used stuff like that to hide roadside bombs. It turned out they were right. There was a bomb. They called in the bomb guys—but the whole thing was an ambush. Everyone in Luke's unit was killed except for him. The whole thing messed him up, and he did some stuff that got him kicked out of the army. He lived with me in New York for a few weeks, and he was a totally different person. He got nervous and paranoid in crowds. He had flashbacks and nightmares and all that stuff. He barely left the house, so I organized a camping trip, to get him out of the city. I thought, you know, nature would be good for him, quiet, peaceful. But then he just snapped over nothing." She shook her head. "After the police took him away, he was kept in custody, and I never spoke to him again—until last night."

"So what did he want?" Tony asked.

"To get back together."

"I'm hoping you told him to go fuck himself."

"I told him we were done, yeah."

"How did he react?"

"Trashed my kitchen."

"Jesus, Char." Tony took her hand across the table, what felt like an oddly intimate gesture because he'd never done it before. "This guy really is a psycho. Where's he now?"

"I don't know."

"You need to call the police."

"He might already be back in New York."

"Or he might be pitching a tent in your backyard."

"What are the police going to do? He hasn't really done anything."

"If he just got out of prison, he'll be on parole. Trashing your kitchen would probably be enough to get him tossed in jail."

Charlotte shook her head. "This is going to sound stupid, but I don't want to get him in trouble. I want him to go, yeah, but I don't want him to go to jail, or to prison, or whatever. I dated him for four years, Tony. We were even engaged. He was a good guy. It's just, what happened to him, it's not his fault. It's the army's fault."

Tony frowned. "The army's?"

She shook her head again. She wasn't going to get into all that. "Anyway, you wanted to know what was on my mind. That's about all of it."

Tony released her hand, sat back. Around them the cacophony of jovial voices and laughter carried on.

Tony finished what remained of his beer and said, "I'm getting another. Want something?"

She had about an inch of the margarita remaining. She nodded.

Tony went inside to the bar. Charlotte stared through the open window at the street, lost in reflection, when someone sat down in Tony's seat. She was about to tell the guy it was taken, but the words died on her lips.

"Hey, Char," Luke said.

# CHAPTER 4

Charlotte barely recognized Luke. Yesterday he had been sober and well-presented. Now he reeked of whiskey and looked as if he'd slept in a Dumpster. His hair was messy and unwashed, his clothes—the same black jeans and pullover —wrinkled and stained. His eyes shone dully from the booze. Beneath the gloss, however, they were dark and hard. They belonged to a stranger.

"Luke?" she said, gratified by how calm she sounded, because calm was the polar opposite of what she felt.

"Fancy running into you here," he said.

"Have you been following me?" she demanded.

"You never used to lie to me, Char."

"What are you talking about?"

"You said you didn't have a boyfriend."

She glanced the way Tony had gone, but she couldn't see into the brewery from where she was seated. "I'll call the police."

"A guy can't sit down with his ex?"

"What do you want? I told you—"

"I know what you told me, Char. Heard you loud and clear. You moved on. I get it. So don't worry. I'm not here to beg you to take me back. I just wanted to tell you that I'm going to kill you."

Charlotte didn't think she'd heard Luke right—though she must have, because she'd gone numb all the way to her bones.

"What did you say?" she said, though she was no longer able to muster the false calm.

"I'm going to kill you, Char."

She stared at him in horror. Then she stood so quickly she almost fell over.

"Whoa, calm down," Luke said, standing too. "I'm not going to kill you right here. I'll give you a few hours to think about it, get it on your brain."

"Luke, you're sick. You need help."

"You were my help, Char. You were what I needed."

"Luke, please, listen to me—"

"What's going on?"

It was Tony. He stopped next to Charlotte, beer in one hand, margarita in the other. He was frowning at Luke.

"Let's go," Charlotte told him.

"Whoa, whoa, whoa," Luke said. "Don't be so rude, Char. How about some proper introductions? I'd like to meet the guy fucking my girlfriend. Sorry, my ex."

Tony set the drinks on the table. "Why don't you take a hike, Luke?"

"Luke?"

"I thought that was your name."

"*Luke?*" Luke repeated, scowling. "You don't know me. You don't know me at fucking all. *Luke?* The fuck you think you are calling me Luke?"

Other customers, Charlotte noticed, were looking at them.

"Come on, Tony," she said. She took his hand to lead him away.

"That's right," Luke said. "Slither out of here on your belly."

"Listen, buddy," Tony said, holding his ground. "She's not into you anymore. Get that into your fucking head—"

Luke threw a right hook. Tony dodged the blow, and Luke's fist deflected off his chin. Charlotte's cry of alarm was echoed by those around her.

Tony punched back, but Luke batted his arm aside, grabbed his hair, and rammed his faced into the table.

"Luke! Stop it!" Charlotte shouted.

Ignoring her, Luke lifted Tony's head from the table and might have drove it down a second time, but Tony snatched the pint he'd recently purchased and smashed it against Luke's ear. The glass shattered, spraying liquid everywhere. Luke stumbled away, a hand going to his bleeding ear.

Charlotte glanced about for help. Everybody appeared as scared and startled as she did, and she didn't think they would jump in, not against somebody Luke's size. Even the three university guys a few seats over were on their feet, backing away.

Luke drove his shoulder in Tony's chest and plowed him into a woman in a blue dress. She fell to her butt. Tony tripped over her and went down as well. Luke rained punches down on him.

"Luke, stop it!" Charlotte cried, throwing herself into the fray, pulling Luke's hair.

Suddenly the bouncer appeared, a massive black man who must have weighed three hundred pounds. He shoved her aside and wrapped his meaty arms around Luke's neck, peeling him off Tony.

Luke, however, steered the bouncer backward, the two of them knocking chairs and tables aside like bowling pins. They crashed into the wall. Luke snapped his head back so his skull struck the bigger man's face.

The bouncer loosened his hold. Luke turned, swinging an elbow that caught the bouncer on the temple. The guy dropped like a sack of rocks.

The whole patio was in a ruckus now, people yelling, threatening to call the police.

Charlotte was crouched next to Tony, helping him to his feet, at the same time not taking her eyes off Luke, who was coming toward her again.

"Luke, I swear to God—" she said, nearly hysterical.

But he brushed roughly past her, mumbling a threat, and disappeared down the street.

Someone called for him to stop, but of course he didn't.

\* \* \*

The police arrived ten minutes later, and the paramedics shortly after that. The concussed bouncer was taken away on a stretcher, while Charlotte and Tony gave their statements to a burly, fair-haired cop named Dunn, who was not much older than they were, maybe twenty-five.

"You sure you don't want to be looked over?" Dunn said to Tony.

Tony nodded. His was holding a dishrag to his nose to stop the bleeding, though he didn't think his nose wasn't broken.

"So what's going to happen now?" Charlotte asked.

Dunn stuffed his notebook and pen into a pouch on his gun belt. "We'll put out an all-points bulletin and hopefully pick him up."

"But what if you don't? What if he comes back to my house again?"

"I'd recommend you stay at a friend or family member's tonight."

"She'll stay at mine," Tony said, his voice nasally.

Charlotte looked at him. "He got my address from the university. He could get yours from them too."

"Shouldn't they have a policy of not giving out the addresses of their students to fucking psychopaths?"

"I'll get in touch with someone there," Dunn said. "In the meantime, you two keep a low profile. We'll get this guy. It's only a matter of when."

\* \* \*

"I can't believe you actually dated that nutcase for four years," Tony said, still holding the dishrag to his nose.

"I told you, he wasn't like this before," Charlotte replied. "It's like night and day."

They were in the backseat of a taxi, heading to Tony's place on College Street. Dusk had settled, cloaking everything outside the window in washed-out blues and purples. The mountains loomed in the distance, black silhouettes.

Tony said, "What was that you mentioned—you know, about what happened to him being the army's fault? I mean, they didn't set up the ambush that killed his unit. How can you blame them?"

Charlotte explained the Chapter 10 Luke was made to sign and the hypocrisy with the way the army was screwing soldiers out of disability benefits.

"It's a bloody travesty," the taxi driver interjected. He glanced at Charlotte and Tony via the rearview mirror. "My grandson was in the army. Went to Iraq for the big hoo-ha in oh-one. Served two tours, made lieutenant, and then was diagnosed with a personality disorder and kicked out without so much as a thank you. He wanted to be a state cop, but with the personality disorder on his record they wouldn't touch him 'cause he was supposedly damaged goods."

"How's he doing now?" Charlotte asked.

"Not good," the driver said, pulling to a stop across the street from Tony's building. "He's in a permanent coma at the hospital."

"My God," she said. "What happened to him?"

"Shot himself in the head last year with his dad's rifle." He stopped the meter. "Sixteen fifty, kids."

\* \* \*

While Tony paid the driver, Charlotte stood on the sidewalk, her arms folded across her chest, looking about nervously. Then the taxi drove away, and Tony took her hand. "Relax," he said, leading her across the street to his building. "There's no way he knows where I live, Char."

"He followed me to the bar, and to do that he had to be following me all day, from when I left my house in the morning. Who's to say he's still not following us right now?"

They reached the opposite sidewalk and stopped. Tony glanced up and down the street. "I don't see him anywhere."

Charlotte almost felt like crying. "What am I going to do, Tony?"

"You'll be fine here."

"But what about tomorrow? You're going to Charleston."

"Oh shit," he said, frowning. Then he shrugged. "Guess I won't be going anymore."

"No, Tony. It's your sister's debut. You can't miss it."

"Of course I can. Luke threatened to kill you, Char. By the way, what was that he said on the way out? Something about running?"

"'Better start running, bitch,'" she said, recalling Luke's words.

Tony shook his head. "Who the fuck does this guy think he is? He's like Dirty Harry's evil twin or something."

"That's why you don't need to get involved in this."

"I already am. He tried to break my nose." He flourished the blood-soaked dishrag as proof.

Charlotte said, "He might try to kill you too."

"You really believe that threat?"

"You saw what he's become like."

"Beating up the guy screwing his girlfriend, to paraphrase his words, isn't the same as trying to murder him."

"I don't think he looks at killing the same way you or I do anymore."

Tony thought about that, then nodded. "Okay, how about this—you come to Charleston with me. You'll be away for the weekend. The police will probably have picked him up by Sunday. And if not, we can stay with my sister longer. She has her own house. She won't mind."

"Really?" Charlotte said, liking the idea immediately.

He nodded. "Actually, why don't we just leave tonight? I have a friend in Colombia who I was going to visit this weekend anyway. I'll give him a call. We can crash at his place tonight. It'll break up the drive, two hours tonight, two tomorrow morning."

"He won't mind?"

"We've known each other since we were kids. He'll be stoked."

\* \* \*

Half a block away Luke sat in the driver's seat of the white van he had stolen in New York and which he had been living in since. He watched Charlotte and the dickhead she'd called Tony talking on the sidewalk. Then they went inside a four-story apartment building, presumably where the dickhead lived.

Luke drank from a bottle of Jack Daniel's and lost himself in his thoughts for a while until someone passed by the van, unwrapping a chocolate bar. That reminded him of how hungry he was, and he was about to cruise around for a fast food joint when Charlotte and the dickhead emerged from the building, the dickhead carrying a red piece of luggage. They went to the adjacent parking area and got in a shitty maroon Ford.

Hunger forgotten, Luke started the van and followed them.

# CHAPTER 5

C harlotte didn't return to her house to pack a suitcase. She didn't know if Luke had gone there to look for her. Instead, she decided to buy whatever she needed when she reached Charleston the following morning. She hadn't done any clothes shopping for a while, and she deserved to splurge on a few new pieces for her wardrobe.

She and Tony were now zipping southeast through the night on Interstate 26. The inside of Tony's Ford Taurus reeked of cigars because the car used to belong to his father who, Tony had explained, had smoked several stogies a day.

Tony was speaking on his phone to his friend, whose house they were planning on crashing. When he hung up he said, "All good."

Charlotte said, "You sure he doesn't mind us just stopping by?"

"Nah. He has a couple pals over anyway. Do you play poker?"

"I know the rules."

"What's better, three jacks or a straight?"

"A straight."

"All right, you can play. Five dollar buy-ins."

"Thanks for the permission, Tony. So what's this guy's name anyway?"

"Ben. He lived a few houses down from mine growing up. His dad's my godfather."

"What does he do?"

"Works for his dad. They own a big pet store."

"What about your parents? They still in the same house?"

"They retired early and moved to Florida a few years ago."

"So no meeting the folks, huh?"

"Aren't you disappointed? What about yours—they still in New York?"

"They're dead," she said.

Tony glanced at her. "Shit, Char. I'm sorry."

"They died a long time ago. I was only eight."

"What happened to them?"

Charlotte looked out the passenger window but saw little except her ghostly reflection. "They were shot during a break-in," she said. "My grandparents raised me."

"I'm really sorry, Char."

"Thanks." To change the topic, she said, "How much longer to your friend's place, do you think?"

"Another hour or so."

"Mind if I put on the radio?"

"Go for it."

The frequency was set to 93.3, a Forest City rock station she listened to sometimes. Kid Rock was rapping about topless dancers and his Motown crew. She liked his country stuff better, but even the gangster lyrics were preferable to talking about her deceased parents.

*  *  *

Tony's friend Ben lived on the outskirts of Columbia in a 1950s bungalow that was nearly obscured by a weeping willow in the front yard. They parked in the driveway behind a pickup truck and knocked on the front door. Nobody answered, so Tony opened the door. The entry hall was dark and filled with sneakers. The living room to the left had a large bay window, ornate cornicing, and timber flooring. It could have been described as charming had it not been for the posters of half-naked Amazonians taped to the walls. Voices floated from the adjoining room, which turned out to be a man cave if Charlotte had ever seen one. A neon Budweiser sign blinked sporadically over a red bar fridge. ESPN played on a large screen TV. And an admittedly impressive chandelier made from upside down beer bottles hung from the ceiling. Three guys wearing a lot of plaid sat around a green-felt table crowded with beer bottles and ashtrays.

"Who's winning?" Tony said, announcing their presence.

His friends welcomed him with expletives and hugs and backslaps. Ben was tall with a hunched posture, as if he was embarrassed by his height. He had curly hair, a turned up nose, and lizard-green eyes. He probably could have passed for the villain in a movie except he had a genuinely friendly smile. The other two were named Steve and John. Steve looked to be of Indian ancestry, was cleanly shaven, and used way too much gel in his short, spiky hair. John had a pasty white complexion, which accentuated the razor burns on his neck, and he was so drunk he could barely stand.

Tony introduced Charlotte.

"What's your name again?" John said to Charlotte all of five seconds after Tony had told him it.

"Charlotte," she said.

"Sharlut," he repeated, nodding astutely. "Listen, Sharlut, I got three words for you. I. Love. Humans."

"Would you shut the fuck up with that shit?" Ben shook his head. "He's been saying that all night. He's not drunk. He actually is retarded."

"Respect," John said, flopping back into his chair. "Show some respect."

"Anyway," Ben said. "Nice meeting you, Charlotte. Now I know why Tony loves Asheville so much."

"Awww," she said, smiling.

"He has to make up for his looks with flattery," Tony said, "or he'd never get laid."

"And it works," Ben said.

"On Jenny maybe," Tony said. "But so would a steak around your neck."

Ben swatted Tony's head, making a face and pointing to the door at the other end of the room.

"Jenny's here?" Tony said, surprised.

Ben nodded. "I told her you were coming by," he said, lowering his voice. "She wanted to see you. She brought Amy too."

Tony's eyes widened. "Fuck off."

"Sorry, dude. I told her you were bringing a new missus, but she didn't care. What was I supposed to do, not let her in?"

"Who's Amy?" Charlotte asked.

"My ex," Tony said, running a hand through his hair. "And she's almost as bad as yours."

❊ ❊ ❊

Jenny and Amy were in the backyard seated on plastic chairs next to a small swimming pool, which was lit eerily with green underwater lights.

They heard the screen door slide open and, at the sight of Tony, jumped to their feet, squawking happily. They hugged him and kissed him on the cheek, careful not to spill the champagne in their flutes.

The peroxide blonde looked Charlotte up and down like she was the anti-Christ. She was wearing a denim jacket over a turquoise top, a short floral skirt that showed off miles of leg, and ridiculously over-the-top four-inch pumps for a friendly neighborhood visit. "You must be Cheryl," she said, offering her hand.

Charlotte shook. "Charlotte," she corrected, "but close enough. And you must be Amy."

"That's right, darling. And this is Jenny." She indicated the brunette, who waved shyly. In contrast to Amy's showy outfit, Jenny was dressed in a slouchy sweater, a frumpy scarf, and loose jeans.

"It's so good to see you, Tony," Amy said, turning her back to Charlotte. "God, how long have you been gone for now? We've missed you here."

"It's good to see you guys too," he said.

"So Ben says you're going to Charleston to see your sister? How's Maria doing anyway? She's still with the theater?"

"Yup."

"And Gregg?"

"They broke up."

"Oh no! He was such a gem. What happened?"

"Guess they just didn't work."

"So what show's she doing now?"

"*Young Frankenstein*," Charlotte said.

"She's fantastic, Tony," Amy said. "She really is. Remember when we watched her in *A Christmas Carol* last year? You absolutely must say hi to her for me."

Charlotte wanted to roll her eyes, or puke. She'd met at least two dozen sorority girls at NYU who could have been Amy's twin sister.

"Sure," Tony said. "I'll give her your best."

"So what's the occasion?" Amy asked.

"The occasion?"

"You're not driving four hours to Charleston just to say hi to Maria, are you?"

"It's her debut in *Young Frankenstein*," Charlotte said.

"If you wanted company, Tony," Amy said, "you should have asked me. I would have loved to go."

Charlotte had had enough of the snub. "Hey, nice shoes, Amy," she said.

Everyone looked at Amy's pumps.

"Thanks," Amy said hesitantly.

"You on your way out?" Charlotte asked.

"Out?" Amy said.

"A night on the town. I mean, they're not your everyday shoes, are they?"

Amy sniffed. "We're meeting friends later."

"Really?" Jenny said. "I thought—"

"Tony, you should totally come!" Amy added promptly. "It will be so fun!"

Tony cleared his throat. "I think we're going to take it easy here tonight."

"Well, where's your drink then? We have *so* much to catch up on."

"I should go catch up with Ben for a bit first. Char?"

"Oh no you don't," Amy said, touching Charlotte's arm. "Tony can go say hi to the boys, but you're staying right here with the girls. I heard you're from New York City. I've never been, and I want to hear about everything I've been missing."

\* \* \*

Hanging out with Legally Blonde was as excruciatingly painful as Charlotte had known it would be. Amy didn't ask a single question about New York. All she wanted to do was blab about Tony—specifically all the things they had done together when they'd dated. Charlotte listened stoically, even though after each story she wanted to ask Amy if she and Tony had been so good together, why'd he dump her?

During a lull in Amy's insecure ramblings, Charlotte said, "You know, I should probably go and check in on Tony."

"Tony's a big boy, dear," Amy said. "I'm sure he's fine without you."

"Actually, dear," Charlotte replied, "we're quite inseparable."

Amy smiled tightly. "How long have you two, you know…?"

"Been dating?"

"I don't know if a few weeks means you're dating."

"We're not dating. We're just fucking."

Amy recoiled as if slapped. Then her eyes flashed daggers. "Watch it, you little tramp. You're not going to last a month with Tony. He's not into skanks."

"I guess that's why he dumped you."

"You bitch!"

"Maybe it's time you let your shoes do the walking straight on out of here."

"Jenny is Ben's girlfriend," Amy snapped. "I have way more right to be here than you do."

"You're right. Excuse me while I go find the bed where Tony and I will be sleeping tonight."

Amy tossed her champagne in Charlotte's face.

"Bitch!" Charlotte said, wiping the champagne from her eyes, then from her shirt.

She looked up just as Amy shoved her hard in the chest. Charlotte cried out, wind-milled her arms, and splashed into the swimming pool. The freezing water almost stopped her heart. She kicked off from the bottom and crashed through the surface, gasping.

Amy was crouched on the pool's coping, smiling nastily. "Hope you have something dry to sleep in, slut."

* * *

"There's no way I'm staying here, Tony," Charlotte said. She was in the guest bathroom off the kitchen, attempting to dry her clothes with a blow dryer. Tony had offered her some of the clothes he'd packed, but she'd refused; she wasn't going to let Amy see her trotting around in oversized men's clothes.

Tony said, "I'll tell her to leave."

"And if she doesn't?"

"She will."

"Forget it. She'll probably sneak back here in the middle of the night and plunge a knife in my heart while I'm sleeping."

"You want to drive the rest of the way to Charleston?"

"Why not? It's only another two hours or so, right?"

"We're already here."

"*She's* here."

"I told you, Char, I'll tell her to go."

Charlotte turned off the blow dryer. Her clothes were still uncomfortably damp, not to mention they smelled like chlorine, but she would cope.

"We're leaving, Tony," she said, and left the bathroom.

# CHAPTER 6

They were back on Interstate 26, the radio playing a song Charlotte had never heard before, the heaters blasting warm air from the vents.

Charlotte had finished venting about Amy, Tony had finished apologizing for the psycho bitch's behavior, and now they were in what might be considered their first non-speaking fight. She wasn't angry at him, of course; he hadn't known Amy was going to be at Ben's. She was just angry in general. First her ex threatens her life, then Tony's ex pushes her in a freezing cold swimming pool. What was next tonight?

"It's probably nothing," Tony said, ending the silence that had stolen over them, "but do you know what kind of car your ex was driving?"

Charlotte frowned. "No, why?" She saw him looking in the rearview mirror and spun around in her seat. A red car was behind them, though it was too dark to see the driver.

"See the white van?" Tony said.

It was a hundred feet behind the red car. "So?"

"I think I saw it parked on Ben's street."

"You think?"

"I saw a white van when we were leaving. I don't know if it's the same one."

She faced forward again. "It can't be Luke."

"Maybe he followed the taxi to my place?"

"And then followed us all the way to Colombia?"

"He drove all the way from New York to find you, didn't he?"

It couldn't be Luke, she thought. No way.

*But what if it was?*

"Pull over," she said.

"Right here?"

"On the shoulder."

"He's not going to be so obvious to pull over behind us."

"Well, if he drives by," she said, "he can't follow us anymore, can he?"

"Good point." Tony flicked on the blinker and eased to the shoulder, slowing gradually. The red car zipped past on their left, followed a few seconds later by the white van.

Charlotte exhaled a breath she hadn't known she'd been holding. "Knew it wasn't him."

"We'll sit here for a minute, to make sure—"

Five hundred feet ahead of them the white van's brake lights flashed.

"Holy shit!" Tony said.

Charlotte's thoughts raced, trying to find an explanation for why the van might be stopping other than the explanation she knew to be true.

*I'm going to kill you, Char.*

"Back up," she said in a voice too composed to be her own.

Tony said, "I'm not backing up on the highway."

"Back up!" she repeated, the composure shattering into panic. "He's reversing!"

"I'm not backing up—"

"What if he has a gun?"

"He has a gun?"

"Go!"

"Go where, Char?" Tony said, shouting now too. "It's like a mile back to the turnoff. I'm not backing up for a mile."

"He's getting closer!"

"Fuck it," Tony said. "I'll outrun him." He goosed the gas. The tires squealed. They shot forward.

As they rocketed past the van, Charlotte caught a shadowed glimpse of Luke behind the wheel.

"He's coming," Tony said, his eyes flicking between the road and the rearview mirror.

"Go faster," she said.

"This isn't a Corvette."

Charlotte looked at the speedometer. The needle was creeping past sixty miles an hour.

"He's gaining on us," Tony said. "Shit—he's going to ram us!"

A moment later there was a loud bang. The Ford jumped like it'd hit a speed bump. Charlotte lashed forward against her seatbelt.

She glanced wide-eyed at Tony. "Slow down!"

"You said go faster!"

"He's going to run us off the road!"

"Shit—hold on!"

The van slammed them again. This time the Ford veered wildly to the right before Tony regained control.

The van pulled even with them. The two vehicles went nose for nose for a few seconds. Then the van sideswiped them. Metal crunched.

They swung onto the shoulder. Charlotte cried out. Tony steered hard to the left, squeezing back onto the road.

Charlotte braced herself in her seat, a voice in her head screaming that she was going to die. The van would out-muscle them next time. They'd shoot off the road and crash into a tree. Given the speed they were traveling, there'd be nothing left of them but dismembered pieces.

Tony braked hard, and they screeched to a terrifying stop. He'd timed it just as Luke tried to sideswipe them again, and instead of colliding with the Ford, the van knifed through empty space to the shoulder. It swung back onto the road, then weaved a drunken S-pattern down the highway before spinning out of control, the smoking tires leaving curlicue skid marks on the macadam behind it.

It came to a rest a hundred yards away, facing them. One

of the headlights had blown out, presumably when it had rear-ended them.

Luke accelerated toward them.

Tony stamped the gas.

"Tony!" Charlotte cried. "No!"

Tony's face was fixed in a grim mask, and he didn't reply.

The van's single headlight grew into a blinding wall of white. Charlotte shut her eyes and waited for the imminent impact.

\* \* \*

It never came. Tony swerved sharply to the right at the last moment, and the Ford nosed into a grassy culvert that lined the highway, where it skidded to a halt. For a few seconds Charlotte couldn't move or think.

Tony groaned and touched his forehead, which he'd apparently hit against the window or steering wheel.

"Are you okay?" she asked him quickly, half expecting Luke to come racing into the culvert after them. "Can you drive?"

Nodding, he angled up the side of the culvert to the highway, which was empty in either direction for as far as they could see.

"Where the hell did he go?" Tony said.

"No idea," she replied. "Let's just get the hell out of here."

Tony accelerated.

Charlotte remained turned around in her seat, looking out the rear window—and spotted Luke emerge on the far side of the road.

"I see him!" she said, pointing. "He must have crashed too!"

"Serves the fucker right."

Tony tooted the horn in farewell while Charlotte watched Luke watch them speed away into the night.

# CHAPTER 7

Charlotte called 911 on her cell phone and asked to be patched through to Officer Dunn in Asheville. After she described to him what happened, he told her he would ask the Colombia police to comb the highway for Luke and his van. In the meantime, they were free to continue to Charleston, given there hadn't been any serious injuries or deaths in the altercation. He ended the call by saying he would be in touch.

She told Tony, "The Colombia police are going to check the highway for Luke."

Tony nodded. "And what about us? Don't we need to give them statements or something?"

"Guess not right now. But if you think the damage to your car is over a grand, he suggested you fill out some forms at the police station in Charleston, for your insurance."

"This fucking car's not even worth a grand." He looked at her. "Hey, you okay?"

She held her hands out before her. "I'm still shaking."

"He's gone. He can't follow us anymore. Forget about him."

"Forget about him? How do I forget about him, Tony? He just tried to run us off the freaking road."

"You still think he's a good guy?" Tony said, repeating what she'd told him back at the Lexington Avenue Brewery. "Don't want him locked up?"

"I don't know," she replied after several moment's reflection.

"I want him to get help."

"You gotta press charges when they catch him. You know that, right?"

"And get him sent back to prison?"

"You gotta do it, Char. You have to."

She nodded, but didn't say anything more.

\* \* \*

At a little past 10 p.m. Charlotte and Tony were driving through Charleston's French Quarter, searching for a hotel. They passed a number of lively restaurants and warehouse buildings before finding a boutique inn that had a vacancy. They checked in under Tony's name, then went to their room on the second floor. Tony raided the minibar for beer and snacks. Charlotte wanted neither. It might not be very late, but she was emotionally drained.

While Tony flicked on the TV, she lay facedown on the bed, fully clothed, and was asleep in seconds.

# CHAPTER 8

**A**my woke in the middle of the night in a dimly lit room she didn't recognize—until she saw the trashy Amazonian women posters taped to the walls. She sat up on the green sofa and felt sick to her stomach. God, why had she drunk so much? She couldn't even recall what time she'd passed out. Steve and John had left by then, she remembered that much. She and Jenny and Ben had remained out by the swimming pool while she ranted about Tony and his slut and—*oh, no*. She'd puked, hadn't she? Yes, by the fence.

Amy groaned with embarrassment and rubbed her temples. She spotted her pumps on the floor a few feet away. Her embarrassment increased tenfold. Who did that bitch think she was, calling her out for dressing up? True, she had worn the skirt and the pumps for Tony—but, jeez, what the fuck? You don't go pointing that out. At least she'd gotten the bitch back by pushing her in the pool.

Giggling to herself, Amy stood. The room spun, and she fell back on her butt to the sofa. She stood a second time and remained on her feet. She made her way to the guest bathroom off the kitchen. She peed, glanced at her tired face in the mirror, then stepped back into the kitchen, where she practically ran over Ben. At least she'd thought it was Ben at first—but she'd never seen the guy standing before her in her life.

"Who the fuck are you?" she said, backing up into a counter.

He moved quickly, squeezing her cheeks between his thumb and fingers and pinning her head to a cupboard. "There was a girl here earlier," he said, his mouth inches from her face, his breath hot and reeking of booze. "Her name was Charlotte."

Amy's eyes widened with fear. "Yes," she croaked, forcing the word from between her puckered lips. "She...here," she added, though it sounded like, *Ee ear.*

"Where'd they go?"

"Charleston."

"Why?"

"Play. Watch play."

"What was the name of it?"

"Please, let...go."

He squeezed harder. "What was the name of the fucking play?"

"*Frank'stein.*"

"*Frankenstein?*"

She nodded.

"Where are they staying?"

She shook her head.

He stared at her for a long moment, and his eyes terrified her. She'd never seen anything like them, anything so hard and cold.

Tears spilled down her cheeks. "Let me go!" *Et ee oh!*

He reached for something on the counter and swung it at her face.

A burst of white filled her vision. She didn't feel any pain and wondered what happened even as she collapsed to the floor. She was still wondering what happened when she died a few seconds later with a paring knife protruding from her right eye.

# CHAPTER 9

C harlotte had haunting dreams all night. During the current one she was at the house party where she and Luke had first met. Luke, however, was sitting on a sofa across the room, chatting with Amy, who was tickling her finger over his chest and trying to kiss him. Charlotte watched them from the corner of her eye and burned with jealously. Finally she confronted them, accusing Luke of being unfaithful. He laughed at her, then dragged her to a swimming pool out back, even though there had never been one at the house in real life. He shoved her in the water, jumped in after her, and submerged her head, drowning her.

Charlotte jerked away, gasping for air.

She nearly swooned with relief when she realized she wasn't really dying. Then she remembered with dread Luke attacking her and Tony in the brewery, trying to run them off the road. Once again she felt sorry for him, for what he was going through, but that pity soon vanished. He had problems, yes, but that gave him no right to take them out on her—least of all try to kill her. Tony was right. She would have to press charges, send him back to prison. She had no other choice. She needed him out of her life.

She looked around the dimly lit hotel room but didn't see Tony. She glanced at the digital clock—7:12 a.m.—then called Tony's name, thinking he might be in the bathroom. There was no reply. She was just getting worried when she spotted a note on the bedside table.

He'd gone for food.

Charlotte got out of bed, opened the blinds to let in the bright morning light, and checked her phone for any missed calls. There were none. The police hadn't called while she'd been sleeping—which, she knew, meant Luke was still out there somewhere.

\* \* \*

Tony returned twenty minutes later with McDonald's, and it was the best breakfast Charlotte had eaten in recent memory, considering she hadn't had a bite since lunch the day before. After she showered and made herself up, she felt almost normal again. Reluctantly she pulled on her crumpled underwear and clothes, which still smelled faintly of chlorine, and exited the bathroom.

"Don't you ever change?" Tony joked. He was lying on the bed, surrounded by junk food wrappers and playing a video game on his phone.

"Get up, geek-boy," she said, collecting her handbag from the armchair. "It's time to take the girlfriend shopping."

"Girlfriend?" he said, grinning. "Is that what you are now?"

"After almost dying together, I figured it was time to up the relationship status."

"Girlfriend," he repeated, as if testing out the word. "Does this mean you're going to start leaving a toothbrush at my place?"

"I already do."

"Well then," he said, hoping off the bed, "girlfriend and boy-friend it is."

# CHAPTER 10

**2**:33 p.m.

Luke sat behind the wheel of the pickup truck on Church Street one hundred feet from the theater, where he could still command a view of the entrance. The truck belonged to the lanky motherfucker who'd been with the brunette the night before. He'd slit both their throats in the upstairs bedroom. They made a hell of a bloody mess before they died, and he had to shower and borrow some of the dead guy's clothes. Nevertheless, killing them was necessary. He couldn't have them find the blonde in the kitchen in the morning. They would call the cops, who would alert Charlotte. She wouldn't go to the musical, and this game of cat and mouse would drag on.

He tilted the bottle of Jack to his lips and spotted Charlotte and the dickhead emerge from a side street. He watched them talking and holding hands. He watched them ask a woman to take their picture in front of the tall brownstone columns along the façade of the theater. He watched them enter the lobby.

Originally Luke's idea had been to wait until the matinee showing of *Young Frankenstein* finished, follow them back to the hotel where they were staying, and kill them there. He'd been looking forward to fucking Charlotte one last time with the boyfriend looking on with a crushed skull. But sitting in the truck, watching the flow of well-dressed people enter the theater, he had come up with something a bit more dramatic, something that would make the news and maybe garner enough attention that guys like him, guys who put their lives on the line for their country, would stop getting royally fucked by the shitheads back on Capitol Hill who'd never done anything for their country except smile for a camera.

Luke opened the glove compartment, found a pen and scrap of paper, and began scratching out a suicide note.

# CHAPTER 11

You live and learn, that was Pandu's motto. You take your beatings, you get back up, and you do better. It was this philosophy that had seen him rise above the Sri Lanka slums in which he grew up by working two jobs to pay for his education while saving enough money to become eligible for a United States green card, which he was granted in 1985. This December would mark his thirtieth anniversary in the country. He now had a loving wife, three successful children, and an equal number of adorable grandchildren.

He'd worked in kitchens and drove taxis for his first ten years in America, getting treated like third-world trash by his superiors, until he purchased the Church Street 7-Eleven franchise and became his own boss. Since then he had seen every type of customer imaginable walk through his doors, and he'd become adept at spotting trouble. Mostly the worst he had to deal with were drunks and shoplifters, but twice he'd been held up. The first time the thief got away with more than nine hundred dollars from the cash register. But you live and learn, isn't that right, and the following day Pandu purchased a SIG Sauer P226. When he was held up the second time, he shoved the pistol in the thief's face. The scumbag ran, but not before Pandu pumped two rounds into his back. The scumbag still managed to flee on foot, but the police arrested him two hours later after he showed up at a hospital missing a quart of blood.

That had been in 2008. Pandu had not had any more attempted robberies since, though he nevertheless kept the pistol at close reach beneath the counter.

He was thinking about all this now because he did not like the look of the large man who had just entered the store. The scumbag was dressed in clean jogging pants and a clean sweatshirt. But everything else about him seemed off. His hard face, his bloodshot eyes, his stiff gait, the way practiced drunks walk.

He came straight to the counter, which meant he either wanted to buy cigarettes—or steal the cash in the register. Pandu lowered his hand to the pistol.

"Good," the man said, smiling at him.

"Good?" Pandu frowned. "I don't understand you, my friend."

"I was hoping you had a gun."

The scumbag yanked Pandu across the counter with surprising speed and strength and tossed him to the floor Pandu had recently spent an hour mopping. In the next moment a combat boot struck him in the face. Pandu saw stars and tasted blood. The strength left his body. The SIG dropped from his hand.

The man retrieved the pistol and aimed it between Pandu's eyes.

Even before he pulled the trigger a second later, Pandu knew he was done living and learning.

# CHAPTER 12

The interior of the Dock Street Theater resembled an eighteenth-century London playhouse. The seats on the main floor were set in long benches, like church pews, while the balcony level featured boxes with individual chairs. Charlotte and Tony shared the first row of one box with an elderly couple.

Charlotte was looking forward to the show. Her parents had been theater enthusiasts, and she must have seen a half-dozen musicals as a child. She had fond memories of *Phantom of the Opera* and *The Lion King* and buying snacks in the concession areas during the intermissions. After her parents died, however, she never went to another production. She didn't know why. She supposed she'd never had a reason to attend one.

The older gentleman sitting next to her leaned close and said, "Have you been here before?"

"No, never," she said.

"Where are you from?"

"Oh, leave them alone, Gregory," said the woman to his right, presumably his wife.

"It's all right," Charlotte said. "I'm from New York. My friend here's from Colombia. We're going to college in Asheville."

"Hi," Tony said.

"What's your name, son?"

"Tony."

"Did you know, Tony, that this is the oldest theater in the country? Well, almost. The original burned down in The Great Fire of—Lord if I can remember. A hotel was built on the same spot, which became the present theater, and it used to employ none other than Junius Brutus Booth. He was the father of John Wilkes Booth. You know who John Wilkes Booth is, don't you?"

Charlotte said, "My high school history teacher would kill me if I didn't."

"The whole family was crazy. Son was the craziest, of course. But his father was missing a few screws as well. Tried to kill his manager in this very building."

For the first time in hours Charlotte thought of Luke, and she frowned.

"Oh, I don't mean to upset you, my girl. That happened a dog's age ago—"

"Shush now, Gregory," said the woman to his left as the lights dimmed. "It's starting."

☀ ☀ ☀

Mel Brooks' reinvention of *Frankenstein* followed a young Dr. Frankenstein (who the actors pronounced "Fronkensteen"), inheriting his grandfather's castle and trying to duplicate the steps of his grandfather and bring a corpse back to life. The bumbling servant Igor ("Eye-gore") and the buxom assistant Inga both got a lot of laughs from the audience. Nevertheless, the real star of the show was Frankenstein's madcap fiancée, Elizabeth, played by Tony's sister, Maria. She was not only a gorgeously exotic woman but wonderfully talented, and Charlotte could barely take her eyes off her.

During the latter part of the play, while the townspeople were hunting for the reanimated monster, a shout originated from backstage. Charlotte was so mesmerized by the production she barely noticed. A second shout, however, caused her to frown. The actors, who were in the middle of a musical number, faltered and looked at each other.

Then, a moment later, Luke emerged on the stage, brandishing a gun.

Charlotte was so surprised she thought she had to be mistaken. She wasn't. Luke was right there. On the stage. *Looking for her*.

She stared in disbelief and fear, a sickening wave of unreality washing over her. She was repeating "no" over and over, though she was barely aware of this.

The actors, Tony's sister included, stopped singing completely. The orchestra fizzled to a halt. Gasps swept through the audience.

Luke aimed the pistol at Igor and said, "No one fucking move, or I blow his brains out!"

More gasps from the audience, some whimpers, though no one tried to leave.

"Where are you, Char?" Luke said. "I know you're here."

Charlotte couldn't move.

Luke stepped threateningly toward Igor. "You got three seconds!"

Charlotte shot to her feet. "Luke!" she shouted idiotically. It was all she could think to say.

Shielding his eyes from the spotlights with one hand, he trained the gun on her. "Will you look at you two," he said. "Ain't you just adorable up there."

Charlotte realized Tony had gotten to his feet next to her.

Luke said, "Tell me, dickhead, she worth it? A few fucks worth your life?"

Tony held up his hands. "Luke…"

"There you go again, pretending you know me. Don't you fucking learn?"

He fired the gun.

* * *

The spell of shocked silence that had fallen over the audience shattered. All at once everyone leapt to their feet, stampeding toward the doors, bumping, shouting. It was instant chaos.

Charlotte tried to catch Tony as he sank to his knees. She ended up on her rear, his upper body slumped in her lap.

From below came the staccato cadence of more gunshots, punctuated by screams of terror. She didn't know if Luke was aiming at her or at the fleeing audience. For the moment, however, she was shielded by the balcony wall.

"Tony?" she said. She couldn't find where he'd been shot. "Tony? Can you hear me?"

His face was deathly pale. "Can't...feel my body."

Those were the four most devastating words Charlotte had ever heard.

"You're going to be okay, Tony. Hang in there. You're going to be okay." As tears filled her eyes she adjusted her position so she could cradle his head. That's when her fingers brushed a warm and sticky clump of hair. She tilted his head and gasped.

She'd found the gunshot wound.

* * *

Officer James Brady and his partner of thirteen years, Murphy Peterson, fought past the swarm of manic people flowing out of the Dock Street Theater. Inside the box office lobby they stopped to assist an elderly man dragging an equally elderly woman by the hands.

"She okay?" Brady barked.

"No, she ain't!" the man snapped. "Some bastard knocked her out of her wheelchair in the panic."

"Murph," Brady said, "help him get her out of here—"

"I got her, dammit!" the man said. "You go get that crazy terrorist on stage! Goddamn ISIS, I bet, gonna blow us all up."

Brady and Peterson drew their guns and slipped through a set of double doors one after the other into the auditorium. Brady's stomach turned upside-down at the sight of what awaited them, and his first thought was that a bomb had gone off after all. Bodies lay everywhere—in the aisles, draped over the benches, perhaps a dozen. A middle-aged man sprawled on his back, a pool of coagulating blood expanding slowly around him. A regal-looking Asian with a clump of salt-and-pepper hair and skull missing, revealing a wedge of brain. A pretty young woman in a one-shoulder red gown, a delicate hand stretched out before her, as if grasping at some invisible lifeline. Suddenly the hand spasmed, an eye opened. But it stared at nothing— dumb, like a butchered animal.

Fighting back nausea, Brady focused on the stage at the front of the room, where, lit up by the spotlights like the star of the show, the perp responsible for the mayhem stood. He was aiming a pistol at the balcony level, shouting at an out-of-sight woman, who was shouting back.

In all his time on the force, Brady had never fired his service revolver. Now, however, he widened his stance, thumbed back the hammer of the Model 28, and squeezed the trigger, praying to hell he hit the son of a bitch.

* * *

A bullet whizzed past Luke's head so close he felt the displaced air. A second one struck him in the left leg. Grunting, he flopped to his stomach.

He spotted the pair of cops at the entrance and squeezed off several rounds, one of which took out the cop on the right. Then the slide on the semi-automatic locked back with a sharp click.

"Fuck," he mumbled. He rolled off the front of the stage and slumped behind the first row of seats. He took a spare magazine from his pocket, which he'd found in the 7-Eleven vigilante's back office, and swapped it for the spent one, seating it with a smack from the heel of his palm. He racked the slide, chambering a fresh round, and peered over the seats.

The cop was gone.

* * *

While gunshots boomed back and forth below, Charlotte was staring at Tony in amazement as he pushed himself to his feet.

"You can move!" she said, fearing he'd been paralyzed.

Tony, looking pale and shaky, took her hand. "Come on—when he's distracted."

Ducking low, shoving chairs aside, they made their way toward the balcony level exit.

* * *

"You still there, hotshot?" Luke called.

"Drop your weapon, asshole!" shouted the cop, who had apparently taken cover behind the last row of seats. "This place will be crawling with police in two minutes!"

Suddenly there was a commotion on the balcony level as Charlotte and the dickhead made a break for the exit. Luke was a decent marksman, and had he been standing he could have picked them off. As it was, however, he didn't have a chance. He would have to intercept them in the lobby, but the fucking cop was between him and it—

He noticed the abandoned wheelchair. It was tipped over in the aisle close to where the cop was laying low. It had one of those portable oxygen tanks attached to it that people with emphysema used.

Luke aimed the SIG at the tank and unloaded the fifteen-round magazine until one of the rounds penetrated the pressurized cylinder.

With a whoosh like a fighter jet flying low overhead, a brilliant violet-and-yellow explosion consumed the auditorium.

\* \* \*

The blast tossed Brady several feet through the air. He hit the ground hard and sucked back a hot, harsh breath of air. His ears were ringing and he couldn't see anything but searing light. He rolled himself onto his side and smelled singed hair and cooked skin. When his vision cleared he groaned in horror. The right sleeve of his uniform had been burned away, revealing pig-smooth skin already turning a mushy, blistering pink. But worse than this was his right leg, which was missing below the knee and squirting blood.

Then the perp was standing above him, silhouetted against devil-orange flames. He pointed a black matte pistol at Brady's face.

"Please..." Brady croaked. "I got kids..."

"More than I got," the man said, and fired.

\* \* \*

Charlotte and Tony had reached the staircase with the divided, symmetrical flights leading to the lobby when a tremendous explosion shook the building, knocking them to their knees.

"What the hell was *that*?" Charlotte gasped. "Does he have fucking *grenades*?"

She leapt back to her feet, though Tony remained on his knees.

"Come on, Tony!" she said.

"I can't."

"Come on!" She helped him to his feet.

The auditorium door banged open below them. A second

later Luke limped into the carpeted lobby.

He saw them and fired the gun.

"Up!" Charlotte said, and they fled up the short set of steps to the second floor, stopping before a ten-foot-tall mirror with an ornate gilded frame. On either side of it were doorways with decorative molding. She and Tony went through the one on the right, though it turned out both led to the same large drawing room with tall windows and antique furnishings.

"That way!" she said, pointing to another doorway at the far end of the room.

"You go," Tony said. "I can't..."

"You have to!"

"Go!" He shook free from her and stumbled to a table draped with a white tablecloth. He collapsed behind it.

"You can't stay there! He'll find you!"

"Go!"

＊ ＊ ＊

Ignoring the burning pain in his leg, Luke limped up the right flight of steps. At the half-landing he stuck his head through the door to the balcony level, to make sure Charlotte and the dickhead hadn't returned there. They hadn't. The entire auditorium had become a scorching inferno.

He continued up to the second floor. As soon as he entered the large room off the hallway he saw Charlotte. She was standing in a doorway to his right, almost as if she had been waiting for him.

He raised the pistol and fired.

＊ ＊ ＊

A gunshot popped, but Charlotte had been ready for it and dashed up a narrow stairway to the third floor. She came to a hallway lined with three doors. She ran past the first two and tried the third. Unlocked! She ducked inside, slammed the door closed, and found herself in a dark, stuffy room filled with old furniture.

And nowhere to go.

\* \* \*

The first two rooms Luke passed had been empty—which meant Charlotte was in the last one. He gripped the door handle. The door didn't budge. He drove his shoulder into it and got it open an inch or so. The bitch had shoved a desk in front of it. Two more shoulders, however, and he was able to slip into the room—just as Charlotte disappeared out a dormer window.

\* \* \*

Charlotte tried her best to ignore the shot of vertigo that threatened to send her tumbling three stories to her death. She wasn't close enough to the edge of the roof to see the theater patrons milling about on the street below, but she could hear them, some shouting, some crying, the pandemonium mixing with approaching police sirens.

Scrambling on all fours, a strong wind blowing at her back, she climbed the steep pitch of the gable roof and pulled herself over the ridgeline a moment before another gunshot popped.

In her haste, however, she lost her balance and tumbled down the leeward side of the roof until it broke horizontally.

Charlotte felt herself falling through air and couldn't fathom that she was about to die. When she struck the ground a couple seconds later, she couldn't believe the fall had been so short. She also couldn't believe she was alive. But then she realized she hadn't fallen forty feet to the ground, only ten or so, to the flat roof of the auditorium.

A moment later Luke landed beside her. She started kicking him with all her strength, shrieking at him to leave her alone. For a wild moment she thought she might overpower him when he backhanded her across the face, then clawed on top of her. Her cheek smarting, her eyes watering, she tried to crawl free, but he was too heavy. He wrapped his arms around her upper body and hissed in her ear, "It's over, Char. It's fucking over."

Grunting, favoring one leg, he lurched to his feet, lifting her with him, and carried her toward the edge of the roof.

She twisted and squirmed, but he was impossibly strong. "Luke! Don't!"

"Where did the dickhead go?" he rasped.

"Luke! Please! Don't do this! I can help you! I'll get you the best doctors!"

"Too late for that now, Char."

They passed a bank of air conditioners and were less than ten feet from the edge of the roof.

Charlotte kept twisting and kicking futilely and felt something hard press into the small of her back.

The gun!

She slipped her hand behind her, fit it over the gun's cold metal grip, and pulled the trigger. The gunshot was deafening. Luke cried out and released her. She stumbled away, still gripping the gun.

Doubled over, holding either his groin or his inner thigh, he lurched toward her, a monster that wouldn't die.

Screaming, Charlotte pulled the trigger over and over and over, and she kept pulling it even when the gun had ceased firing bullets and Luke was lying on his chest, unmoving, bleeding out.

# EPILOGUE

It was December 13, the last day of finals before the Christmas break. Charlotte was walking home from the university along North Lexington, her head down against the icy mountain wind.

She'd spotted the guy following her two blocks back, when she randomly glanced over her shoulder, something she'd been doing a lot lately.

She'd crossed the street. He'd crossed it too.

Now she came to a red traffic light at Walnut Street. She glanced over her shoulder again.

He was twenty feet back.

It wasn't Luke, of course. Luke was dead. It wasn't a nameless stalker either. It was just some guy walking home from the university, who'd happened to cross the street shortly after she did.

Nevertheless, it was easier to tell herself this than believe it.

He stopped next to her. He wore an olive bomber jacket and a knit hat. His eyes were a frosty blue, his cheeks red from the cold.

"Charlotte, right?" he said, grinning crookedly at her. "I'm in your marketing class."

"Hi," she said. The light changed to green. She began walking.

He kept pace beside her. "I'm Bill."

She smiled.

"I, uh, I know about what happened," he said. "You know, a

couple months ago. Well, everyone does, right? But I'm sorry. That's sucks, you know. That guy…"

"I don't like talking about it."

"Yeah, I know, of course. So, you live up this way?"

"No," she said, which was true. She'd already passed the turn-off to her house a ways back.

"So where you going?"

She pointed to the Lexington Avenue Brewery a little ways ahead.

"The LAB?"

"Yup."

"Good beer there."

"It's a brewery."

"You, uh, meeting someone?"

"Yes," she said.

"Ah, okay," he said awkwardly. "Well, see you in class, right?"

He cut across Lexington while she continued to the brewery. Inside, she didn't see Tony anywhere and sat by herself at a two-person table.

She checked her phone. Tony hadn't messaged her. She turned the phone over in her hands a couple times distractedly. She hadn't planned on getting a drink, but now she waved the waitress over and ordered a margarita.

She frowned to herself. She'd been doing pretty good today not thinking about Luke and Charleston. Now, thanks to Bill, it was all fresh in her mind's eye.

Fourteen people had died at the Dock Street Theater. The massacre made headlines all over the country, but what gave the story legs and kept it in circulation to this day was Luke himself, and the slow fuse that led to the powder keg, namely his mental health. This was due in part to the suicide note found in his pocket, which had been addressed to his commanding officer, the medical examiner who'd failed to diagnose his PTSD, and "all you other shitheads (you know who you are)." The message was short, only six words: "You break it, you fix it."

Inevitably questions were raised. Why had someone as

psychologically traumatized as Luke been released back into the public? Had he been purposely misdiagnosed? If so, were such misdiagnoses standard practice? Was there a massive cover up going on, a way for a cash-strapped military to save billions of dollars in disability pay?

It's been a PR nightmare for the Pentagon, and a number of top military hawks had been forced to resign, including the head of the Department of Veteran Affairs.

Currently there was an ongoing Congressional investigation into the matter.

Gooseflesh marbled Charlotte's skin as she pictured Luke in his coffin six-feet underground, a big dead grin on his face.

The front door to the bar opened and Tony entered. She waved him over.

"Hey," he said, kissing her on the cheek with ice cube lips. "Feels like the end of days out there."

The waitress delivered her margarita, and he ordered a pint of beer.

"Any media requests today?" he said, and she knew he was only half joking.

"Just some guy in my marketing class telling me about how what happened in Charleston sucked."

"Sucked?"

"His word."

"You need a disguise. Maybe those glasses with the mustache attached."

Charlotte felt an abrupt burst of affection toward Tony. Although he had lost Ben and Amy and Jenny, he had been a rock these past couple months, and she didn't know what she would have done had she lost him—and she almost had. An MRI scan revealed that Luke's bullet had skated the base of Tony's temporal fossa, a shallow depression along the side of the skull, and a neurosurgeon needed to perform a procedure called debridement to remove the bullet, bone fragments, and scalp tissue. That Tony didn't end up blind, paralyzed, or a vegetable was a miracle. If fact, his only observable side effects were a skewed sense of balance for a couple days and a small scar.

"Listen, Tony," she said, taking his hand. "I think I need to get out of here."

"Sure," he said. "We can go to my place, watch a movie."

"I mean Asheville."

He stared at her, surprised.

She said, "It's too close to Charleston, too many memories."

"Where would you go? Back to New York?"

"No, I'm done with winters. I'm thinking maybe LA."

"What about your degree?"

"I'll finish it at UCLA or somewhere."

"Oh," he said, and he looked devastated.

She squeezed his hand. "I don't mean just me, Tony. Us. I want you to come with me."

He brightened, but seemed far from enthusiastic. "I don't know how easy all that will be, Char. I have student loans and—"

"I have money."

He frowned. "You have money?"

She nodded.

"Did you just knock over a bank?"

"My parents were well off," she told him. "My dad owned some factories in China. They left me a trust fund in their will. I received it last year when I turned twenty-one."

"What kind of trust fund?"

"One with a lot of money in it."

"How much?"

"Enough," she said simply.

He looked skeptical. "You use coupons at the supermarket, Char."

"My grandparents were thrifty. It's how they raised me."

Tony sat back. "So if you have this big trust fund," he said, apparently still not convinced she wasn't having him on, "why the hell are you doing a degree in hospitality management?"

"You don't remember, do you?"

"Remember what?"

"I told you I'm going to open my own restaurant." Grinning,

she produced from her handbag a real estate listing of a Sunset Boulevard restaurant she'd printed off the internet. "I've been talking to the agent, and I'm thinking of submitting an offer. I'll hire someone to run it while we finish our degrees and get the hang of the whole management side of things. So—what do you think?"

Tony shook his head silently for a few seconds, then said, "Wow, Char, I mean, Christ. *Wow.*"

"Wow in a good way?"

His grin matched hers. "In the best way. Only thing is," he added, "you got to change the joint's name. I mean, Sunset Pizzeria and Pasta? It sounds like a retirement village."

"I'll leave that to you then—something with an Italian feel."

"I got one already." He paused dramatically. "Tony's Pizza."

"Heck no," she said, laughing.

"Charlotte's Pies?"

She groaned. "That's not even Italian. Maybe we'll stick with Sunset Pizzeria and Pasta after all."

"You're the boss, Char," he said, leaning across the table to kiss her on the lips. "Whatever you want."

* * *

Standing at the bathroom urinal Tony shook, zipped, then went to the sink. While washing his hands he caught his reflection in the mirror and gasped. His skin was gray and peeling. His eyes were bloodshot and sightless. Clumps of his hair were missing in places. Where the bullet had struck him in the left side of the head, and where there should only have been a small scar, was a hole oozing blood and maggots.

Tony closed his eyes, counted to three, and opened them again.

His regular reflection, albeit scared white, stared back.

"Goddamn," he mumbled. He bent over the basin, cupped cold water into his hands, and splashed his face repeatedly.

He'd been having hallucinations ever since he'd been released from the hospital in Charleston. They were usually like this most recent one, a ghastly image of him dead and rotting, but sometimes they were of Charlotte in an equal state of decay, or Ben, or Jenny, or Amy.

He'd been having nightmares too, bad ones. They always involved Luke coming after Charlotte and himself—and sometimes his parents in Florida—and they would always end with Luke killing everyone and Tony jerking awake a moment before he was killed too.

Nevertheless, the hallucinations and nightmares he could deal with. It was the anxiety that was eating him alive. It churned in his gut nonstop, from the moment he woke in the morning to the moment he went to sleep at night.

He'd seen a doctor a few weeks back, who'd prescribed him Zoloft. That was doing jack all. Booze, it turned out, worked better. Tony wasn't getting shit-faced every day, but he'd begun taking nips from a flask morning, noon, and night.

Charlotte didn't know about any of this. He hadn't told her, and he wasn't planning to. She had her own demons to deal with.

*Besides*, he thought, turning off the tap and taking a deep breath, *we're going to LA. It's a new environment, a fresh start. I'm not Luke. I'll get better.*

Tony dried his hands and face with paper towel and returned to the table, giving Charlotte a carefree smile as he sat down across from her. Then he waved over the waiter to order something stronger than a beer.

# NEIGHBORS

# PROLOGUE

B uddy saw the smoke from half a block away. It streamed up into the morning sky lazily in thick black billows. A siren wailed in the distance, punctuated by the deep blast of an air horn.

Buddy broke into a sprint, only slowing when he reached the crowd gathered in front of the burning apartment building. "Move!" he shouted, elbowing through the rubberneckers. "Move! Outta my way!" People cursed, a few cried out. Then he was at the front of the throng, next to a fire truck studded with a dozen flashing auxiliary lights. An American flag affixed to the back of it flapped in the warm air.

The building's double front doors were wide open, likely left that way when the residents fled. Beyond them a furnace blazed, nothing visible except a wall of blustering flames. A firefighter in a tan Nomex suit with reflective stripes—"Boomer" written across the back of the jacket—was attacking the fire with a thick hose spraying a jet of water.

Buddy charged toward the building. Two burly cops blocked his way and seized him by the arms.

"Get back!" one of them snapped.

"My ma's in there!" Buddy said. "She's in a wheelchair!"

"You can't go in," the other one said.

"My ma's in there!" he repeated, trying to twist free.

The cops led him away through the crowd, stopping at the

rear of an ambulance. The cop on the right said, "Now take it easy, okay? You gonna be all right?" The ambulance's cherry tops flashed rotating red light across his face. Grainy chatter from two-way radios seemed to originate from everywhere. A second fire truck rumbled to the scene, and someone on a bull-horn ordered everyone to move to the far side of the street.

"My ma's in there," Buddy said numbly. "She's in a wheelchair. She's trapped. She's—" The words died on his lips. He was star-ing into the cargo area of the ambulance, where his neighbor, Dil Lakshmi, lay on a stretcher, an oxygen mask covering her nose and mouth. "No..." he mumbled, barely a whisper.

In the same moment Dil opened her eyes. For a second she stared at nothing, then her eyes fell on him. Something shifted in them, and she screamed.

The cops jumped. Buddy stumbled backward a step.

Dil tore off the mask and pointed a shaking finger at Buddy. "Him!" she said. "Him! Him! Him!"

"Miss, calm down," one of the cops said, going to her.

"He kills people!" she wailed. "He kills them in his apart-ment! He tried to kill me!"

Both cops whirled to stare at Buddy. Their hands went to their holstered pistols.

Buddy was shaking his head. "Me?" he said, and his shock at seeing Dil gave way to anger. "*Me?* She's a psychopath! She killed her boyfriend in Kentucky. That's why she moved to New York. She did this! *She killed my mother!*"

Buddy lunged forward, to get to her.

The cops wrestled him to the ground, flipping him onto his chest and pinning him in place with their knees. The cold, sharp metal of handcuffs locked around his wrists.

"Not me, you fuckers!" Buddy shouted, his mouth squashed against the asphalt. "Her! Arrest her!"

The cops heaved him to his feet and shoved him into the back of a nearby patrol car.

# ONE DAY EARLIER

H olding back the blinds with one hand, Buddy Smith peered out the window at the yellow moving truck parked at the curb below. A wide ramp extended from the back of it to the road. Two men wearing matching red shirts were carrying a dresser between them up the path to the apartment building's front entrance.

"What's going on, dear?" his mother asked him. She was plunked in her wheelchair in front of the TV as usual, watching old movie reruns. When she was in her twenties, before Buddy was born, she'd starred in a few small budget movies herself. Critics had compared her to Kathryn Hepburn—her looks, not her acting. Her acting stank. Buddy had watched her old films. But he agreed that in her prime she'd resembled Kathryn Hepburn with her androgynous face, razor sharp cheekbones, and perfectly coiffed curls. She held onto her looks well into her fifties, but went downhill, fast, after her stroke at fifty-nine, which aged her decades in a month. Now, two years post stroke, she was a shrunken, wrinkled, decrepit old woman.

"Someone's moving in," he told her.

"Into Mrs. McGrady's?" she asked.

"I don't know."

Buddy dropped the blinds and turned away from the window. He glanced at his wristwatch. 7:15 a.m. He had to get a move on if he didn't want to be late for work.

In the kitchenette he opened the space-saver refrigerator and retrieved his lunch. It was packed in two Tupperware containers, which in turn were wrapped in a plastic bag from the dingy C-Town supermarket a block over. There were plenty of cafés and fast food joints near the bank where he worked. But Buddy was a simple guy, he preferred simple food, and he ate the same thing every day. A sandwich with meat, tomatoes, and mayonnaise; a raw carrot; a banana; a handful of almonds; and a hard-boiled egg. He would have been content with only the sandwich, but he wanted to make sure he checked off all the ticks of a well-balanced diet. The carrot was great for vitamin A, the banana for potassium, the almonds for vitamin E, and the egg because, the way he saw it, if it had all the ingredients inside it to make life, it had to be good for you. Yeah, some argued it was high in cholesterol, but he was twenty-five and in perfect shape. Fuck cholesterol.

Buddy stuffed his lunch into his leather attaché and returned to the living room. He stopped in front of the mirror hanging on the wall to study his reflection. He looked good, professional. His chestnut hair was cut short and combed smartly. His blue eyes were clear and bright. His skin was blemish free. He perfected the knot of his yellow tie. Then he leaned closer to the mirror, pulling his lips into a grimace to make sure there was nothing from breakfast stuck between his teeth.

"Today's a big day, Ma," he said, shifting his gaze in the mirror from himself to his mother. Faced away from him as she was, he could only see her sagging shoulders and the back of her head, all white curls. *Romancing the Stone* was playing on the tube. "I think I'm going to be getting that promotion."

"You think?" she said.

"I can't read minds, Ma. But Gino's told me I've been doing a good job. Everyone thinks I'm doing a good job." Also, though Buddy didn't say this, only one other employee at the bank had applied for the position, an asshole named Fernando, which gave him a fifty-fifty shot.

"I'm proud of you, dear. You work hard. You deserve a promotion."

"I do, don't I?" He glanced at his wristwatch again. "Okay, I gotta get going. Can't be late, especially today."

He secured a button on his single-breasted suit and went to the door.

"What time will you be home?" his mother asked.

"The usual," he told her. "Love you, Ma."

"Love you too, dear. Good luck today."

Buddy stepped into the hallway, pulled the door closed behind him, and jogged the handle, to make sure it had locked securely.

* * *

The door to what used to be Mrs. McGrady's unit stood ajar. Buddy stopped before it, noting the triangular block of wood wedged beneath the sweep to prop it open. He looked inside. A mattress leaned against one wall. Several cardboard boxes formed a rough pyramid in the center of the living room. "LAK-SHMI" was scrawled onto each in black marker.

"Bullshit," Buddy muttered to himself as he continued to the stairway. Mrs. McGrady had been the perfect neighbor. She'd been somewhere in her eighties and never made a peep. She never had guests either, not even family. He only saw her every few weeks or so when she was coming or going from one of her doctor's appointments. Then last month she'd had a medical emergency in the middle of the night. Luckily she wore one of those bracelets that could summon an ambulance with a push of a button, or she might have gone unnoticed, dead in her bed, until she started smelling up the floor. The firefighters made a racket banging on her door before they busted it open. Buddy stuck his head into the hallway and asked what was going on, but nobody wanted to tell him. He waited and watched as Mrs. McGrady was wheeled away on a stretcher, then he closed the door and went back to sleep. He learned the details the following day from the landlord, Mr. Wang, an industrious frog of a man who always seemed to be fixing something around the building. He'd been replacing Mrs. McGrady's door when Buddy came home from work, and he gave Buddy all the details. Heart attack. Massive. No way she could go back to living on her own. If she survived the ICU, she'd get shipped to a hospice, so said the doctor Mr. Wang had spoken to when he rang the hospital to inquire whether Mrs. McGrady would be able to pay her rent on Tuesday.

Anyway, Buddy had been hoping her unit would remain vacant for a while. The last month without a neighbor had been great. Not that he blasted his music or threw a big bender or anything like that. It was just nice to know he had the entire third floor to himself.

So who was moving in now? he wondered. Some burnout who'd have his buddies over all the time? Some immigrant couple with half a dozen noisy kids?

The name on the boxes had been Lakshmi. That was Pakistani or Indian, wasn't it?

"Bullshit," Buddy repeated, descending the staircase. One flight down he ran into the movers. He stepped into the second-floor hallway to let them pass. They were carrying a partially dismantled metal bed frame. They didn't say anything to him, didn't thank him for moving out of the way, and he was fine with that. He thought it was ridiculous you had to say something to someone else just because you came to within speaking distance. When people did this he always thought of grunting apes. He grew up in Calabasas, California, which had been full of grunting apes. You couldn't walk down the street without one grunting at you. They always said the same thing too. "Hi, Buddy" or "How's your mother?" or "Hot today, isn't it?" That last one pissed him off the most. He had a few pet peeves, but talking about the weather was number one. He knew when it was hot or cold, sunny or rainy. He didn't need someone pointing this out to him, thank you very much. Yeah, they were just breaking the ice, but that underscored the whole problem with small talk. The ice didn't need breaking. Silence was fine. Don't grunt at me, I won't grunt at you.

This was one of the reasons New York was great. People didn't grunt. They didn't even look at you. If someone did, they were either panhandling or selling something, and it was all but expected of you to ignore them.

Buddy reached the first floor. The double mahogany doors to the front of the building were propped open with more of those wood blocks. He squinted as he stepped outside into the morning sunlight. Then he sneezed four times. It was always four times, never five, never three, and always when he stepped from somewhere dark to somewhere bright. He used to think he had some freak allergy to the sun. But when he looked up the condition on the internet he discovered it was due to his brain getting its wires crossed, a nerve in the nose getting mixed up with one in the eye. Some weird shit like that. Completely harmless, but pointless.

"Bless you," a woman said.

Buddy had been so busy sneezing he hadn't seen her until he was on the sidewalk a few feet away.

"Thanks," he said, continuing on.

"Hey," she said. "Do you live here?"

Buddy stopped and turned. The woman was brown-skinned, his age, or maybe a couple years older. She had a beauty mark on her left cheek, which made him think of Marilyn Monroe. The rest of her features could have been cut from a magazine: large brown eyes, sharp lips, strong yet feminine jawline.

Not a panhandler, he thought. Selling something then?

She wasn't holding a clipboard.

"Yeah," he said hesitantly. "Why?"

"Cool! I'm Dil."

"Dil?"

"Dilshad. But call me Dil." She stuck out her hand.

Buddy stared at it for a moment, the long, bony fingers, then shook. "Buddy."

"Nice to meet you, Buddy," she said. "I was worried there

wasn't going to be anyone my age in this place."

Buddy glanced at the moving truck, then at the silver Prius parked beside it. The car hadn't been there when he'd looked out the window earlier. The hood and windshield were dusty, the bumper muddied. Kentucky plates.

"You're moving in?" he said.

"Don't sound so overjoyed," she said with a smile.

She had straight, white teeth. Buddy liked that. He had a thing for nice teeth, a nice smile. Too bad about that beauty mole though. Some people liked them; he hated them. She should probably get it removed. Then again, what did he care? No way he was going to fuck her. Getting involved with a neighbor? Worst idea ever. Would never happen.

He said, "I was expecting... I don't know."

"Are there any roaches?"

"Huh?"

"Cockroaches. I hate them."

"None that I've seen." Buddy decided not to tell her about the mice. He'd caught one a while back, which he now kept in a cage and called Spot because of a black patch of fur on its back.

"Good," she said. "I don't know anything about this place. I found it online. Saw the pictures. The price was right. Spoke to the landlord, Mr. Wong...?"

"Wang."

"Right. I spoke to him. He was nice. Or sounded nice. So I took a leap of faith. I was supposed to move in last night, but the movers delayed last minute, so I had to stay at a crummy hotel. I wasn't going to sleep on the floor." Just then the two movers emerged from the building. "Hey, that's them. Hold on, Buddy, I'll be right back."

Buddy made a show of glancing at his wristwatch. "I actually have to get going to work. I'm going to be late."

"Oh, right. I didn't even think about that—but the suit and everything. Okay, well, listen, I'm in 3A. Knock on my door when you get home. Pizza and beers on me. Just chitchat, you know. I'd love to hear about the neighborhood."

"I'm, um, probably going to be pretty late."

"Sure, no problem. Swing by whatever time you get back."

She gave him another smile and a wave, turned, and immediately whipped up a conversation with the movers.

Buddy watched her for a long moment, then he continued on his way to work.

\* \* \*

Buddy worked at a TD Bank branch on Fordham Road a few blocks from his building. He'd studied finance at college even though he'd had no idea then what he wanted to do when he graduated. But he figured if money made the world go round, then he should know something about it. He definitely never saw himself as a loan officer. Yet that was the first job he'd applied for, was hired for, and the rest was history. Four years now he'd been at it. Not a great gig, but not a bad one either. He had his own desk, a computer. He had to bullshit with a few applicants every day, explain to them the different types of loans and credit options that were available, but mostly he completed paperwork and updated files, stuff he didn't mind doing. The best part, he could bunker down in his office and not deal with his moronic coworkers, who could be just as bothersome as neighbors, always wanting to grunt about one thing or another.

And speaking of neighbors, what was up with that Dil girl? She had a yapper on her, that was for sure. Didn't shut up. She was going to be trouble. Probably come knocking on his door asking to borrow sugar and shit, or asking him to fix her blocked sink. Like he knew anything about fixing blocked sinks. Fuck. And inviting him over for pizza and beers? They'd known each other all of two minutes. Maybe Hickville, Kentucky, was like Calabasas, where everybody said "Hello neighbor!" to everyone else. But not New York. In New York you didn't go inviting strangers into your apartment. Not unless you wanted to get raped and cut up and left for dead. There were psychos in New

York, lots of them. Neighbors included. After all, psychos had to live somewhere too.

Buddy had been walking with his head down, preoccupied with these thoughts, when he looked up to discover the bank twenty yards away, a bland, functional building in the middle of an empty parking lot. And there was Wilma Walters between him and the bank, ambling up to the front doors in that hippo shuffle of hers, giant ass flagging this way and that. She was in her sixties, a teller, been with TD since before there were computers. She was the only teller allowed to sit down behind the counter. She had a nice tall stool, with a nice cushion. It wasn't fair to the other tellers. What, just because you let yourself go you got special privileges? But Gino was too chicken shit to do anything about it. If he made her stand, and she toppled over and burst open like a gelatin-filled piñata, he'd cop the blame. Which meant his only option would be to fire her. Yet, in his words one evening when Buddy had stayed late and they got to grunting, how did you fire someone from a job they'd been doing long before you were even born?

Chicken shit.

Buddy thought about stopping and waiting until Wilma pulled farther ahead, because if he kept up his current pace, he was going to arrive at the bank doors right when she did. Then he would have to walk through the lobby with her, all the way to the teller counter.

Then again, if she glanced over her shoulder, or saw his reflection in the glass front of the building, and he was just standing there, she'd know he was trying to avoid her.

Buddy kept walking and reached the front doors exactly when she did, like they'd goddamned choreographed it.

Wilma swiveled her head slowly toward him and smiled. She had a relatively thin face. Her neck and shoulders weren't that fat either. All her weight had simply parked itself in her trunk. "Good morning!" she sang—literally. *Guuuuuud morning!* She greeted everyone at the bank this way, all ten employees, five days a week. What was that? Twelve hundred singing good mornings a year? It was surprising she hadn't blown her head off with a shotgun by now.

"Morning, Wilma," Buddy said pleasantly, helping her with the door. She waddled past him inside. He followed, slowing to keep pace beside her. How she ever got anywhere, he didn't know.

"A bit chilly, isn't it?" she said. "And it's supposed to be spring!"

Buddy wasn't going down that road, so he merely nodded, and they walked in silence. The bank's layout was one big square. Teller counter straight ahead. Info booth and waiting area to the right. A string of four glass-walled offices to the left. Buddy's was the last one. Between it and the teller counter a door led to a staff-only area that contained a kitchenette, a stationary room, Gino's office, the vault, and the building's rear entrance.

Wilma said, "I hope they've fixed the photocopier. You know it hasn't been working for two days now. Did you know that? How long does it take to fix something around here—? *Guuuuuud morning!*"

Betty, a teller half Wilma's age and size, had emerged from the staff area. She had a nest of black Medusa curls and a permanently angry face. "Morning, you two."

Wilma said, "Now tell me this weather isn't normal for spring. Is it normal?"

"It's pretty cold, Wilm. Gotta wear a jacket."

Although only halfway across the lobby, Buddy felt Betty's arrival meant he could take his leave, and he veered away from Wilma toward his office. He flicked on the lights, powered on his computer, then went to the kitchenette. He opened the fridge, to deposit his lunch inside, and frowned. Betty had placed her lunch on the top shelf next to the butter and jam. Right where he always put his lunch. For four years now, every day. She had to know that. Was she just fucking with him? Or was she really that clueless? He moved her lunch—a plastic container filled with leftover spaghetti bolognaise—to the bottom shelf, beside the milk, cream, and a two-liter bottle of Coke. He put his lunch in its place.

Back in his office Buddy slumped into his chair—and frowned again. His Empire State Building paperweight, which he'd bought from a going-out-of-business souvenir shop on the Upper West Side, was facing the wrong direction on his desk. As he swiveled it forward, he noticed the pencils and pens in his stationary cup were all upended, their tips pointed skyward.

"What the hell?"

Just then the front door to the bank opened and Fernando entered. He was Buddy's age, Hispanic, a major ass-kisser. If he got the promotion over Buddy today, it was only because he was sucking Gino's dick in his free time.

Wilma sang her idiotic welcome. Fernando grunted with her and Betty for a good minute before swinging by Buddy's office.

"Buddy!" he said, grinning. "What's up, chico? And what's up with those pencils? They all upside down or something."

"I didn't notice."

"Fuck you didn't, you OCD freak!"

Laughing good naturedly, obvious to the fact Buddy wanted to cut his head off and shove it in a microwave, he went to his office, which was adjacent to Buddy's.

Buddy left the pens and pencils how they were, to show Fernando his stupid gag didn't bother him. Then he accessed the internet. Usually he would use the time before the bank opened to check his emails or to read the news online. Now, however, he logged into Facebook with his alias, Jennifer Walsh. He'd chosen a female name because he figured people, both men and women, would be more receptive to friending a female rather than a male they didn't know. He also chose a hot no-name Filipina actress for his profile picture because the majority of the population was ugly, and everyone wanted good-looking friends to boost their self-esteem.

Buddy typed "Dil Lakshmi Kentucky" into the search box and pressed Enter.

And there she was, number one on the first page of results. He clicked her profile and jumped to her timeline.

Her most recent post read:

Going to the movies tonight. Twisted Jordon's arm to see a rom-com.

It was dated March 14, 2014, more than a year ago.

Buddy chewed his lip, wondering at this. Had she started a new account? He was about to do another search for her name when a message popped up. It was from Fernando.

Hey! Long time. How have you been?

Buddy glanced at the moron through the glass wall dividing their offices. He was leaning close to his computer screen, one hand on his mouse, waiting for a reply.

Buddy had sent friend requests to everyone he worked with so he could spy on them, see what made them tick. Virtual stalking—it was a hobby of his. Most had accepted, and their lives were as boring as he'd imagined they would be. Fernando had been harassing "Jennifer Walsh" for a date ever since they friended.

Buddy typed: "I'm great, Fernando, thanks."

"Listen..." he replied. "I was wondering if maybe you want to get a drink sometime?"

Buddy glanced at Fernando again. Still leaning close to the screen, but now tapping his foot anxiously.

Buddy finally turned the pens and pencils in his stationary cup tips down—they had been bugging the hell out of him—and typed: "When are you thinking?"

"Any time."

"How about today? Say, five?"

"Perfect! Where's convenient for you?"

Buddy thought for a moment, then typed: "Do you know the Mercury Lounge? Lower East Side. Great live music."

Fernando didn't hesitate, even though the bar was at least an hour away by train. "Works for me. But can we make it five thirty?"

"I'll be wearing a red dress. See you then."

Fernando hooted from his office. Then he was on his feet, doing a little dance and pumping his fists in the air. He saw Buddy watching him and added a few groin thrusts to his jig.

Buddy gave him a thumbs-up, then returned his attention to finding out more about his new neighbor. He performed a second search, but it didn't appear she had any other Facebook accounts. He tried a Google search next with the same keywords—Dil Lakshmi Kentucky—to see if she was active on any different social media platforms.

Buddy's eyes widened as he scanned the first few results. He clicked the top link, jumping to a story from the Cincinnati *Inquirer*:

### Court in upheaval after woman found not guilty in death of boyfriend

A jury tasked with deciding the fate of a woman accused of stabbing to death her boyfriend with a pair of garden shears has been found not guilty of both murder and manslaughter. The twelve jurors deliberated for more than seven hours before acquitting Dilshad Lakshmi, 27, in the 2014 slaying of restaurant manager Jordon Scott, 29.

Dilshad Lakshmi admitted to stabbing Jordon Scott six times, but pleaded not guilty to murder on the grounds she acted in self-defense.

Much of the packed courtroom in Newport, Kentucky, was filled with the victim's family, including his parents and younger brother.

Relatives of Mr. Scott broke down into tears after the jury's verdict was read.

"I hope your children die the same way!" Mr. Scott's mother, Naomi Scott, yelled at Ms. Lakshmi as she was led out of the courtroom, her face impassive. Mrs. Scott collapsed a few minutes later and was taken to a hospital in an ambulance.

Speaking outside the court, Mr. Scott's aunt, Silvia Carey,

said: "It's a travesty. It sends out the message that it's okay to kill someone if you have an argument with them. How can that woman walk free while my nephew is dead and buried underground? He had so much to live for."

Ms. Lakshmi's attorney, Monty King, claimed that Jordon Scott became aggressive toward his client after the couple returned home from a friend's birthday party, accusing her of flirting with other partygoers. After a heated argument, he followed her to the backyard, where she'd gone to smoke a cigarette. When he began to physically assault her, she stabbed him with a pair of garden shears.

Prosecutor Mary Lindberg presented an entirely different version of events, asserting that Ms. Lakshmi was the one who turned violent when Mr. Scott attempted to end their relationship. Relying on the testimony of forensic experts, the prosecution argued that Mr. Scott was stabbed while sitting down at the patio table. "The first wound destroyed the left ventricle in his heart," she said. "There was no justification to continue stabbing him. That is cold-blooded murder."

Monty King, however, invoked the "stand-your-ground" defense, arguing that because his client felt threatened she was not obligated to stop attacking Mr. Scott until she felt certain she was safe.

"Bullshit," Buddy said, filled with a zany kind of energy. He had never met a killer before—not even an acquitted killer. For a moment he wondered if it could be a different Dilshad Lakshmi. But how many Dilshad Lakshmis were there in Kentucky? And twenty-seven—twenty-eight now—would be roughly the age of his newest neighbor.

He returned to the search page and clicked on the second link:

After spending hours selecting a jury, attorneys for both sides in Dilshad Lakshmi's murder trial delivered opening arguments in Campbell County Circuit Court.

Police say Dilshad Lakshmi stabbed boyfriend Jordon Scott six times out back of their East Row home in 2014.

Dilshad Lakshmi's defense attorney, Monty King, began his opening statement by describing his client as a former honor student at the University of Kentucky with "no criminal record and a good head on her shoulders." He also said that testimony from neighbors who heard Jordon Scott shout at her threateningly, and photographs of bruises on Dilshad Lakshmi's arms and legs, will support Lakshmi's assertion that she stabbed him in self-defense.

But according to WLWT News 5 investigative reporter Martin Armstrong, prosecutors aren't buying it. Assistant Commonwealth Attorney Don Cormic said, "We believe the evidence will prove that any perceived abuse against Ms. Lakshmi did not rise to levels justifying stabbing someone six times."

Prosecution also allege that Dilshad Lakshmi's former cellmate at the Campbell County jail in Newport will testify to the court that Ms. Lakshmi showed no remorse over the death of her boyfriend, often joking about the stabbing. She will testify that Ms. Lakshmi originally planned to plead insanity, but when she realized she would come across as too intelligent, she decided to plead battered girlfriend syndrome instead.

"Bullshit," Buddy said again, staring at the photograph that accompanied the article. No makeup, and a slack, expressionless face, but definitely the Dil Lakshmi he'd met this morning.

He returned to the search page and brought up a third article:

Detectives have charged a woman with murder following the death of a twenty-nine-year-old man on Saturday in the East Row Historic District of Newport, Kentucky.

A police media representative announced she was expected to appear in the Campbell County Circuit Court on Monday.

Talking to the media outside the taped-off home, Detective Milo Hoover said the man died under suspicious circumstances but was tight-lipped about details surrounding the death. He said the woman was assisting police with their inquiries.

A commotion caused Buddy to look up. Betty had just opened the front doors to the bank and the line of people who'd queued up poured noisily into the lobby, some going to the withdrawal tables, others to the teller counter.

Reluctantly Buddy closed the web browser, pushed thoughts of his psycho-bitch neighbor from his mind, and started preparing for the day.

* * *

The morning was busier than usual. Buddy approved one loan applicant and rejected another. The latter was a thirty-something woman who gave him a sad sap story about needing ten grand to finance a trip to Denmark, to visit her ailing mother. Nevertheless, her debt-to-income ratio was way too high to meet the eligibility requirements, and his hands were tied. That was the thing, these people thought Buddy was God or something, could just grant a loan out of the goodness of his heart. But it wasn't up to him. He was just the smiling face of the bank, the guy who filtered out the losers with low credit scores. He forwarded all applications to the underwriting department, which made the final decision. Checks and balances to make sure bleeding hearts with puppy dog eyes didn't get loans they couldn't pay back. And he only forwarded what he thought would be approved, otherwise he ended up looking like a chump.

At noon Buddy ate his lunch at his desk as usual, then spent the afternoon looking busy reviewing account records in case Gino stopped by to tell him about the promotion. He also managed to squeeze in an hour of brainstorming his next novel. He was a writer, but he didn't tell anyone that because he hadn't published anything yet. And he knew what people thought of unpublished writers. They dismissed them immediately as hacks or "aspiring authors"—the latter insinuating that they were attempting something they could never achieve. Which was bullshit. After all, you didn't call a med school student an "aspiring doctor."

Buddy had started writing seriously after he graduated college, and by seriously he meant every day. He'd completed three manuscripts so far in as many years. He didn't write full drafts like they did in the old days. That was a consequence of the limitation of typewriters: you had to put down what you wanted on the first go because there was no Backspace or Delete key. With word processors, however, it was a different ballgame. Buddy, for instance, would get an idea for a chapter, dump as much nonsense onto the page as he pleased, mainly to feel as though he'd accomplished something, before going over the dribble, rewording it, erasing entire paragraphs, adding new ones, until it was close to how he wanted it. Then he'd move on to the next chapter. By the time he got to the end of the story he had a near perfect final draft.

Buddy's first novel was called *Fallen*. It was about a husband and wife who die in a car crash together. The man goes to heaven, while the woman, a former hooker, goes to hell. Nevertheless, the man still loves her, wants to spend eternity with her, so he returns to Earth and goes on a massive killing spree to piss off God and impress the Devil. In the end he gets condemned to hell—where he learns there's no such thing as love, only carnal desire, and spends eternity watching his wife fuck an endless supply of miscreants.

Buddy sent off query letters to a dozen agents and received form rejections from all of them save one, who mentioned he liked the idea, but fifty-thousand words was too short for a full-length novel. He encouraged Buddy to beef it up to eighty- or ninety-thousand words and resubmit.

Buddy didn't heed the advice. The story was perfect how it was. Anything he added would be fluff. Besides, by then he was already several chapters in to his next novel and wasn't looking back. The name of it was *Monsters*, and it started with a bang—a

Boeing 747 goes down mysteriously in the Himalayas. A US-led search-and-rescue operation is put together, because the majority of the passengers were American, and they find the wreckage in remote mountainous terrain, as well as the cause of the crash: the remains of a fifty-foot-long dragon. The US secretly dispatches an eclectic group of scientists and soldiers to find and capture a living, breathing specimen. They succeed and bring a large male back to the States, where, naturally, it escapes and wreaks havoc on LA.

Buddy pitched the story as a modern-day *King Kong* with dragons. A handful of agents liked the idea enough to ask for sample chapters, but in the end they all passed.

Buddy didn't understand why. The story was a real corker. It had everything you could want. Action, mystery, science, folklore, even a romantic subplot for the female readers, because they comprised the largest reading demographic.

In the end the rejection only made him more determined to succeed with his third novel, *Prey*. The plot was dark and gritty, the most realistic yet: an American soldier stationed in Okinawa gets arrested for raping and killing a local Japanese girl. The US Army can't do anything to help him; he's beyond their jurisdiction. So while being transported to stand trial for his crimes, the soldier kills the guards and goes underground. But he soon learns there's no way to escape the island—ninety-nine percent of the population is Japanese, and his white face is all anyone's talking about—so he decides to make the most of his freedom before his inevitable capture by raping and killing as many locals as he can. The story has a Rambo-like vibe—one man against an entire police force—and ends with an equally spectacular climax.

Buddy was so confident it was a winner he initially sent query letters to only three agents at the top literary agencies in New York. When they passed, he sent queries to another six agents. When they passed, he began to freak out and spammed no less than fifty agents, pretty much everyone in New York that represented suspense and thriller novels.

No one was interested. It was a huge blow to Buddy's confidence, because he suddenly felt as though his career was moving backward. He became depressed and stopped writing for about a month, during which time he did a lot of soul searching, eventually deciding his writing had grown too ambitious. After all, what did he know about dragons or covert government missions or Japan or soldiers? The old adage was true: you had to write what you knew about. Lawyers wrote legal thrillers; doctors wrote medical thrillers; cops wrote police procedurals. Problem was, Buddy wasn't an expert on anything. That's why, a couple weeks ago, he made the switch to the horror genre, because horror writers didn't need to be an expert on anything. Look at Stephen King. He bullshitted about kids finding a dead body, and rabid dogs, and crazy fans. The best horror was the mundane, stuff that could happen to anyone. All you had to do was know how to scare people. And that was something Buddy could do, no problem.

So far he had a few good ideas for his fourth novel, yet he was partial to a story he'd tentatively titled *The Pizza Guy*. The protagonist, Mac, is a pizza delivery driver. One night he delivers a pie to a very attractive woman named Desiree, and soon after he begins to stalk her. When she orders a pizza the following week, he laces it with Rohypnol, delivers it to her, then waits in his car outside her home. Thirty minutes later he knocks on her door. When she doesn't answer he breaks in through the back and finds her passed out in the bedroom. He strips her naked and is about to rape her when the front door opens. Some guy—her boyfriend most likely—catches him in the act and goes nuts. During the ensuing fight, Mac drives the heel of one of Desiree's stilettos into his eye, killing him instantly.

Mac decides he has to dispose of the body, so he pulls his car into the driveway, then goes back inside to collect the asshole—only to find Desiree awake and spazzing out over her dead boyfriend. Mac sees no choice but to kill her too, and he strangles her to death with her laptop power cord.

He loads both bodies into the trunk of his car, and he's about to get the hell out of there when four more people arrive in a convertible, blocking him in the driveway. Mac tells them he's Desiree's friend from high school, she's gone to the liquor store, and invites them inside, where he kills them one by one in gory slasher movie fashion.

That's as far as Buddy's outline went. He still needed an ending. But he was stumped. Because now there would be blood throughout the house. Simply getting rid of the bodies would no longer be enough. When Desiree was reported missing, the police would treat the house like a crime scene. Mac's fingerprints would be everywhere, his hair would be in the carpet, all that *CSI* stuff.

Buddy was toying with the idea of having Mac bring Desiree and the boyfriend back inside and torching the place. The blaze would take care of the DNA problem nicely. Nevertheless, he wasn't sure whether this was original enough. He needed an ending that would blow the nerds at the literary agencies out of the water. Something really amazing. He was getting sick of rejection letters and didn't want to waste another year on a book that wasn't going to get picked up.

At three thirty in the afternoon, Buddy, running dry on inspiration, stretched and yawned. He closed the notepad in which he had been scribbling his ideas and glanced out his door at Betty and Wilma and the two other tellers. Gino was nowhere in sight, and Buddy wondered why he hadn't come to see him yet.

Had he simply forgotten about the promotion?

Was he waiting until the end of the day to deliver the news?

Buddy tapped his pen against his knee for several long moments. Then he got up and went to Gino's office.

The door was closed. He knocked.

"Yeah?" Gino called.

"It's Buddy."

"Yeah?"

"Can we talk for a sec?"

"Yeah, yeah. Come in."

Buddy entered. Gino's office was about twice the size of Buddy's, still not very big. Office Depot furniture, a calendar on the wall, a bottle of hand sanitizer on the desk, next to a framed photograph of his daughter. Gino himself was as insipid as his office. Middle aged, Italian, coarse gray hair parted far on the left side of his skull, bangs swept across his forehead. He wore thick-rimmed eyeglasses that did little to improve his pudgy, gnomish face, and an ill-fitting double-breasted navy suit with gray pinstripes. He was slumped in his Executive's chair, a cell phone stuck to one ear. His legs were crossed, the top one showing a hairy ankle between pant hem and sock. By the sound of the conversation, he was speaking to his wife.

"I'll be back around five," he told her, rubbing the back of his head. "Want me to pick up a pizza for dinner...? What do you want on it...? How about mushrooms...?"

Buddy waited patiently, hands clasped in front of him, while Gino spent another minute taking his wife's order. When Gino hung up he shook his head, saying, "Anchovies. I married the only person in the country who likes goddamn anchovies. What's on your mind, Buddy?"

Buddy glanced at the chair he wasn't offered to sit in, then back at Gino. He shifted his weight from one foot to the other and said, "You mentioned you'd be deciding on that promotion today. Just wondering if you have any news?"

Gino sat straighter, adjusted his brown tie. "Actually, Buddy, I do. I've chosen Fernando."

Buddy blinked in surprise. His insides sank beneath an invisible weight.

"It was a tough decision," Gino went on. "You were both qualified. But there was only the one position. Tough decision." He gave Buddy a lame shrug.

"I've been at the bank for four years," Buddy said evenly.

Gino nodded. "You're a valuable member of the team, Buddy, no doubt about that."

"Fernando's been here for, what, one year?"

"Yeah, well, my decision wasn't based solely on experience."

He cleared his throat. "Look at the big picture with me, Buddy. All banks have pretty much the same rates, right? So you have to ask yourself: why does someone come here? Why do they choose us? Some, because they live in the neighborhood. Others, because of relationships. They get to know us. Like us. Trust us. Not just Betty and the other tellers. You and Fernando too. Especially you and Fernando. When it comes to something like a loan, they want to know you're doing your best for them. Answering all their questions. Explaining all their available choices."

"I do that," Buddy said.

"I know you do, Buddy. I know you do. But there's more to it. Like I said. Relationships. You need to...open up a bit. Give off friendlier vibes. A smile now and then wouldn't hurt."

"You don't think I'm friendly?"

"Sure I do, sure. But Fernando, you know, you've seen him. He makes his clients feel at home, jokes with them, makes small talk. Consumer loans are one thing, Buddy. But mortgage loans, there's a lot more on the line. A lot more money. Clients want to know they're making the right choice. They need good gut feelings about their loan officers. Relationships, Buddy. Relationships. Do you understand what I'm saying?"

Buddy balled his hands into fists. "You're saying I'm not getting the promotion because I don't grunt enough?"

Gino frowned. "Grunt?"

"Make small talk! Jesus."

Gino stiffened at Buddy's tone. "I've made my choice, Buddy. I think I've explained myself adequately."

"Clients like me," Buddy said. "Everyone at the bank likes me."

"How many times did you leave your office today?"

"I was busy."

"During lunch? Your breaks?"

"I eat at my desk, and I work through my breaks."

"Look, Buddy. This isn't the end of the road. There are plenty of options for advancement within the bank. Perhaps you could investigate transferring to a larger branch—"

"You want me to transfer?"

"That's not what I'm saying—"

Buddy stepped forward. "Is he sucking your dick?"

Gino's cheeks bloomed red. "What did you say?"

"Is that spic Fernando sucking your fucking dick?"

Gino's face hardened. His jaw clenched. "You've just gone way overboard, Buddy," he said in a quiet voice, adding, "You should go home now." He paused. "And you know what, I don't think you should come back on Monday."

"You're *firing* me? You can't fire me. Due process—"

"Go home, Buddy."

"You can't fire me!"

"Get out of here!"

Buddy wanted to smash something. Instead he snatched the photograph of Gino's blowfish daughter and launched it against the far wall. Glass exploded.

"Out!" Gino howled. "Get the hell out of my office right now!"

Buddy left.

\* \* \*

While walking home, Buddy composed in his head a dozen different ways to get back at Gino. These ranged from erasing his face with sandpaper, to breaking every bone in his body with a frying pan, to skinning him with a hunting knife. In every scenario he kept the asshole alive and conscious for as long as possible, so he would experience every excruciating second.

"Motherfucker," he mumbled, turning down the walk to his apartment building. "Cocksucker, motherfucker, lowlife piece of shit."

Buddy clomped up the stairs to the third floor and barely glanced at his psycho-bitch neighbor's door when he passed it. At his unit he fumbled the key into the lock and stepped inside. It was dark, shadows piled upon shadows. The only light came from the gap between the blinds, a strip of white filled with dust motes. His mother said from her wheelchair in front of the TV, "You're home early, dear."

"I didn't get the promotion," he grumbled, dumping his keys and wallet on the small deal table, then going over to her and sagging to his knees. *Batman* was playing on the tube, the original one starring Michael Keaton and Jack Nicholson. Buddy took his mother's frail hand in his. Tears welled in his eyes, but he fought them back.

"What happened, dear?" she asked in the soft rasp that passed for her voice. "Why didn't you get the promotion?"

"I was fired."

"Fired?" she said, surprised. "Whatever for?"

Buddy only shook his head. "What am I going to do, Ma?"

"You'll start looking for another job on Monday, that's what you'll do."

"What if no one wants to hire me?"

"Why wouldn't anyone want to hire you? You're young, you're smart—"

"I'm not social."

She paused. "Is that what that manager of yours told you?"

Buddy shrugged. "In a nutshell."

"Ptooey! What does he know anyway?"

"I can't use the bank as a business reference."

"Does that matter?"

"If I want to work in another bank it does."

"Do you want to work in another bank?"

"What else am I supposed to do?"

"You can do whatever you want, dear."

"And start from scratch again? I already have four years of experience."

"Better starting over now than in ten years from now."

"But I liked the bank."

"Did you?"

"Well, it was easy." He shrugged. "I had a lot of time to do my writing."

"You know, Buddy, maybe getting fired was a blessing in disguise, because now you can write fulltime."

"But I need money now, Ma. I need to pay the rent next month."

"I'm sure Mr. Coolabah at the C-Town will give you a job. He always has different boys in there stocking the shelves."

"I can't stock shelves! I'm twenty-five."

"You could do it part-time, just enough to pay the rent. And it would only be temporary. Until you finish your new book. How far are you along on it?"

"I haven't started yet. I'm still working out the plot. And I need an ending—"

A knock at the door made Buddy start. Frowning, he stood and cocked his head, waiting, listening. Another knock. He went to the door cautiously and said, "Who is it?"

"Dil!"

Cursing to himself, Buddy opened the door a wedge. He squinted against the brightness of the hallway, then sneezed four times.

"Bless you!" Dil said, giggling. "That's the second time today! Are you allergic to me or something?"

"It's the light—going from dark to light. A nerve in my nose..." His eyes narrowed suspiciously. "How did you know I lived in this unit?"

"Mr. Wang told me. He came by this afternoon to make sure I was settling in okay. He's such a sweet man."

Buddy nodded but didn't say anything. He was hoping the awkward silence would scare her off.

Undeterred, Dil said, "Um, so what are you up to?"

"I just got home," he said. "I was going to take it easy tonight."

"Oh." Her face dropped. "So you don't want to come by for a beer or anything?"

"I've had a long day."

"Yeah, right, okay. I understand... Next time."

Buddy closed the door, locked it, and returned to his mother, though he remained standing.

"Who was that?" she asked him.

"The new neighbor," he said. "You were right this morning. She moved into Mrs. McGrady's."

"She sounded nice. You should go spend some time with her."

"No way, Ma. I don't want her thinking we're friends or something. She'll be knocking on the door all the time."

"Would that be so bad?"

"Yeah, it would be bad. It would be terrible."

"You could use a nice girlfriend—"

"Don't start, Ma," he growled.

"I'm just saying, if you had a nice girlfriend, you might not need all those other women that want you to pay for—"

"She's a murderer! Yeah, your nice little neighbor is a murderer! She killed her boyfriend. You still think she'd be good for me?"

"Whatever are you talking about?"

Buddy told her, summarizing everything he'd read online.

"My oh my," his mother said when he'd finished. "That's something, isn't it?"

"I know. I should write a book about it. Psycho neighbor moves in and—"

"What is it, dear?"

But Buddy barely heard her. He felt as though someone had just plugged a live wire into his brain. His mind raced, the story coming together with effortless ease.

The protagonist would be a writer—a frustrated writer. Even better, an eccentric hermit. Yeah, make him complex. He hides away in his apartment all day, trying to write the next Great American Novel or some bullshit. Then, out of the blue, he gets a new neighbor. That's where Buddy could start the story. Just like it happened today. The protagonist is peering out the window, sees her moving in. Then, later, he bumps into her somewhere around the building. Maybe she knocks on his door to ask for sugar. She invites him over for pizza and beer. He doesn't want to go, he's a loner remember, but she's persistent. Finally he says okay, to shut her up. But before he goes he spies on her on Facebook—no, that's no good. The hero needs to be sympathetic. So maybe he tries to friend her for real? Yeah, that's better. He tries to friend her, but she's stopped using Facebook for a year. He looks her up on other social media and comes across a story about her trial in Kentucky. No, gotta change that. Cleveland or Seattle or somewhere. Doesn't matter. So he learns she's a killer. Murdered her boyfriend. Stabbed —no, shot him right in the face. More dramatic that way. But she got off. Not like Dil. Can't make her innocent. More like OJ. She got off on a technicality. She has to be a real killer. Anyway, even after reading this, he goes over for pizza and beer, because he's curious, he's never met a killer before, so he goes over, and he ends up sleeping with her—yeah, a romantic subplot for the women readers. But then what? Conflict, need conflict... Okay, she starts acting strange—*Single White Female* strange. Sure. Maybe some of the pets go missing around the building, the dogs and cats? Then the *landlord* goes missing. Yes! Nobody suspects anything—nobody except Buddy, or at least the character based on Buddy. Damn right! Then what? He goes to the police, but they won't do anything without evidence of a crime. They think the landlord's just gone away on a vacation or something. So it's up to him, good old Buddy—no, he needs a name. Dave? Don? Sure, Don. It's up to Don to save the day, to uncover proof that Dil killed him. Or not Dil, whoever. Wendy. Yeah, Wendy's an okay name. All right, this is good, it's great, but there needs to be a twist too. Maybe *she* knows that *he* knows she killed the landlord. Maybe...maybe in the big finale, while he thinks he's laying a trap for her, she's actually laying a trap for him? Nice one, Buddy! The climax will have to involve something big, something dramatic. Maybe a car chase. Or maybe a fight on the roof of the building. Yeah, that would work. He could knock her over the edge. She could be hanging there, fifty feet above the ground, and he could offer her his hand, because some part of him still loves her—? No, too cliché.

Nevertheless, it didn't matter. Buddy didn't need the ending right now. He had the rest of the story. And what a corker of a story it was!

"Buddy?" his mother was saying. "Buddy, what's wrong? What's the matter?"

"I have a new idea for my book, Ma!" he exclaimed. "It's The One. I know it is!"

❊ ❊ ❊

Buddy spent the next two hours at his desk in his bedroom, in front of his laptop, writing like a demon. Words had never come so easy to him before. He wasn't simply dumping crap onto the page either, to make him feel productive. It was all top notch stuff, final draft quality stuff. And he already had close to five thousand words. Five thousand!

He was up to the point where Don goes to Wendy's for pizza and beers. He typed:

Don walked down the hallway to Unit 3A, the floorboards creaking ominously beneath his weight. He stopped in front of his new neighbor's door and raised his fist to knock. He wasn't sure why he had agreed to come. He liked his privacy. He didn't want her coming by and asking for sugar and shit. He didn't want her thinking they were friends. But she had been so persistent. He didn't want to hurt her feelings.

He knocked, three times, loudly. The silver skull ring on his middle finger added a sharp wrap sound, like a bone striking wood.

Wendy opened the door and gave him a winning smile. "Don! Thanks for coming."

"I can never say no to beer and pizza," he said.

She ushered him into the living room, which was impersonal, like a prison cell. The walls were practically begging for a picture. They probably wouldn't even mind a ratty poster. The sofa was the only piece of furniture. It sat alone in the middle of the room, like somebody wondering where all their friends had gone. Cardboard boxes were piled high on the floor. Don didn't blame her for not unpacking them. After all, she had only just moved in this morning.

"I didn't think you were going to come," Wendy said, still smiling at him. "You seemed hesitant when I invited you earlier."

"Not at all," he lied smoothly. "I was probably just thinking about the novel I'm working on."

"You're a writer?" Her eyes bugged out of her head with admiration. "I've never met a famous writer before!"

"Well, I'm not really famous. Writing takes a lot of practice

Buddy slammed the keyboard without finishing the sentence. The dialogue wasn't right. It was stilted, fake.

He deleted the last few lines, rewrote them, deleted them again, tried a third time.

Still crap.

"Bullshit!" he said, shoving himself to his feet and pacing back and forth in the small room. For the first time since he'd sat down two hours before, writing had become an effort again.

What happened to his muse, his creative juices?

He thought he knew.

Up until that point in the story, everything he'd written had actually happened. Seeing the moving truck out his window. Bumping into Dil outside the building. Checking her up on Facebook. Hell, he'd practically rehashed the newspaper stories about her verbatim.

Nevertheless, now he was back to making shit up. And that was no good. It wasn't real.

"I need more material," he muttered to himself.

Buddy glanced at his wristwatch. It was a bit past seven o'clock. Not too late to still go by Dil's place? He didn't have to stay long. Just have a look around, bullshit a bit, get the material he needed to continue writing tomorrow...

Decided, Buddy yanked off his tie, his dress shirt, his pants, tossing them all on the bed. He rolled a stick of deodorant beneath his armpits, then pulled on a pair of jeans and a white tee. In the bathroom he splashed cold water on his face and brushed his teeth.

Back in the bedroom, he closed the laptop lid, plunging the room into darkness. He went to the living room, which was equally dark save the eerie glow from the television. He padded quietly across the floor so as not to wake his mother. He thought about slipping on shoes but decided there was no need. He was only going down the hall. He collected his keys from the deal table, then his wallet too, in case he had to pay for the pizza. He stepped into the hallway and sneezed four times. A fifth sneeze tickled his nose but retreated. He closed and locked the door, then went to Dil's unit.

He knocked.

"Coming!"

A moment later the door swung inward, and Dil stood across the threshold, all dark hair and big black eyes, wearing nothing but a smile and a white terrycloth towel.

"Buddy!" she said. Then, addressing his roving gaze, she added, "I was just about to have a shower. What's up?"

"I'm feeling a bit better and was wondering if you still want to have a beer?"

"Definitely!" she said. "But I've already had a couple, so you're going to have to catch up."

"Do you want me to get some more? I can—"

"No, no, I bought a whole case from that supermarket a block over. How convenient is that? I think I'm going to love New York. Come in."

Buddy followed her inside and looked around, amazed. Her place was like nothing he'd imagined; in fact, it was as if she'd been living here for months, not hours. There were laminated prints on the walls—Van Gogh, Matisse, Rousseau—books on the bookshelf, a vase of flowers on the coffee table, a basket of fruit on the kitchen counter, two potted palms bookending the sofa. A scattering of candles, all lit, perfumed the air with a vanilla scent.

"You've been busy," he said.

"I just finished, and I smell like a pig. I still need that shower. But make yourself at home. Beer's in the fridge. I won't be long."

She disappeared into her bedroom.

Buddy went to the kitchenette. Through the glass-fronted cupboard doors he could see stacks of plates, bowls, mugs, glasses. They made his cupboards seem barren in comparison. He opened the fridge and found it bursting with food. Eight bottles of Carlsberg lined the door shelf. Another six or so shared the crisper with a bunch of celery, a bag of baby carrots, and a variety of leafy green vegetables.

Buddy made a mental note of all this—when it came to writing, the devil was in the details—then retrieved a beer. He twisted off the cap and took a sip. Next to the basket of fruit, he noticed, was a wood knife block from which protruded seven handles. He withdrew a seven-inch cook's knife and turned it over in his hand. Stainless steel, hollow handle, well-balanced. He replaced it, already wondering how he could incorporate it into his story.

Buddy returned to the living room. He shuffled through the magazines on the table. *Seventeen, People, National Inquirer.* A large picture frame stood beside the TV, displaying four individual prints. They were all of Dil and what appeared to be family. No friends, no dead ex.

He went to the bookcase, reading the spines of the books. There were a lot of romance novels by authors he'd never heard of, a few cooking books, and some biographies.

Buddy decided he'd load Wendy's bookshelf with horror titles instead, maybe even add some true-life crime. Hint at her homicidal side.

Whistling gaily—his mood had done a full one-eighty from what it'd been after his blow up in Gino's office—he went to the easel in the corner, on which sat a blank canvas. No, not blank, he realized. Dil had sketched a pencil outline on it. So was she an artist? Another great detail. A killer with an artistic side. How could he work this into the story? Maybe Don finds drawings

Wendy did of her ex-boyfriend, sick, gruesome ones celebrating his death?

Goddamn! Buddy thought. This was so much easier than staring at a computer screen and making everything up. It was all laid out right before him.

The door to the bedroom opened and Dil appeared, now wearing a red satin robe over a matching slip, the hem of which stopped a little above her knees. She unwrapped the towel from her head and shook her dark, damp hair out, so it cascaded over her shoulders.

Buddy felt an awakening in his groin and mentally doused it with cold water. He wasn't there to get laid. Research. That was all. Then he was gone.

"So what do you think?" she asked.

"Good color on you."

"Not me, Buddy!" she said, closing the robe and tying the sash. "The apartment. Not bad, huh? It was just so sterile, cold. I need a homey place."

"You draw?" he said, indicating the canvas.

"I paint—oils. I sketch the picture first in pencil. That's a spot in the country where I liked to go to."

"Yeah?" he said. "What did you do there?"

"Just sat around. It was quiet, beautiful."

"You went by yourself?"

"Sometimes," she said. "Do you have a spot like that?"

"Where I go to be by myself? Not really."

"Not really?"

"I don't know. Sometimes I go to the roof."

"This building's roof?"

He nodded. "If you continue up the stairs one more flight you come to this little storage room. There's a door that leads to the roof."

"We should totally bring some chairs up there! Make a chill-out zone. Hey, I know this is out of the blue, but do you smoke pot?"

"Pot?" Buddy repeated, surprised. "No, not for a while."

"I thought everyone in New York did?"

"I don't know about that."

"Well, whatever, do you want to? I brought some from Kentucky."

Without waiting for his reply, she went to the kitchenette, opened the freezer, and produced from behind a box of frozen blueberries what must have been an ounce of marijuana in a Ziploc bag.

"So?" she said, holding it up for him to see.

"Sure," he said.

"Awesome! Now where did I put it?" She opened the cupboard below the sink. "Ah!" She set an electric coffee grinder on the counter and plugged it into a wall socket. "Way better than scissors." She dumped a few green-brown buds into the grinder, clapped the top on, and twisted it. The whirling blades made a hungry buzzing sound. After a few seconds she removed the top and tapped the finely ground marijuana onto the counter. "Neat trick, huh? My ex taught me it."

"Were you guys together long?"

"Four years or so."

"He's still in Kentucky?"

"Yeah. Sort of."

"Sort of?"

"Yeah, he's still there." She'd taken a pack of rolling papers from the Ziploc bag, stuck two together in an L shape, and was now in the process of rolling a massive joint.

"Why'd you break up?"

"I don't like talking about him, Buddy. He was an asshole, and he totally screwed up my life. I shouldn't have mentioned him."

Buddy was watching her closely. Anger, definitely. But where was the remorse? The sadness?

Dil must have felt his eyes on her because she looked up from the joint and held his gaze.

Buddy smiled, finished his beer, and got another from the fridge. "You want one?" he asked her.

"Yes, please," she said.

Buddy twisted off both caps and set her bottle on the counter. She licked the strip of glue on the paper, then lit the joint with a yellow Bic lighter that had been amongst the apples and oranges in the fruit basket. "Man," she said, exhaling toward the ceiling. "I've been waiting all day for this."

She took another toke, then handed the joint to him. He pinched it between his thumb and forefinger and inhaled deeply, watching the cherry flare. He held the smoke in his lungs for all of two seconds before lurching forward in a fit of coughs.

Dil giggled. "When was the last time you smoked?"

"College," he managed, passing the joint back.

"What subject did you take?"

"Finance."

"God, why would you take *that*?"

Buddy chugged a mouthful of beer to soothe his throat. "Seemed like a good idea at the time."

"What do you do?" she asked. "Wait, let me guess. You work at a bank or something?"

Buddy frowned. "How'd you know that?"

"Lucky guess," she said.

"I'm serious."

"Come on, Buddy. You studied finance. You wear a suit. Where else would you work?"

"I could have been a manager somewhere, like at a travel agency."

"Well, a manager of a travel agency's not what came to mind. A bank did. Here."

They passed the joint back and forth a few more times, Dil doing most of the talking, before she tapped it out in the sink.

"Anyway," Buddy said, gripping the counter. He definitely felt the effects of the pot: woozy, giddy, relaxed. "I don't work at a bank anymore. I was fired today."

Dil's eyebrows went up. "Fired?"

"I called my boss a cocksucker."

"Shut up!"

"Yeah," he said, smiling at the memory. "Then I tossed a

photo of his daughter across the room."

"You did not."

"Yeah, I did. Fucking gnome deserved it."

"Why would you ever do that?"

"He passed me up for a promotion."

"So you called him a cocksucker and busted a picture of his daughter?" She seemed like she wanted to laugh but held it inside instead. "Shoot, Buddy...that really sucks. Fired...wow..." She chewed on this for a moment, then added, "Hold on, we need some music to lighten the mood." She went to a stereo system that sat on a low table beneath the window. Buddy watched her, noting the way the thin fabric of the robe hugged her thighs, her butt. She scooped up a handful of CD cases and shuffled through them. "Do you like Michael Jackson?"

Buddy didn't but said he did.

Dil slipped a disc in the stereo and pressed Play. A moment later the opening drumbeat of "Billie Jean" blared through the speakers. She turned down the volume slightly. Then she moonwalked into the middle of the living room, her feet sliding magically over the floor.

The spectacle was so absurd Buddy chuckled.

"What?" she said. "This is how I walk." She moonwalked to the bookcase and grabbed a romance novel, which she pretended to read. Then she moonwalked back to him, looking over her shoulder to make sure he was paying attention.

"Not bad, huh?" she said, grinning. "When I was in grammar school, my best friend used to have these really waxy floors in her basement. Every time I went over to play with her, we'd practice moonwalking. I could do it better if I had socks on."

"It was good," he assured her.

Dil picked up her beer, then clinked it against his. "Cheers, neighbor," she said.

"Cheers," Buddy said—even as a voice in his head told him to stop dicking around and get down to business. He needed material for the book.

After all, he wasn't going to write an entire chapter about the two of them standing around getting high in her apartment.

Nevertheless, before he could think of a suitable question, Dil opened the fridge and said, "Hey, do you remember that scene in *Ghostbusters* when Sigourney Weaver opens her fridge and it leads to a different dimension? How trippy would that be?"

"I had a dream like that once," he told her. "But my fridge didn't lead to a different dimension. It led to hell."

"Holy shit, Buddy! That's not trippy. That's freaky. Did you see the devil?"

"In my fridge?"

"In your fridge in your dream."

"I don't remember. I think I just saw flames."

"Well, that's still freaky. Are you hungry? I'm starving."

"Didn't you want to order a pizza?"

She made a face. "Oh, right…"

"You don't want to?"

"Do you?"

"Up to you."

She shrugged. "It just feels like a lot of work."

"A lot of work?"

"Do you know any pizza numbers off by heart?"

"No."

"Well, that means we have to find the number for one. Then we have to call them and tell them what we want on it."

"That's not that hard."

"Yeah, but then you have to give them your address, and they always repeat it like three times, spelling out everything. Then you have to wait like thirty minutes, maybe longer, for it to arrive. Then you have to pay the delivery guy. And you have to leave him a tip. I hate leaving tips. He's going to know I'm high. No—forget it. I'm not calling."

Buddy mulled that over. "I guess it is a lot of work, isn't it?"

Dil's eyes lit up. "What about a cake? Do you want to bake a cake?"

"That's way more fucking work than ordering a pizza."

"Come on, let's make one! It'll be fun. I bought flour and sugar and everything today too."

Dil went to the pantry cupboard to gather what they would need. After a moment, Buddy joined her.

While they went about mixing the ingredients together in a large glass bowl, Buddy contemplated the surreal course the evening had taken. A couple hours ago he'd wanted nothing to do with his psycho-killer neighbor, and now here he was in her kitchen, blitzed out of his mind, listening to Michael Jackson, and baking a goddamn cake.

Even so, Buddy had to admit he was having a good time. In fact, he couldn't remember when he last had this much fun.

When the cake was in the oven baking, he said, "So what do we do now?"

"Lick the spoon, obviously." Dil held up the large wooden spoon they'd used, which was covered in gunky chocolate cake mix.

"Forget it."

"Didn't your mom ever let you lick the spoon when you were a kid?"

Buddy shook his head. "My mom was a progressive liberal actress. She thought a woman cooking and baking and cleaning and all that crap was too nineteen fifties."

"An actress!" Dil said. "Was she in anything I would have seen?"

Buddy shook his head again. "Just some real old stuff before I was born. You wouldn't know it."

"Did she used to live in LA?"

"That's where I was born," he told her. "My dad was a production assistant. He met my mom on the set of one of her movies. They got married and were pretty good together until he was busted sexually assaulting some underage actress. He went to prison. My mom and I moved to New York to live with her sister. She didn't work because the child support she was getting was enough for both us to live on. When I turned eighteen, and the money stopped coming, she mooched off her sister while I went to college. I didn't see her much after that until she had her stroke."

"Oh, Buddy..."

"Her sister put her in a nursing home. Medicare covered the first hundred days, but when that ran out some administrative asshole said they had no permanent beds free and she had to leave. Her sister didn't want to take her back, so I moved her in with me."

"Does she still live with you now?" Dil asked, surprised.

Buddy nodded but didn't say anything more. The memories were bringing up all sorts of emotions he didn't care for. And what the hell was he doing telling Dil his goddamn life story? This was exactly why he hadn't wanted anything to do with her. He was getting too close. She was going to think they were friends or some shit. She would start coming by. Soon they'd be fucking BFFs...

"I should go," he said. "I have stuff I have to do."

Dil touched his arm. She was looking at him with her big black eyes, sadly, sympathetically, and then she was stepping toward him, and to hell if she was going to do it... She was! She leaned in, tilting her chin up—and then they were kissing. He heard the wooden spoon clatter onto the counter, felt her breasts press against his chest.

After a moment, Buddy ran his hands over the smooth satin of her robe, up and down her thighs. They were firm. So was her butt, firm, toned, like she worked out.

A voice in his head was telling him this was wrong, this was bad, and he was about to put an end to it when Dil undid his jeans, slipped her hand down the front of his boxers.

He fumbled opened her robe, peeled it off her shoulders. She was breathing hard, her cleavage heaving, fucking *heaving*, like they were acting out something from one of those romance novels on her bookshelf. His hands took on a life of their own, exploring everywhere, squeezing, pinching, plying. He was rock hard now. She knew that. She was arcing her crotch into his. And right then he wanted to fuck her more than he'd ever wanted to fuck anyone.

Their mouths locked, their tongues danced. He drove her backward into the counter, hiked her onto it. She moaned, which made him all the more frenzied. He tried pulling the slip over her head, but she mumbled something that sounded like "no." He stepped back, his heart pounding. Her eyes sparkled like chips of obsidian, wild, carnal. Her lips curled into a grin.

She slid off the counter, took his hand in hers, and led him to the bedroom.

※ ※ ※

Buddy dreamed he was in court, standing behind the bar table, addressing the judge. "We were baking a cake, Your Honor," he said, "and she became angry and stabbed me with a knife. It was in a wood block on the counter."

"The police never found the knife," the judge said.

"It's still inside me."

"The knife's inside you?"

"She stabbed me really deep. I didn't want to take it out because I thought it would make the wound worse."

"Did you start the fight?"

"No, she did."

"Liar!" Dil shouted from where she sat next to her lawyer.

"It's true," Buddy insisted.

"He doesn't even have a job, Your Honor," Dil said, jumping to her feet. She was completely naked, Buddy noticed for the first time, her skin a flawless nutmeg brown, her perfect breasts defying gravity, nipples at attention. "He told me this!" she went on. "He was fired. He's a bum. Don't believe him."

"What was the fight about?" the judge asked.

"I just went over to his unit to borrow sugar," she said, "and he went totally crazy. He started attacking me, so I stabbed him in self-defense."

"That's bullshit, Your Honor!" Buddy said. "She stabs everyone, and she always says it's in self-defense. She's a psychopath."

"You are!" Dil said. "You still live with your mom!"

"Fuck you!"

"Fuck *you*!"

The court went wild. The judge banged his gavel repeatedly

—

Buddy snapped open his eyes. It was dark, he couldn't see, but he immediately recognized the alien feel of Dil's bed beneath him, the fresh smell of her linens. He recalled the sex they'd had with a burst of excitement, though this was quickly replaced with dread and regret.

*He'd slept with his neighbor. His fucking neighbor. It was the beginning of the end—*

A black silhouette stood by the window. Dil? Yeah, had to be. She was just standing there…staring at him? And where was her arm? Was it behind her back? Was she holding something behind her back?

"Dil?" he said.

"Oh, you're awake," she replied, turning toward him. She hadn't been staring at him after all. She'd been looking out the window. He'd been viewing her profile.

"What are you doing?"

"I couldn't sleep," she said. "It's not you," she added quickly. "I just don't sleep much these days."

Buddy's eyes adjusted to the gloom, and he now saw she wore her red satin robe. Nothing was in either of her hands.

"What's outside?" he asked.

"I was looking at the stars. Or trying to. You can barely see any. I guess that's something I'm going to have to get used to in this city." She came to the bed, slipped under the covers, slid a knee over his legs. The robe was cool and smooth on his skin. "I just like looking at them. They remind me how small and insignificant Earth is, how insignificant I am, how much more stuff is out there that we can't even begin to fathom."

"Did you smoke another joint while I was asleep?"

She hit his shoulder playfully. "I'm serious, Buddy. I mean, people get so stressed about their lives. Their boss, or paying their telephone bill on time, or...this or that. But when you understand you're an eye blink in something that's billions of years old, you realize how silly all your worries are, how meaningless they are. Seriously, there're billions of billions of planets out there, worlds and life forms beyond imagining, and I can't sleep because..."

"Because what?"

"Nothing," she said. "Anyway, I'm glad I met you, Buddy."

He didn't say anything.

"And I want you to know," she went on, "I don't usually do this."

"Do what?"

"You know," she said, rubbing her leg against his. "*This*. I've just been...lonely lately... I don't know..."

She set her head on the pillow. Her hair brushed his cheek, smelling of flowers and grapefruit.

Buddy thought she might keep talking, but she didn't. He closed his eyes and listened to her steady breathing until he drifted back to sleep.

* * *

Dil woke to light streaming through her bedroom window. She rubbed the sleep from her eyes, and a warmth filled her chest as she remembered the night before. She rolled over, expecting to find Buddy sleeping next to her. He was gone.

Frowning, she sat up. The bedroom was stark and unwelcoming. Unlike the living room, she hadn't gotten around to fixing it up yet. She had a number of prints and picture frames ready to hang, but she held off yesterday, deciding she wanted to paint the walls first. She was thinking retro pink or tangerine, maybe even sky blue. All three would go well with the bed's salmon upholstered headboard and dove-white duvet. She also needed more pillows. She loved pillows. Today or tomorrow she'd stop by a Wallmart and purchase a dozen colorful pillows—

Actually, screw that, she thought. She'd visit Macy's or Bloomingdale's.

After all, she was in New York freaking City.

The door to the bathroom was open, though she didn't hear the water running. "Buddy?" she said.

No reply.

She glanced about for a note but didn't see one. She got out of bed and pulled her robe closed tighter against the chill morning air. Arms folded across her chest, she entered the living room. The cake, which they had forgotten about until they'd smelled it burning halfway through their lovemaking, sat on the kitchen counter, a charred, inedible square.

Dil smiled as she recalled leaping off Buddy and dashing to the kitchen, stark naked, in the hopes of saving it.

Nevertheless, her mood was already dampening. Because why had Buddy left without waking her or leaving a note? Did he think neither action was necessary given he lived next door? Or did he regret staying over? Was last night a one night stand and nothing more?

Dammit, what had she told him when she'd returned to bed in the middle of the night? That she was lonely? God, had she come across as clingy, pathetic? Had she scared him off?

She hoped not. He might be odd, aloof, even a bit bigheaded, but like she'd told him, she was lonely, really lonely, and he was company. Also, it didn't hurt he was fit and handsome and something of a stallion in bed.

Dil hadn't been with anyone since Jordon. A relationship had been the last thing on her mind during the trial, of course. But after she was cleared of all the baseless charges against her, she thought she might be able to resume her life as normal. That proved not to be the case. Her trial had been the talk of Newport for more than a year, and thanks to the prosecution's portrayal of her as a manipulative, cold-hearted murderer, much of the town had formed their opinion of her long before the innocent verdict was read. The real estate company where she worked didn't want her back, and her so-called friends didn't want anything to do with her. Jordon had been a popular guy, and some no doubt wanted someone to blame for his death, while the others simply didn't want to be seen in public with someone of her notoriety. Not that she blamed them. She couldn't walk down the street without attracting profanities shouted from passing vehicles, or hostile looks from shopkeepers. The manager of one restaurant had outright refused to serve her, and she had to get up from her table and leave, humiliated, two dozen judging eyes on her. After that incident she rarely left her house, instead spending most days inside teaching herself to paint. Finally she made the difficult decision to leave Kentucky —difficult only because it meant leaving her father, mother, and brother behind, the only people she'd felt close to in the world.

Dil went to the purple electric kettle next to the microwave. She lifted it by the handle and discovered it was half full with water. She clicked it on and started toward the fridge, to retrieve the milk, when she noticed a black wallet on the floor, pressed against the baseboard molding beneath the cupboards.

She picked it up. A couple of twenties were tucked into the sleeve, a variety of cards in the card slots. She pulled one out— a TD credit card issued to Buddy Smith. Dil realized the wallet must have fallen from one of Buddy's pockets while they'd been making out after baking the cake.

Her first impulse was to call him on the phone, but she didn't have his number. Besides, he was right next door. It made more sense to drop off the wallet. Not to mention it would also provide her the opportunity to read his face, see if last night meant anything.

After fixing her hair in the magnetized mirror stuck to the fridge, Dil went next door and knocked. She waited a good ten seconds, then knocked again.

Buddy didn't answer.

Was he sleeping? she wondered. Or had he gone out?

Without his wallet?

Dil thought about returning to her apartment and waiting

for Buddy to put two and two together and pay her a visit. Yet she found she didn't want to wait. She wanted to see him now.

She tried the door handle. It twisted in her grip. She pushed the door open and poked her head inside. It was dark, the lights off, the blinds closed. The TV, however, cast a flickering glow on someone sitting before it in a wheelchair—someone with curly, white hair. For a moment Dil couldn't fathom who the person might be until she remembered Buddy telling her his mother lived with him.

"Uh, hi, there!" Dil said awkwardly, wondering why the woman hadn't attempted to answer the door. "I'm your neighbor. I just moved in. Buddy, uh, forgot his wallet at my place last night. I'm just going to leave it on the table here."

Buddy's mother didn't answer.

Dil set the wallet on the table and was about to leave—but hesitated.

Why wasn't the woman answering her? Was she hard of hearing? Deaf?

*Had she had another stroke?*

"Hello?" Dil said, louder.

No reply.

A ball of dread formed in Dil's gut. Something was not right. Her instincts told her to turn around, leave, but she didn't listen to them. Instead she crossed the room, slowly, tentatively. She detected an unpleasant musty smell.

When she reached the wheelchair she gasped. The woman sitting in it was little more than a clothed skeleton sheathed in shriveled, leathery skin. Her unseeing eyes were painted with garish eyeliner, her sunken cheeks powdered with blush, her cracked lips smeared with bright red lipstick. Her hair was too white and glossy to be anything but a wig.

Dil's first thought was that it was a prop, a Halloween prop, one of those expensive ones you rent rather than buy.

Her second thought: *It's real. My God, it's real, it's a corpse, it's a real corpse.*

Even as Dil stumbled backward in horror, she noted the dust

coating the metal arms of the wheelchair, the rubber tires, the spokes.

For a moment she thought the dead woman was moaning before realizing the sound had originated deep within her own throat.

She turned to flee—and sensed a presence in the bedroom doorway.

Buddy stood there, his hair wet, a crimson towel wrapped around his waist. He was watching her impassively.

"I knew you were going to be trouble," he said.

\* \* \*

Dil ran. Buddy caught her before she reached the door. His hands curled around her shoulders. She opened her mouth to scream, but in the same instant Buddy's right arm pressed against her throat, choking her, silencing her. All she could muster was a strangled croak.

She scratched and tore at his arm, her nails digging into his flesh, drawing blood. Buddy swung her around, moving her toward one of the bedrooms. Inside it she glimpsed a number of glass bottles on a shelf, each containing—

*Oh God no.*

Dil kicked, squirmed, flailed.

Buddy grabbed a fistful of her hair and removed his arm from her throat. She sucked back air. Before she could do anything else he slammed her head into the doorframe.

Light exploded across her vision. Her face went numb.

He drove her head into the doorframe a second time.

Stars and blackness ferried her into unconsciousness.

\* \* \*

Buddy spat a litany of curses as he carried Dil's limp body

into what used to be his mother's bedroom. He couldn't believe his bad luck. He'd locked the front door every day for the last two years, and the one time he forgets to, his goddamn nosy neighbor busts in.

He had excuses for not locking it. He was still loopy from the pot when he left Dil's place earlier. He was flustered by his lapse in judgment to have sex with her. He was overeager to wash her smell off him, to get into his writing, and to forget the night ever happened.

Not that any of these excuses mattered. The damage was done.

She'd seen his mother.

Buddy set Dil on his mother's bed, which she hadn't used since he'd slipped a plastic bag over her head while she was watching an old Sean Connery movie twenty months before. She had only been living with him for six weeks then, but it had been six weeks too long. When he'd agreed to care for her, he'd had no idea what he was taking on. He'd figured a bit more cooking, cleaning, ironing, that kind of stuff. The reality was she pissed her bed every night, which meant he had to wash her linens and shower her each morning. Then he'd get home from work only to find she'd pissed herself again, often shitting herself too. Another shower, more laundry. Come dinner he didn't get a break because the stroke, which had paralyzed much of her body, prevented her from feeding herself. So he'd have to pound her dinner into mush and spoon it into her mouth. In the evening she might signal she needed to use the bathroom instead of letting loose in her diaper. Nevertheless, getting her undressed, on the toilet, cleaning her up—fuck, it was easier to let her soil herself and hose her down in the shower.

Needless to say, caring for her simply became too much. But killing her wasn't the answer. Buddy knew that right after she took her last, agonized breath. Flooded with guilt at what he'd done, he began talking to her, apologizing to her, changing her, bathing her, all the old routines. When her stench became overpowering, he removed her lungs, stomach, liver, intestines, heart, and brain, and treated her body with salt for forty days until no moisture remained. Then he filled the cavities with sawdust from a local cabinetmaker and sewed her back up.

Buddy knew what he was doing wasn't right, wasn't healthy. In fact, according to WebMD, he was demonstrating all the symptoms of a schizophrenic disorder. Even so, he didn't feel comfortable seeing a doctor, and he didn't have the cash to see a shrink, so he ordered a variety of antipsychotic medication from an RX pharmacy in India. They worked in the sense they stopped the voices in his head and made it very clear to him that his mother was a mummified corpse in a wheelchair. Yet he found he didn't like this reality at all. He was much happier with the voices and his mother alive and well. Besides, the drugs made him feel depressed and suicidal and even more antisocial than he already was.

He flushed them down the toilet shortly after he began taking them, and he had been doing just fine ever since.

Four lengths of blood-speckled rope, each three feet long, were tied to the bed's four corner posts. Buddy used them to secure Dil's hands and legs, as he had done many times before to the prostitutes he brought back to his unit. He didn't hire them from pimps or madams or other intermediaries, nor did he contact the self-employed ones via their Facebook pages. He picked them off the street so there was no way they could be traced back to him. Chinatown or Soho one month. Midtown, between Forty-eighth and Fifty-ninth, another month. The Bronx. Murray Hill. Tribeca. He's killed thirteen in total since his mother's death. They were all the same. Confident and sultry when they were fucking him and thinking they were in control. Weeping and moaning when they realized who was really in control, when they woke from their beating tied to the bed, their tongues cut out.

Buddy's collection lined the shelf on the wall directly before him. Thirteen wide-mouth, one-liter glass bottles, each containing a ten-percent formaldehyde solution and a perfectly preserved segment of tongue, each labeled with a piece of masking tape and a corresponding name: Selma, Angel, Tara, Zoe, Crystal, Tawny, Tiffany, Brandy, Lola, Ginger, Candy, Jade, Devon.

Buddy would have liked to have added Dil's tongue and name to the collection, given how much of a grunter she was, and how much trouble she was about to cause him. But he couldn't do that. Her death had to look like an accident.

She was his goddamn neighbor after all.

\* \* \*

With Dil secured and gagged in case she regained consciousness, Buddy spent the next twenty minutes transferring his collection of tongues to his car, which was parked in the small lot behind the apartment building. He carried the bottles three at a time, in his orange backpack, and placed them in the vehicle's trunk.

Back in his unit Buddy untied and ungagged Dil—he hadn't needed to worry about her after all; she was out for the count—and carried her to the living room, where he set her on the floor. Then he gathered the four lengths of rope and stuffed them in his backpack, so as not to leave anything suspicious behind for the fire investigators to find.

Kneeling next to his mother, taking her frail hand in his, he said, "I'm sorry about this, Ma. But you know I have to do it, right? It's the only option."

"I know that, dear," she said. "I understand."

"And, well, maybe it's for the best. Because sooner or later your sister, or someone from the city or state, would have started asking about you. And I couldn't just say you died. They'd know you'd been dead for a while. They'd know what I did to you. But if they think you died in a fire, a really big fire, and there's nothing left..." He blinked back tears. "I love you, Ma. I love you so much."

"I love you too, dear. Now, stop wasting time talking to me, and go do what you have to do."

Buddy kissed his mother's papery lips, then scooped Dil into his arms. He carried her to her unit, set her in her bed, and pulled the duvet over her body, tucking it beneath her chin.

In the kitchen, he turned on the stove's bottom left element and placed a cast iron skillet on it. He filled the pan with a dozen greasy strips of bacon from the fridge and sandwiched it with a roll of paper towel and two dish clothes.

Soon the grease in the skillet began to smoke. It popped and sprayed before eventually bursting into flames, which leapt to the adjacent combustible items.

A short time later the kitchenette was a full-blown inferno.

❊ ❊ ❊

When Dil opened her eyes she thought she was falling through a cluster of storm clouds. In the next moment she rolled onto her side in a paroxysm of coughs. Eyes stinging, throat scorched, she tumbled out of the bed to the floor, where the air was cleaner but still toxic.

*What was going on? What was burning? What happened—?*

Buddy!

But there was no time to think about him.

The apartment was on fire.

She had to get out of there.

Now.

Although Dil couldn't see—the smoke was too thick, creating nearly blackout conditions—she was able to crawl to the living room.

And became completely disorientated.

She attempted to make her way to the front door but somehow got turned around and ended up bumping into her easel, which was against the opposite wall.

She tried screaming for help but all that came out of her mouth was a dry wheeze. The fire had stolen all the oxygen from the air, making each subsequent breath feel as though she were sucking back glass.

Heart pounding, woozy as if drunk, she dragged herself forward with arms that had stopped cooperating. The heat blistered her skin, cooking her alive.

Her only hope, she knew, was the window, but where was it? How far away? She no longer had any sense of perception. She didn't even know if she was actually moving. She wanted to believe she was. Yet maybe it was in her head, maybe—

Her hand knocked something—a table.

The stereo!

Mustering the last of her strength, she pressed her hands against the wall, slapped it, grasping for purchase—and gripped the window ledge. She pulled herself to her feet. Faced pressed against the warm glass, she hooked her fingers beneath the finger lifts and tugged the bottom sash up.

Wonderfully cold, spring air sprung in. Dil stuck her head through the opening, heaving, coughing, then flopping onto the steel gratings of the fire escape.

In a disorientated blur she descended two flights of stairs to the lowest platform, released the ladder, which swung down along a track, and continued to the ground.

As soon as her feet touched the sidewalk her legs gave out and she collapsed. People and noise swarmed around her, but she was already giving into the overwhelming urge to close her eyes, and everything faded to dark.

❋ ❋ ❋

Buddy saw the smoke from half a block away. It streamed up into the morning sky lazily in thick black billows. A siren wailed in the distance, punctuated by the deep blast of an air horn.

Buddy broke into a sprint, only slowing when he reached the crowd gathered in front of the burning apartment building. "Move!" he shouted, elbowing through the rubberneckers. "Move! Outta my way!" People cursed, a few cried out. Then he was at the front of the throng, next to a fire truck studded with a dozen flashing auxiliary lights. An American flag affixed to the back of it flapped in the warm air.

The building's double front doors were wide open, likely left that way when the residents fled. Beyond them a furnace blazed, nothing visible except a wall of blustering flames. A firefighter in a tan Nomex suit with reflective stripes—"Boomer" written across the back of the jacket—was attacking the fire with a thick hose spraying a jet of water.

Buddy charged toward the building. Two burly cops blocked his way and seized him by the arms.

"Get back!" one of them snapped.

"My ma's in there!" Buddy said. "She's in a wheelchair!"

"You can't go in," the other one said.

"My ma's in there!" he repeated, trying to twist free.

The cops led him away through the crowd, stopping at the rear of an ambulance. The cop on the right said, "Now take it easy, okay? You gonna be all right?" The ambulance's cherry tops flashed rotating red light across his face. Grainy chatter from two-way radios seemed to originate from everywhere. A second fire truck rumbled to the scene, and someone on a bull-horn ordered everyone to move to the far side of the street.

"My ma's in there," Buddy said numbly. "She's in a wheelchair. She's trapped. She's—" The words died on his lips. He was staring into the cargo area of the ambulance, where his neighbor, Dil Lakshmi, lay on a stretcher, an oxygen mask covering her nose and mouth. "No..." he mumbled, barely a whisper.

In the same moment Dil opened her eyes. For a second she stared at nothing, then her eyes fell on him. Something shifted in them, and she screamed.

The cops jumped. Buddy stumbled backward a step.

Dil tore off the mask and pointed a shaking finger at Buddy. "Him!" she said. "Him! Him! Him!"

"Miss, calm down," one of the cops said, going to her.

"He kills people!" she wailed. "He kills them in his apartment! He tried to kill me!"

Both cops whirled to stare at Buddy. Their hands went to their holstered pistols.

Buddy was shaking his head. "Me?" he said, and his shock at seeing Dil gave way to anger. "*Me? She's a psychopath! She killed her boyfriend in Kentucky. That's why she moved to New York. She did this! She killed my mother!*"

Buddy lunged forward, to get to her.

The cops wrestled him to the ground, flipping him onto his chest and pinning him in place with their knees. The cold, sharp metal of handcuffs locked around his wrists.

"Not me, you fuckers!" Buddy shouted, his mouth squashed against the asphalt. "Her! Arrest her!"

The cops heaved him to his feet and shoved him into the back of a nearby patrol car.

# EPILOGUE

Six months later Buddy was sitting in a reclining chair on his balcony, the sun on his face, proofreading the final draft of his novel, *Neighbors*. He tipped a Sam Adams to his lips, taking a long, cold swallow. A smile curled his lips as he finished a particularly enjoyable paragraph in which Wendy moonwalks across her living room. The smile turned into a chuckle, and he reread the paragraph two more times. The book had really come together. The characters weren't your typical two-dimensional clichés, and the climax on the roof was a definite winner. He'd sent off query letters to three agents this morning because he figured by the time they got back to him requesting the full manuscript, he would be done with the proofreading. He could already see himself in one year's time, bullshitting to fans at bookstores and writing conventions across the country, hanging out with other famous authors, living the dream.

Ironically, Buddy owed much of this soon-to-come fame and fortune to Dil, for if it hadn't been for her sticking her nose where it didn't belong, he wouldn't have set fire to the Bronx apartment building, he wouldn't have collected on his renters insurance—which was paying his current rent and would continue to do so for another six months—and, consequently, he wouldn't have had the opportunity to write fulltime. Well, almost fulltime. He was working two days a week at a Subway restaurant to pay for everyday expenses. But what was two days? Not to mention he could eat as many free subs as he wanted, which were not only delicious but checked off all the ticks of a well-balanced diet.

Nevertheless, Dil didn't deserve all the credit, because if Buddy had cracked during his arrest after the fire, he would no doubt be sitting in the slammer right now. But he hadn't cracked. Quite the contrary, he'd been smart enough to invoke his right to silence. And if you're guilty of something, and are unfortunate enough to get arrested and taken into custody, that's what you have to do, invoke your right to silence, otherwise your goose is cooked. Because when it comes to interrogations, detectives have all the knowledge, experience, and power, while the suspect only has paranoia and fear. That's why the *Miranda* warning was introduced some thirty years ago. The government knew the odds were skewed against the accused, and they wanted to level the playing field in the name of justice. Most people, however, are too stupid to know when it's in their best interest to zip their traps, and instead they get suckered into confessing their crime. The really stupid ones even confess to crimes they didn't commit. That's how good detectives are at psychological manipulation. So you don't want to go up against them mano a mano. You want to invoke the Fifth Amendment privilege against self-incrimination and arrange for a criminal defense attorney, or public defender, because they know the game inside out, they know the detectives' playbooks, which means they know how to win.

Buddy's attorney pretty much told the detectives and the prosecution to go fuck themselves, pointing out all the weaknesses in their case before they filed a single charge. Most important was the fact there was no evidence of any crime. No tongues were unearthed in the charred remains of Buddy's apartment (Buddy had disposed of them in a Dumpster eight blocks away before parking his car and walking back to the building to "discover" the fire). And his mother, while not reduced to ash and bone bits in the blaze, had been burned too badly to determine her time or cause of death. So in the end it was a case of "he said, she said" that rested solely on Dil's testimony—and she was about as unreliable a witness as you could get, considering she had been accused of murder herself. It didn't matter she had been cleared of the charges; she had stabbed her ex-boyfriend six times. No jury in their right mind would take her word over Buddy's, a man who had no criminal record and who had loved his mother enough to volunteer to become her primary caregiver after her stroke.

When Buddy was inevitably given a written release and allowed to walk free, Red Cross put him up in a hotel for a couple days with a hundred fifty dollar daily stipend while he negotiated with Allstate his future living arrangements. He could have remained in New York, of course. But he decided it was time for a change and got on a Greyhound and traveled cross country to California. Not Calabasas—no fucking way—but LA, where, like New York, there weren't many grunters, and he could once more blend into the background.

Buddy tilted the Sam Adams to his lips and drained what beer was left in the bottle. Then he went inside to get another. The new apartment was a tiny studio, three hundred square feet, but pimped out, thanks again to his renters insurance, which had also covered all his personal belongings, including furniture, electronics, even his wardrobe.

In the kitchenette Buddy opened the fridge, but discovered no more beer. He considered making a coffee instead, but decided fuck that. He was celebrating finishing his manuscript; he deserved to get a little shit-faced, even if it was only ten thirty in the morning.

After all, he was going to be a famous writer soon, and famous writers could get shit-faced at any time they pleased; it all went part and parcel with being a tortured artist, a creative genius, an eccentric loner.

Grabbing his keys and wallet, Buddy left his unit, making sure to lock up behind him. He might not have to worry about someone discovering his mother anymore, but the building was full of minorities and college burnouts, and he didn't trust a single one of them.

Halfway down the bland white hallway he stopped in front of a unit with its door left open. Two women, a black and an Asian, were inside. They were roughly his age and wore loads of makeup and short shorts. The black one was holding a paint swatch to the wall, while the slim Asian was sipping a Diet Coke through a fluorescent pink straw.

"Uh, hi?" the Asian said, seeing him. She'd styled her hair in idiotic pigtails.

"Hi," Buddy said. "I live on this floor."

"Yeah?" she said, acting pissed off for no reason.

"I'm just saying, I'm your neighbor."

"I'm Nicole," the black one said. "This is Izzy."

"So—you just moving in?"

"Yup," Nicole said.

"Cool," he said.

"Umm... Did you want anything?" Izzy said, still pissed off.

"No, I'm just saying hi. I guess I'll see you guys around?"

"Sure," Nicole said.

"Whatever," Izzy said.

While continuing down the hall, Buddy heard Izzy mumble "creep" under her breath before the two of them burst into juvenile laughter.

Nevertheless, Buddy didn't care, was barely listening. Because he'd just been zapped with a new story idea, a sequel to *Neighbors*. He could call it *Neighbors 2: A New Nightmare*. Or *Neighbors 2: The Next Chapter*. Or maybe even something like, *The Girls Next Door*. Yeah, he liked that one. Anyway, the plot would go something like this: After his ordeal with Wendy, good old Don moves to LA, and he's liking it there, really digging it, until these two girls move in next door. They're real bitches, right off the bat. He does his best to ignore them, but all their partying and loud music and shit starts to piss him off, so he goes to their place one night, to tell them to turn down the music. Only one of them is home, the angry Asian—sure, the bitchiest one—and she says the wrong thing, something that sets him off...and he kills her? Damn right he does! Get a murder happening within the first few chapters, get the reader hooked right away. Maybe make it an accident though? Need to keep old Don sympathetic. So it's an accident, but the Asian's still dead. Don freaks out and...what? Brings her back to his unit? Okay. He brings her back and dumps her body in his bathtub or something. There could be a really intense scene in which the black roommate comes over looking for her friend—good one, Buddy, keep the suspense high!—and after this Don knows he has to get rid of the Asian's body. Not only does the roommate continue to suspect him of foul play, the corpse is beginning to stink. But— *conflict, Buddy, conflict*—there are CCTV cameras in the elevator, the lobby, so instead he...well, shit, he embalms her! Stuffs her with sawdust, keeps her in his bedroom!

*Write what you know about, right?*

"You better believe it!" Buddy said to himself as he skipped down the staircase, never feeling better. "You better fucking believe it."

# AFTERWORD

Thank you for taking the time to read the book! If you enjoyed it, a brief review would be hugely appreciated. You can click straight to the review page here:

Dark Hearts - Amazon Review Page

Best,
Jeremy

# ABOUT THE AUTHOR

## Jeremy Bates

 USA TODAY and #1 AMAZON bestselling author Jeremy Bates has published more than twenty novels and novellas, which have been translated into several languages, optioned for film and TV, and downloaded more than one million times. Midwest Book Review compares his work to "Stephen King, Joe Lansdale, and other masters of the art." He has won both an Australian Shadows Award and a Canadian Arthur Ellis Award. He was also a finalist in the Goodreads Choice Awards, the only major book awards decided by readers. The novels in the "World's Scariest Places" series are set in real locations and include Suicide Forest in Japan, The Catacombs in Paris, Helltown in Ohio, Island of the Dolls in Mexico, and Mountain of the Dead in Russia. The novels in the "World's Scariest Legends" series are based on real legends and include Mosquito Man and The Sleep Experiment. You can check out any of these places or legends on the web. Also, visit JEREMYBATES-BOOKS.COM to receive Black Canyon, WINNER of The Lou Allin Memorial Award.

Made in the USA
Coppell, TX
15 October 2021